BODIES AND BOWS

BODIES AND BOWS

Elizabeth Penney

St. Martin's Paperbacks

This is a work of fiction. All of the characters, organizations, and events portrayed in this novel are either products of the author's imagination or are used fictitiously.

First published in the United States by St. Martin's Paperbacks, an imprint of St. Martin's Publishing Group.

BODIES AND BOWS

Copyright © 2021 by Elizabeth Penney.

All rights reserved.

For information, address St. Martin's Publishing Group, 120 Broadway, New York, NY 10271.

www.stmartins.com

ISBN: 978-1-250-25798-7

Our books may be purchased in bulk for promotional, educational, or business use. Please contact your local bookseller or the Macmillan Corporate and Premium Sales Department at 1-800-221-7945, ext. 5442, or by email at MacmillanSpecialMarkets@macmillan.com.

Printed in the United States of America

St. Martin's Paperbacks edition published 2021

10 9 8 7 6 5 4 3 2 1

For Mum and Dad, who taught me to love books

Acknowledgements

Writing *Bodies and Bows* was so much fun, and I hope the series fans eagerly awaiting its publication love it. For me, visiting Blueberry Cove is like spending time with friends in a beautiful place I cherish. A huge thank you to my editor, Nettie Finn, and the team at St. Martin's, including copyeditor John Simko and the publicity team of Allison Ziegler, Kayla Janas, and Sarah Haeckel. Plus, as always, a shout-out to my agent, Elizabeth Bewley. All you do is so appreciated!

Maine lighthouses are so iconic I had to feature one. In an odd coincidence, Blueberry Cove's lighthouse looks exactly like the one at Pemaquid Point, where a real beauty guards a wild and rocky section of the Maine coast. And like my character Florence Bailey Ricci, before automation, families lived in lighthouses, dedicated to keeping ships safe. Chester Chapman's Korean War experience is also based on the true story of American soldiers who were shamefully kept prisoner beyond the end of the war. My father also served in the Korean War, perhaps the least known of all our armed conflicts. Here's to Dad and all our dear veterans, both living and sadly gone. Last, and least, the Beast is an homage to our '99 Jeep Cherokee, one of those vehicles that seems to live forever.

Finally, here is a *Bodies and Bows* bonus, a recipe for the Blueberry Cove cocktail. Sara Bond, an author friend of mine, created this drink for one of her book and cocktail pairing blog posts. I of course had to try it, and it is delicious! She's also a wonderful writer, and you can check out her books at www.saratbond.com.

The Blueberry Cove by Sara Bond

1 oz gin
½ oz Lillet Blanc
¼ oz simple syrup
Prosecco
Blueberries

In the bottom of a shaker, muddle a handful of blueberries. Add ice, gin, Lillet, and simple syrup. Shake vigorously. Strain into a Collins glass. Add prosecco to the top. Garnish with a few more blueberries.

Enjoy!

CHAPTER 1

A loud *bloop bloop* from the fish tank made me jump, the three-year-old *Reader's Digest* almost slipping from my grip. But the pretty angelfish still swam serenely in their underwater lair, showing no concern for any humans waiting to be tortured.

I was at the dentist's office, alone in the waiting room except for the fish, on a gorgeous morning made for anything but this. Through the big window facing downtown, I could see a deep blue bay dotted with islands. Sailboats and lobster boats tracked across the water, leaving creamy froth in their wake. Summer was almost over, I realized wistfully, and I'd barely had a chance to enjoy it. For good reasons, but still.

A child screamed in a back room, followed by pleading reassurances from his mother and the lower, calmer tones of Dr. Pedersen. "This won't hurt a bit, Timmy. I'm just going to take a peek. Open wide . . . that's a good boy."

"You'll get a lollipop if you listen to the dentist," his mother said.

Twenty years ago that would have been me, cowering in the big chair and staring wide-eyed at the tray of scary-sharp implements. Dr. Oslo Pedersen had been taking care of my teeth since I moved to Blueberry Cove at age eight to live with my grandparents after my parents tragically died in a car accident. I put a hand to my cheek, wondering if the filling that had landed like a chunk of tinfoil on my breakfast plate was one of Dr. Pedersen's. I don't have many fillings, fortunately, mainly because my grandmother had limited sweets and stood over me until she could trust me to brush and floss.

Instead of turning back to the magazine, I thought about my to-do list. At nine, Grammie would open Ruffles & Bows, the vintage apron and linens shop we owned together on Main Street. We had fall inventory to unpack, and then, after the shop closed, volunteer duties at the lighthouse.

Tonight, a group of us planned to go through old trunks left behind by the last keepers, who left in the early 1950s when the light was automated. The new lighthouse museum was scheduled to open on Labor Day weekend, thanks to various local fundraisers. Our committee was in charge of creating exhibits depicting life as a lighthouse keeper, and it was shaping up to be a really fun project.

"Iris?" a voice inquired from the doorway.

I looked over to see Gretchen Stolte, dressed in a smock-and-pants uniform. "Hi, Gretchen. I didn't know you worked here." Not that I knew her well. She was a recent transplant to the area, an attractive woman with tawny hair and green eyes. Today she wore her hair up, held in place by an antique dragonfly clip.

She gave a soft snort as we started walking down the hallway to the examination rooms. "I'm a licensed dental hygienist," she said. "Over ten years of experience."

"Wonderful," I said, feeling scolded for my innocuous remark. She was one of those prickly people who took offense easily, I remembered.

My glance fell on a photograph depicting a small sailboat heeling over in tumultuous seas, one of many lining the hallway.

"Dr. Pedersen must be so glad to have Lance back in town," I said, attempting another pleasantry. His son, a world-class sailor and Olympian, had recently retired from the pro circuit with a great deal of fanfare. With his good looks, bad-boy reputation, and outstanding performance, Lance was a media—and local—darling. My friend Bella Ricci had gone on a few dates with him this summer, and the rest of our posse was vicariously enjoying the situation.

Her shoulders stiffened and she sped up, forcing me to racewalk down the carpet. Oops. I'd done it again. Too late I recalled that Gretchen didn't like Bella, so any mention of Lance would salt the wound. She had gone out with Bella's ex-husband, Alan, for a while, and when they broke up, she blamed my friend, which was totally unfair. But I had learned that people were rarely rational in matters of the heart.

"Have a seat," Gretchen ordered when we entered the tiny treatment room. She sat at a narrow desk that held a computer while I set down my handbag and climbed into the big chair. "What brings you here today?"

Why do we always have to repeat medical information despite relaying the problem while making an appointment? With a sigh, I leaned back in the chair and studied the ceiling panels, which displayed an aerial map of the Maine coast. "I lost part of a filling from a right bottom molar this morning. While I was eating breakfast."

Gretchen clicked keys, bringing up my chart and studying it. "You have one restoration in that quadrant."

"That's it." I obediently opened my mouth when she came to take a peek. I also closed my eyes against the bright light she pulled down to shine right into my face.

She studied my tooth for a long moment and then I felt the heat of the lamp move away. "Dr. Pedersen will be with you shortly. Dr. *Peter* Pedersen."

"Oh. I usually have Dr. Oslo," I said, disconcerted by this news.

"Dr. Peter is taking over the practice due to Dr. Oslo's pending retirement," she said, that snippy tone back in her voice. "We're gradually transferring all the patients over." That made sense, since Dr. Oslo was well into his seventies. He'd already seemed ancient to me when I'd started coming here.

She bustled out and I was left to wait, my anxiety building with every moment. Even staring at the map on the ceiling trying to find landmarks didn't calm me. I wanted the procedure to be over so I could get out of here. Lollipop or not.

Hope soared when I heard footsteps, but it was only Mrs. Oslo, clasping a sheaf of files in one arm. "Gretchen—" she began, but seeing the hygienist wasn't there, she huffed and withdrew before I could ask where her son was.

Finally a tall man with cropped dirty blond hair and a goatee, dressed in a white coat, strode in, Gretchen right behind him. *Dr. Pedersen, I presume.* He resembled his famous brother in height and facial structure, but while Lance dazzled the eye, the same features were merely ordinary on Peter. Until today I hadn't really clued in to the fact that Dr. and Mrs. Oslo had another son. Every family picture in the office featured Lance.

He peered at my chart then at me. "Iris? I'm Dr. Pedersen." Without waiting for an answer, he handed the chart to Gretchen then reached for the lamp. "Open wide for me."

I closed my eyes again, and so it began. After examining me with hums and muttered exclamations, he injected my gum with something that numbed the whole right side of my mouth. Saliva pooled immediately, and I prayed I wouldn't choke on my own spit. *How often did that happen?* I wondered.

"So, Iris, where do you work?" He asked this and a variety of other questions I couldn't answer while he fiddled about, drilling and packing and probing.

When I finally dared to open my eyes, they were both staring down at me with serious expressions. Why do dentists do that? "Am I okay?" I asked, trying to push myself upright.

Dr. Pedersen patted my shoulder. "You're fine. Lovely set of teeth." He handed me a piece of articulating paper. "Bite for me, please."

Soon after, I staggered out into the sunshine, blinking, my mouth still numb and my bank account quite a bit lighter. Halfway across the parking lot to my car, I noticed Lance, shirtless and in shorts, rinsing down his Porsche with a hose. The Pedersens lived on the property, with the dentist's office in one wing of a huge Colonial house. At the back of the paved area used for parking stood a former carriage house, now a four-car garage.

With a grin, he shut off the spray. "Hey, Iris. Beautiful day, isn't it?"

I mumbled something, my lips still not working right. But between my mouth gaping open and the drool, I probably looked like ninety-five percent of the women he encountered. Trying to smile, I fumbled for the keys to Beverly, the white '63 Ford Falcon my late grandfather had restored for me.

Lance whistled. "Nice car. Maybe you can take me for a spin some time."

My face flamed with heat, despite knowing that he was only being friendly. It wasn't his fault that he was sex on a stick, as my bestie Madison called him. Besides the fact that he was dating another friend, Bella, I was also very happily seeing someone, a great-looking carpenter named Ian Stewart. Rather than respond, I settled for a wave and climbed into my car. By the time I was backing out of my space, he had the hose spray on again and was intent on washing down the headlights.

Bella lived down the street from the Pedersens in a cute Craftsman bungalow. As I approached, I saw a tow truck from Quimby's Garage in the driveway, with Bella's gray Volvo wagon up on the flatbed. Oh no. That wasn't good.

I signaled and pulled over to park on the side of the road, then shut the car off and hopped out. Bella was standing on the lawn watching Derek, the tow truck driver, finish raising the flatbed to level. Noticing me, she gestured me over.

"What a bummer," I said, trotting across the grass. "What's wrong?"

Bella grimaced. "I don't know yet. It wouldn't start." She folded her arms across her slim body, the ocean breeze lifting a lock of her long brown hair. "But whatever it is, I'm sure it will be expensive. And take a while. Good thing Derek can give me a loaner."

I groaned in sympathy. Car repair bills always seemed to strike when you could least afford them, both financially and time-wise. "Need a ride to the garage?"

Her face lit up. "Would you? Derek offered me a lift but . . ."

"Say no more." Derek Quimby was a talented mechanic but a total slob. I'd seen the inside of his tow truck, and it was a mess of fast-food wrappers, old coffee cups, and random paperwork. Bella must have been on her way to work at Mimosa, her boutique; she was wearing a pink silk skirt and matching top, with an open-front fine-knit cardigan over it. I wouldn't trust that outfit to Derek's truck, either.

A man of medium height and about our age came around the hedge from the adjoining house, a Victorian that had been made into apartments. He had a thatch of dark hair and a heavy beard and was wiping greasy hands on a rag. "Hey, Bella. Putting Derek to work, are you?"

"Not by choice," Bella said. "Kyle Quimby, this is my friend, Iris Buckley. Kyle teaches sailing down at the yacht club. Derek is his cousin."

"Nice to meet you," I said, noticing Kyle's great tan and an athletic build set off by faded jeans and a tight T-shirt. Both were as grease-stained as his rag. "Are Bella's kids in your class?" Alice and Connor were taking sailing lessons at the club this summer, a rite of passage for many local children.

"They are." He gave me a big grin. "Naturals, both of them." He turned to Bella and gestured with his rag. "Need a ride? Give me a minute to clean up and I can take you on my way to the club." The grin flashed again. "Bella's not the only one with car troubles. My seventy-four TR6 is giving me fits, as usual."

Thanks to my grandfather, I actually knew what a TR6 was—a small sports car made by Triumph between 1968 and 1976. "It has a two-point-five liter in-line six engine and a manual transmission, right? Those babies are fast."

His dark eyes held mingled surprise and respect.

"You got it. Come take a look if you want. We can go for a ride some time."

"I'd love to. But right now I'm taking Bella to the garage. And then I have to get to the shop." At his quiz-zical expression, I added, "I own Ruffles & Bows, the apron shop on Main Street."

"Oh yeah, I've seen it," he said. "Nice place." He looked at Bella. "So you're all set, I take it?"

"I am, Kyle, but thank you," Bella said. "Iris and I have a lot to talk about."

We did? All I had to share was my Lance sighting a few minutes ago. Other than that I thought Bella and I were up to date. The members of the posse—Bella, Madison, Sophie, Grammie, and me—either spoke to or saw one another practically every day.

"That's cool," Kyle said. "But if you ever need my help, you know where I live."

How nice that Bella had such a considerate neigh-bor. I also thought that he might have a crush on her, which would be totally understandable. A native of Milan, Italy, Bella had natural elegance, olive skin, and the face of a Renaissance Madonna.

The whining noise from the tow truck hydraulics finally ceased, restoring blessed silence to the neigh-borhood. Derek checked to be sure the Volvo was secure, then walked over to join us. He greeted Kyle and me with a nod. "We're all set, Bella. Ready to head out?" Like his cousin, Derek was dark-haired—although clean-shaven with a fade—and he was about the same height and weight.

"Iris is giving me a ride to the garage," Bella said. "We'll meet you there."

Derek nodded. "All righty then. See you in a few." As he headed for the tow truck, Kyle tagged along to give him the update on the TR6.

"Let me grab my things and we'll go," Bella said. I waited on the lawn while she dashed into the house, but when Kyle went back around the hedge, I strolled up the sidewalk to check out his TR6. The British racing green paint job and tan interior appeared to be in mint condition, and I could imagine the joy of racing along winding roads in that sporty little beauty.

Behind the wheel of the tow truck, Derek gave a honk and began to pull slowly down the drive. Bella emerged from the house as Derek turned onto the street, and I hurried to meet her at Beverly. Enough daydreaming.

Quimby's Garage was located on the state route that skirted town, so rather than go down to Main Street and out that way, I decided to cut through the residential side streets up on the hill.

"Guess who I saw at the dentist's office?" I asked as we set off. I couldn't repress a grin. "Lance. He was washing his Porsche."

Bella continued to look straight ahead but a tint of pink flushed her cheeks. "We went for a ride in that Porsche last night, after we had dinner at the Lighthouse Grille." The Grille was one of the best restaurants around, with excellent food and a romantic atmosphere. "It was fun."

"I'll bet. How are things going with him?" I was curious, not only because he was a sports celebrity, but because she hadn't really dated since her divorce. After ten years of marriage, she'd caught her husband cheating and immediately thrown him out. She'd barely recovered from the life-disrupting trauma. His dating other local women, like Gretchen, hadn't helped.

She lifted one shoulder in a shrug. "They're fine." She threw me a smile. "Keeping it casual." The smile faltered slightly. "Did I tell you that Alan is staying in town this week?" Her ex-husband.

"Get out of here. Why? And where?" Horror swept over me. "Not with you, I hope." Usually the children went to his place in Rockland on alternate weekends and school vacations.

Bella laughed. "Iris, calm down. He's staying at the Sunrise Resort with his grandmother so they can both spend time with the kids. And by the way, I just found out that Florence used to live at the lighthouse. Her maiden name was Bailey."

"Seriously? That's fantastic. I hope she'll let us interview her." We'd been hoping to track down members of the Bailey family, but after almost sixty years, we had thought the likelihood was slim. Florence coming to town right now was a gift. "How old is she?"

"Eighty-five and still going strong. She told me that she's very excited about the lighthouse museum. She even brought photo albums with her."

I groaned in excitement. "Pictures of the lighthouse in the 1950s? I can hardly wait to see them." Our exhibits would have so much more depth if we could talk to Florence and find out what life in the lighthouse was really like. Maybe she'd even let us film an interview. We could set up a monitor and play it on a loop.

We had reached the intersection with U.S. Route 1, and naturally had to wait for passing traffic to thin before pulling out. Summer traffic on the Maine coast was horrendous, which we locals resented but welcomed at the same time. Catering to tourists was how most of us made a living. Grammie and I had sold a lot of aprons and linens to visitors this summer, and better yet, we had captured their e-mails for future marketing efforts. Customers could order from our online store—or ask us to stitch up custom aprons. That new sideline was taking off.

"Iris, there is something I need to tell you." Bella's tone was tentative.

I jerked my head around to face her, fear making my heart lurch. "What is it? Are you okay? Are the kids okay?"

She gave a little laugh. "No, it's nothing like that. We're totally healthy." She pressed her lips together, studying me and obviously thinking about how to tell me whatever it was.

A horn beeped behind me. Now, of course, traffic was clear but I couldn't focus on Bella and driving at the same time. I waved for the driver to go around us.

"It's Alan," she finally said, as the other vehicle roared past. "He wants to give our marriage another try."

CHAPTER 2

Mindful of my earlier blurt, I bit back the objections crowding to my lips. Although Bella and I were fairly new friends, I'd seen the hurt Alan had caused, witnessed the devastation resulting after her family was ripped apart. And those sweet kids . . . how much damage would it do to raise false hopes? Because leopards didn't change their spots—and cheating husbands would certainly stray again, right?

Someone honked behind us again, and this time I checked traffic and pulled out, giving myself a moment to frame my words. Once we were safely in the southbound lane, I said, "Bella, it's really none of my business if you get back together with him or not. I just want you and the kids to be happy. Period."

"But?" Her smile was rueful. "You're worried he might blow it again. Rip open barely healed wounds and hurt us bad."

I couldn't have said it better. "Yeah, something like that. Doesn't he realize that he can't waltz back in as if he didn't do anything?" And I'd hurt *him* bad if he messed up a second time. Definitely no do-overs.

She turned to stare out at the passing countryside. "He knows that. And he knows I'll make him work for it. He said he's already in counseling." She threw me a glance I couldn't quite read. "Honestly, Iris, he seems different. Humble, for one thing. And Alan was never ever humble."

"I'll take your word for it," I said, vowing to keep an eye on the situation whether it was my business or not. Next time I saw Alan, I would pay more attention, see if I could evaluate his sincerity.

Quimby's Garage loomed up on the left, so I signaled and slowed for the turn. The tow truck was already there, and Derek was backing into a spot with the Volvo still on the bed. After an SUV with out-of-state plates passed heading north, I zipped across the lane and pulled into an empty parking spot. "Want me to come in with you?" At her nod, I shut off the engine.

By the time we reached the office area on the left end of the building, Derek was ambling across the blacktop toward us. Beyond the open bay doors, metal clanged and an air wrench fired in percussive bursts. It was a noisy place. Derek's uncle, Roy, ran the garage, and they had a couple of employees.

Derek held open the office door. "After you."

We entered a space barely big enough for a short counter with a stool and a computer and a row of old vinyl chairs along the wall. In here, sounds from the garage were muffled, helped by the lively oldies song playing from hidden speakers.

Derek sidled past us and around the counter. He clicked away on the computer, muttering to himself. "Ah, there you are. We'll be able to get the Volvo in later today, see what's up."

"How long do you think the repairs will take?" Bella asked. "Any idea what's wrong?"

He pursed his lips. "We'll need to hook it up to the diagnostic. Once we do that, I'll give you a call.

We won't proceed with anything until you give the okay."

That was one reason why I went to this garage. They didn't go ahead and do a bunch of work and then present you with a giant and unexpected bill.

Bella rolled her eyes with a sigh. "I'm praying it's not anything too serious. It's almost at the point where I should get a newer vehicle. But I'd rather keep this one going for a while, if I can."

"We'll keep you safe and on the road, Ms. Ricci," Derek said. He peered at the screen. "Is this your cell number?" He started to read off the digits.

An advertising jingle blared over the speaker, much louder than the music had been. *Pirro Auto . . . we're on fire—* Derek lowered the volume with a grumble. "How many times a day do I have to hear that? They need to stay in Portland, not go after our customers up here." He rolled his shoulders with a huff. "Let me try that again." He started over with the cell number.

"That's the right number," Bella said. "Now, about that loaner . . ." She was starting to fidget, as was I. The Goodyear Tire clock on the wall read quarter of ten. Her boutique opened in fifteen minutes. If we left now, we'd barely make it downtown on time.

Derek pulled a set of keys off a rack behind the desk. "It's out back. Come with me."

In the far corner of the lot behind the garage sat a battered black Jeep Cherokee of antique vintage. With its oversize tires, grille guard, and coating of grime, it looked as if its last outing had been off-road. "Mudding," they call it in Maine, where they even named a time of year after the gooey, black, wheel-sucking stuff: mud season.

Derek chuckled fondly. "The Beast, we call it. Don't be fooled by its appearance. Runs good."

Bella glanced down at her silk skirt then at the Jeep. With a sigh, she held out her palm. "Wish me luck."

Still smiling at the image of fastidious Bella behind the wheel of the Beast, I pulled into the alley behind Ruffles & Bows. Grammie's Bronco was already parked there, since she and my cat, Quincy, had opened today. Believe it or not, we had people who stopped by the store on a regular basis just to see him. Of course, Quincy wasn't surprised by that. Who doesn't love a friendly and supersmart orange tabby?

I gathered my things and climbed out, allowing myself a moment to bask in the sunshine before I went inside. Then, as my to-do list started to cascade through my mind, I took one last breath of briny sea air and headed for the back door.

The rear entrance led directly into a small hall, once tobacco-brown dingy but now bright with fresh paint. For decoration, we'd hung a few prints of French Impressionist paintings depicting women and girls in aprons. My favorite, hung next to a row of hooks, was a Mary Cassatt showing a mother sewing while her daughter leaned on her lap. So much like Grammie and me when I was little. With a nod at the Cassatt, I stopped to slip on a pinafore store apron over my pale green '50s retro dress. I almost always wore mid-century clothing since it suited my curvy figure. Now this style was the store's signature look.

Ready for work, I stepped into the main area of my beautiful store. This building had once been a dry goods store owned by my ancestors, and it still retained its tin ceiling, hanging globe lights, and carved mahogany counters and woodwork. Grammie and I had added distressed vintage cabinets and shelves to hold linens, and colorful aprons were displayed on rotary clotheslines and mannequins. "Delightful and inviting, with a touch of whimsy," *Coastal Lifestyles* had said. I'd take it.

Wearing a pinafore over a pink dress similar to mine, her gray bob gleaming, Grammie stood behind the main counter leafing through sales slips. She looked up and smiled. "There you are. How did it go?"

I deposited my bags behind the counter and touched my cheek. The numbness was almost gone. "You know how I feel about the dentist." Quincy padded over and rubbed against my ankles, insisting I pick him up. So I did. "I had Peter Pederson today. Dr. Oslo is retiring." I nestled my nose into Quincy's soft fur and he started purring. "They should have therapy cats at the dentist's office."

Grammie snorted. "Surely it wasn't that bad."

"It pretty much was." I released Quincy, then tugged my apron into place. "I ran into Bella after, and guess what? I have news." I said this last in a singsong voice to tease her.

"What is it?" Grammie asked, clasping her hands in exaggerated entreaty. "Please don't make me guess."

I moved to the coffee station to pour a cup. "It's a little convoluted, but bear with me. Bella's ex-husband's grandmother is Florence Bailey, who used to live in the lighthouse. And she's in town this week, staying at the Sunrise Resort."

Grammie sucked in a breath. "That's fantastic. Do you think she'll let us interview her?"

"I hope so." I found milk in the mini-fridge and added it to my mug. "Bella said she brought photo albums with her. I can't wait to see those."

Grammie brought her mug over for a refill. "Me neither. I was a baby when the lighthouse went automated. Photographs will really help us a lot with the displays."

Due to her strong interest in local history, Grammie had volunteered to lead the exhibit committee. She'd then recruited my friends and me to help. We'd spent the past couple of weeks cleaning the keeper's cottage, sorting through items left behind, and planning displays. Donations of lighthouse equipment and memorabilia were starting to come in, too.

"That's what I thought." Carrying my coffee, I wandered over to the counter. A piece of paper caught my eye and I picked it up for a closer look. "Someone ordered *five* aprons? Holy cow."

"I know," Grammie said with a chuckle. "The order was in the store e-mail this morning. She wants aprons for her daughters and daughter-in-law, for Thanksgiving."

I set the note aside and flipped through my planner, trying to figure out when we could fit in this job. Grammie and I sewed the aprons whenever we could—between customers, at night, and on Sundays, when we were closed.

"I'm glad she gave us that much lead time," I said. "We're going to have to start telling people they have to wait." I cringed at the idea, knowing that in this era of overnight shipping and huge megastores, people expected instant delivery.

Grammie sighed. "I hate to do that," she said, sounding bone-tired. "But I really don't see any other solution. We both work six days a week."

I regarded Grammie with alarm, seeing for the first time how exhausted she looked. When we'd opened the business three months ago, we'd been buoyed by excitement and the sheer adrenaline of taking a risk. Our timing had been good, with a launch on Memorial Day weekend right before the summer season kicked off. Like everyone else in town, we'd worked like crazy to maximize sales in the busy season—so we could make it through the slow ones.

"We need to hire someone," I said, my tone brooking no argument. "And when we do, you are taking a vacation."

Despite my bold words, my belly fluttered in trepidation. Could we afford it? Employees cost more than just their wages, since there were insurance and payroll tax considerations. I'd have to go through the budget line by line, see where we could cut. Plus, if we continued to sell custom pinafores—I had a brilliant idea. "It needs to be someone who sews. They can help us produce aprons." I pulled at the skirt of mine. "These aren't terribly complicated."

Grammie's mouth twisted with skepticism. "You think we can find someone who is good with customers *and* can sew? I mean, listening to everyone else, they feel lucky if they find people they can trust." We were members of the local chamber of commerce along with the other retailers and yes, thanks to low unemployment, finding good retail help was more difficult than ever.

"We won't know until we try." I went to the computer on the counter and pulled up the *Blueberry Cove Herald*'s website. Job classifieds could be posted both online and in the print edition, so I chose the former option. The *Herald* only came out once a week and I wanted to jump-start the process. "Downtown business needs help. Ideal candidate is someone who loves aprons and linens, is good with people, and loves to sew. Ruffle & Bows is looking for the perfect person to help us grow. Compensation is commensurate . . ."

With fifteen minutes, I had posted an ad, sent in a print ad request for good measure, and created a filter to capture the applications in our regular account.

Hopefully we'd get some good responses—otherwise I would widen the net to the surrounding towns.

Meanwhile, Grammie was unpacking a box of inventory she had brought in from the storeroom. "I love these aprons," she said, smoothing a blue cotton half-apron appliquéd with apples and rickrack trim. Next in the pile was a red-and-white child's polka-dot apron with tiny pockets for crayons. "They're perfect for a back-to-school display."

"That's what I thought," I said, watching as she continued to pull aprons out of the box. All summer I'd been buying whatever caught my eye, and then I'd organize the aprons by style or theme. I pointed to the child-size mannequin dressed in one of our pinafores. "If I buy another one of those, we can do a teacher-and-student display in the window." We had an old-fashioned student desk in the barn at home. It would be perfect for our window.

"This reminds me," Grammie said. "We need to find some mannequins for the lighthouse museum. Then we can display clothing and gear." One outfit we'd found was a set of bright yellow oilskins, complete with a hat. Exactly like the man on the fish sticks box.

I turned back to the computer. "Let me see what I can rustle up." People were always selling old mannequins as they either upgraded or went out of business. We didn't care if they were new or even in great condition. Just something we could dress in vintage clothing, which was the main draw anyway.

While I plunked away, searching for options and e-mailing vendors, Grammie finished unpacking the box. She'd set up an iron in the side room where we stitched aprons and, hopefully soon, planned to hold classes. Late fall would be a perfect time to start those up, once people were driven indoors by bad weather.

The front door opened, making a bell tinkle, and I glanced up to see two familiar and very cute children entering. Alice and Connor, Bella's children.

"Hey, guys," I called. "Is your mom with you?" Quincy, of course, went running over to them and they both bent down to pet him.

Alice shook her head, long silky hair swaying. "No, Daddy and Nonna. Mom is at work."

Of course, but I thought maybe she'd taken a break to visit with us. The door opened again and an older woman entered, ushered in by Alan, Bella's ex. The last person on earth I wanted to see today.

CHAPTER 3

Steeling myself, I kept my gaze on the woman who must be Florence. Tiny and thin, almost bird-like, her flyaway white hair cut in a cute cap. She wore Capri pants, sneakers, and a sleeveless blouse, with a sweater tied around her shoulders. Elegant, yet casual.

"Hey, Iris," Alan said, his voice gravely and deep. I finally met his gaze, which was sheepish, as if he knew what I thought of him and his efforts to woo Bella back. He then noticed Grammie, who popped out of the side room. "Hello, Anne. How are you?"

"I'm fine, thank you." Grammie's smile was genuine as she briskly crossed the hardwood floor, hand extended. "I'm Anne Buckley," she said to Florence.

"And I'm Florence Ricci." Florence shook Grammie's hand firmly, equally matched in deportment and style. Two very formidable women, indeed. After letting go of Grammie's hand, Florence gazed around with a sigh. "What a lovely store. Believe it or not, I haven't been to Blueberry Cove in years. But when I heard about the lighthouse museum opening, I just had to change that." She sent her grandson a fond glance. "And darling Alan rented us the loveliest suite at the Sunrise Resort. What a treat." She rolled her shoulders. "I had a back massage right in my room this morning."

Alice and Connor, still fussing over Quincy, exchanged glances with a snicker. They were at the age when almost anything adults said or did made them laugh.

"I've got cookies," I said. "Are you two hungry?" I glanced at their father for permission—he nodded.

The children presented themselves at the counter, declaring that they were absolutely starving. Besides a bag of chocolate chip cookies from the Belgian Bean—Sophie's business—I had juice boxes on hand. Carrying their treats, they went to sit in the side room to snack. Grammie poured a mug of coffee for Florence, then gave her a tour of the shop.

That left Alan and me alone at the counter, both of us extremely uncomfortable. He immediately pretended great interest in a spinning rack of funny cards next to the counter. While he was thus occupied, I took the opportunity to study him covertly. Alan wasn't terribly tall, but he had the trim fitness and tan of an avid golfer, which he was. His features were lean, his mouth usually curled in a slight smile, and his short hair had an adorable cowlick in front. I could see why Bella—and a bunch of other women—found him attractive. His smooth charm promised courtly attention and a good time.

"It's nice that you brought your grandmother to see the kids," I finally said. Despite my reservations about Alan, I didn't need to be a jerk to him. "Are they having a good time at the resort?"

His face lit up with a grin. "They sure are. I have to drag them out of the pool for dinner every night. And they're loving their sailing lessons, too." Then the smile dropped slightly, and I could guess why. A mention of sailing led inevitably to thoughts of Lance, who was dating Bella.

Oh, how tempted was I to tell him it was his own fault. And that of course Bella wasn't going to be alone indefinitely. But instead, I said, "I took those same sailing lessons." During my first summer in Blueberry Cove, Madison had taken me under her wing. One of the most popular girls in our age group, she was bright and funny, a daredevil who had a soft spot for a grieving and confused peer. We'd been best friends ever since.

Grammie and Florence had made the rounds and were now back at the counter. "Guess what, Iris? Florence is going to lend us her photo albums. We can make copies of whatever we want."

"That is so good of you," I told Florence, both awed and touched. Family photographs were precious. "We'll take really good care of your pictures, I promise."

"No problem," Florence said, smiling shyly. "They've been sitting in my attic for decades. Alan had to shovel the dust off the boxes."

We all laughed at her gentle humor.

"We're going to be working at the lighthouse tonight," Grammie said, glancing between Florence and Alan. "You're welcome to come by. Bring the kids and they can climb the tower. It's perfectly safe."

Alan shifted on his feet. "Maybe we will. Thanks for the offer." He turned to his grandmother. "It's up to you, Nonna."

"Maybe it's time," Florence said, her expression sad. "I haven't been in the lighthouse since the day we moved out." She sucked in a breath, shaking her head. "Over sixty years ago. Do you believe it?"

"Whatever you decide is fine," I said. "We'll be there after five." We were going to pick up sandwiches for the committee and head over after the store closed.

Perhaps seeking a change of subject, Florence's

attention was caught by the child's pinafore. "Oh, how darling." She looked us up and down. "It's exactly like the ones you're wearing."

"Exact replica." Grammie took her arm and drew her closer to the mannequin. "They're stitched by hand. And we take custom orders."

"So you could do one in Alice's size?" Florence eyed her granddaughter, who was chasing Quincy through the shop. He kept stopping to allow the children to catch up before darting away again. He was something else.

"We certainly could," I said, reaching for an order form.

"Alice, come here," her great-grandmother called. Alice came running, followed by her brother and Quincy. Florence checked the tag inside Alice's shirt and told me the size. "I want to order one for me and one for Bella, too," she said. "We can wear them at Thanksgiving." Alan perked up when his grandmother mentioned the holiday, probably hoping he would be included.

"That's what a lot of people are doing," I said, picturing how cute it would be for women and girls to wear matching aprons while preparing a meal together. And we really should design something for boys and men, too. Maybe I should ask customers to submit photographs. We could feature the families on our website and social media . . . with an effort, I forced myself to set aside this great idea. But I did scribble notes for later, so I wouldn't forget.

I took down the order details, with Alan volunteering Bella's size before blushing so furiously I actually felt sorry for him, and then the Ricci clan took their leave.

"He still has a thing for her, doesn't he?" Grammie

asked as the door slammed behind them, the bell tin-
kling.

Leave it to Grammie to uncover the truth in five seconds flat. No wonder I never got away with anything
when I was a kid. Or even now, come to think of it.

After we closed at five, Grammie took Quincy home
and I picked up the sandwich order at the Mug Up Deli.
Then I drove out to the lighthouse, windows down,
an oldies station playing and a warm breeze blowing
through my hair. Late-afternoon light gilded rippling
waves in the bay and transformed the tumbled, rocky
shoreline into gold. Oh, how I loved summer.

The lighthouse stood at the very end of Hemlock
Point, a classic white tower attached to a two-story
keeper's cottage. As I drove up the access road to park
near the cottage door, I saw Ian and Sophie's fiancé Jake
standing beside an aerial lift next to the tower. They noticed me and waved.

I hopped out and hurried over. "Hi, sweetie," I said,
giving Ian a kiss. "Hey, Jake."

"Hey, Iris," Jake said, running a hand over his red
brush cut. He worked as a lobsterman and, like Ian, was
tanned and fit. Two hardworking men ready to tackle a
big painting job.

"I see you got the lift," I said. "Starting the job tonight?"

Ian pointed to a piece of equipment. "We're pressure
washing first, which will take us a couple of evenings.
The structure is in good shape, so we'll be able to start
painting pretty much right away."

Tipping my head back, I studied the forty-foot
tower, thankful I wasn't the one who would be riding
a lift into the air. Heights and I don't get along. "When
you're ready for a break, come join us. I got you each

a sandwich and a cold drink." I lowered my voice to a whisper. "And whoopie pies."

Both men gave hoots of delight. All Mainers loved the treat, which was basically a puffy chocolate cookie sandwich with a white cream filling.

Ian pecked me on the lips. "Thanks, babe. See you in a bit." As I walked away, they began to talk about power washing.

Ian and I had been dating since late May, when we'd reconnected after not seeing each other since high school. Not that we were an item then, but I'd certainly had a crush on him. And he'd confided that he'd noticed me, too. Everything had been wonderful this time around, although I'd been tempted to jump the gun a little instead of moving slowly as we'd agreed. Now we'd both pulled back slightly, leaving a little breathing room in our relationship. But it was still great, easy and fun and drama-free.

Grammie was driving up the access road, so I grabbed the paper sacks containing our meal from Beverly's back seat. Grammie tooted a greeting before sliding into the next parking place. Through her open driver window, she called, "I brought paper plates, napkins, and plastic utensils, in case we need them."

"Perfect." I waited for her to gather her things and lead the way to the cottage, where she unlocked the door. The lighthouse museum would be run by a newly organized nonprofit, and Grammie was on the board.

We stepped into a long entryway with a white beadboard ceiling and walls. A lone yellow rain slicker hung on the wooden pegs lining the inside wall, and old boot trays still held traces of mud.

Grammie glanced up at the cobwebs festooning the corners. "After we sort through everything, we'll get a crew in here to clean."

"It's not too bad," I said. "At least there isn't a lot of junk."

"True. The Coast Guard kept the place in good shape." She thumbed a latch on the kitchen door and stood back to let me enter first. The place was like a time capsule, with its rounded fridge; L-shape bank with Formica counters, porcelain sink, and tall bead-board cabinets; and an ornate wood-fired cook stove in front of a brick hearth. I parked the bags containing dinner in the fridge, which had been cleaned and was running.

"Talk about a million-dollar view," I said, moving as if magnetized to the windows overlooking the water. An old maple drop-leaf table and four chairs sat under the windows, and I imagined the many meals the keeper and his family had enjoyed there. After tearing my gaze away, I took in the rest of the room—dull brown lino-leum flooring, a fluorescent ceiling ring, and faded but cozy wallpaper illustrated with a motif of spices, bak-ing supplies, and kitchen tools.

"We can do a lot with this," Grammie said with en-thusiasm as she flicked on the overhead light. "The original features haven't been spoiled with renovations."

I agreed, although the linoleum could go. Maybe there was hardwood flooring underneath. I'd ask Ian to check. We wandered into the living room, which also overlooked the water. Here, only a wooden rocking chair remained as furnishings, property of the light-house station. The Baileys had taken all their own fur-niture away, of course. The empty built-in bookcases on either side of the fieldstone fireplace were perfect for displaying books and other small memorabilia. With some period furniture, we could help people imagine how it was to live here. The wallpaper in this room was a design of roses climbing over trellises.

The final room on the ground floor was the keeper's office, and this still held stacks of the logs, documents, and records the keepers had been required to maintain. Kept closed up, the room held a pleasant scent of old books, ink, and dust. A green pull shade covered the window facing the drive and I tugged on it, sending it flying up with a snap.

"This room is a treasure trove for historians and researchers," Grammie said. "I had two college students approach me about doing a project cataloguing everything this fall. They're going to digitize it for the university library, which will probably take the physical materials too, for their archives."

"That's excellent," I said. Once the historic records were safely removed, we could set up a display in here, too. I imagined an open logbook on the high table, a pipe, pen, and coffee mug close at hand.

Out the window, I saw Madison's Mini Cooper zipping up the access road. "Oh good, our committee is arriving. Let's go meet them." Madison was bringing Sophie, who would catch a ride back with Jake after we wrapped up tonight. Bella was also scheduled to show up. I hoped she would make it with everything else she had going on.

Madison hopped out of the driver's seat, long, lean, and bursting with energy. A headband restrained her curly black hair, and she wore faded jeans and an orange peasant blouse that suited her golden-brown complexion. "Hey, ladies," she called. "I see the dream team is already hard at work." Her wide grin was infectious.

Sophie had noticed Ian and Jake as well, and was watching them wield the power washer, a dreamy expression on her face. Her long blonde hair was tied in a ponytail and she wore jeans and a gauzy blouse.

"Earth to Sophie," I said. "What's new?"

She reluctantly turned from the alluring display of masculine prowess. "Oh, hi. I'm sorry. What did you say?"

The rest of us burst out laughing. Ever since their engagement last month, the pair had been acting like lovestruck zombies. It was sweet.

"Nothing," I said. "I thought we could work inside for an hour or so and then eat." I pointed to a nearby picnic table on the bluff. "That looks like a good spot."

Grammie patted Sophie on the arm. "Your young man will be joining us for dinner, so maybe you can tear yourself away for a while."

Sophie gave Grammie a quick hug. "Oh, Anne. I wish you were the one helping me plan my wedding." Sophie, like all my friends, loved Grammie for her levelheaded advice, kind heart, and wicked sense of humor.

Grammie tilted her head, studying Sophie with concern. "Are those tears in those pretty blue eyes?" She slipped an arm through Sophie's. "Why don't you tell us about it?"

While we strolled into the cottage, Sophie told us about her mother, Helena. "Okay. First thing you have to understand is, with two brothers, I'm the only girl in my family. So this is Mom's big chance to plan a dream wedding. And hey, I admit that it's my dream wedding, too. The problem is, our tastes are total opposites. Her ideal is Princess Kate and William and mine is barefoot on the beach."

I could see the conflict. Sophie and Jake were both very down-to-earth. "Does she want to have the wedding in Connecticut?" We had paused in the kitchen, and I opened the fridge to grab bottles of iced tea to sip on while we worked.

Sophie shuddered. "Thankfully no. We insisted on Maine and won. But the first obstacle is the reception. I've been tasked to find a suitable spot. And if I fail, she'll be up here in a flash to take over."

"So we'll help you." Madison popped the cap off her tea. "Locally, the Sunrise Resort is great. So is the yacht club."

Before Sophie could respond, the relentless throb of the pressure washer cut off suddenly, allowing the sound of a throaty engine to be heard. I knew that sound. "Speaking of which, here comes Bella."

Madison grimaced. "What's she driving? If that's her Volvo, she needs an engine check."

"Come look," I said with a laugh, herding them back out the kitchen door and through the mudroom.

"And what did you mean by 'speaking of which'?" Madison, my very bright and curious best friend, asked.

"Tell you in a sec," I said.

Bella pulled up in the Beast and turned off the engine. The heavy vehicle rocked, rattled, and shook, giving a final explosive puff of black exhaust. From their perch on the lift, Ian and Jake watched with smiles.

"Nice rig," Grammie said dryly when Bella slid out of the driver's side. "Car's at Quimby's, I take it?"

"One hundred percent correct." Bella reached in and pulled out a tote bag. "Alan said I could use his BMW, but I said no thank you." Her smile was crooked. "I'm not ready for that level of commitment."

Madison and Sophie both looked at me, mouthing, *Alan?* in disbelief.

"Yes, that Alan," I muttered. But that was all I was going to say. It was up to Bella to share updates about her ex—or not. We all fell into step, heading toward the cottage door.

"Are Alan and the kids coming over tonight?" Grammie asked. "I brought a big container of chocolate chip cookies just in case."

"Homemade cookies?" Madison said. "You've been holding out on me."

Grammie squeezed Madison's forearm. "Be a good girl tonight and I'll see you get a couple."

Madison played along, heaving a huge sigh. "All right, if I must." Then, brows raised, she asked Bella, "*Are* Alan and the kids coming?"

"Yes, I believe so," Bella said, tossing her loose hair back. "Didn't Iris tell you? Alan and his grandmother are staying at the Sunrise Resort this week."

"I didn't tell them anything," I said. "But guess what? Alan's grandmother was a Bailey and she used to live here in the lighthouse."

The change of topic diverted everyone's attention, and between Grammie and me, we got everyone up to speed on Florence's involvement. "I'm hoping she'll allow us to interview her on camera," I said. "It would be awesome for people to hear what living here was actually like."

"It sure would," Madison said. "And we can use clips for promotion." She ran her own small marketing company and had volunteered to do the museum's social media. I could tell by her distant expression that the wheels were already turning.

We were all standing in the kitchen now, and Sophie asked, "What's my assignment tonight, Anne?"

Grammie pulled a planner out of her tote bag, which was sitting on a kitchen chair. She flipped it open to the right page. "Sophie, I'd like you, Madison, and Iris to sort through the storage room upstairs. See if there is anything we can use for our displays. Bella, I'd love to have you help me in the keeper's office. We have students coming soon and I want to start getting it organized."

"What time are we stopping to eat?" My belly rumbled. "I'm already getting hungry."

"Shall we say in an hour?" Grammie grabbed the promised container of cookies out of her bag and pried open the lid, releasing sweet aromas of sugar and vanilla and chocolate. "Take one to tide you over. After dinner, we can work another hour or two, if we need to."

We all took a cookie and iced tea and wandered off to our assignments. The storage room was on the second floor, the smallest of the three bedrooms. This level also included a very basic bathroom with a clawfoot tub.

Madison opened the door and all three of us stared into the room. "We'll need more than a couple of hours to deal with this," she said.

The room was crammed with boxes, trunks, mysterious pieces of equipment, coils of rope, and a mermaid figurehead from a ship. "Wow, that is beautiful," Sophie said.

Although battered and faded, the wooden figure was sleek, with long carved hair that gave the impression of movement. "We are definitely using that in a display," I said. Madison already had her phone out and was edging through tight spaces to get closer.

"Where do we begin?" Sophie asked, hands hanging at her sides in discouragement. The task really did seem daunting.

I opened a door across the landing. This was the largest bedroom, and the plan called for creating more exhibits up here. The third bedroom would become an office and volunteer room. "I think we're going to have to take everything out and decide if it's to keep, throw away, or exhibit," I said. "There's room in here to stash everything."

By the time Madison made her way back from photographing the figurehead, Sophie and I had a plan of attack worked out. The three of us set to work, carting items into the big room and organizing them in rows. Things that were too heavy would have to wait for more muscle power and a dolly.

Then I found a hope chest. The wooden trunk was pushed back against the wall, submerged under crooked stacks of dusty old books.

Madison rubbed a hand across the glossy finish. "What a pretty trunk. Why would the Baileys leave this?"

"No idea," I said, throwing open the lid. I expected to find linens and clothing tucked neatly into tissue paper, and there was some of that below, but it looked like someone had tossed random clothing on top. I found an olive green cardigan with a darned elbow and one loose button, a pair of men's canvas trousers, and an apron, the type you hooked over your neck and slid your arms through. "Farmhouse," the style was called. This one was white cotton, with blue tatted edging and an embroidered bouquet of flowers below the neckline.

Something rustled when I held it up and, fishing around in the pocket, I found a folded piece of white paper. Expecting a shopping list or something else equally mundane, I unfolded the page: a letter, dated January 1953.

My darling girl,
How's my baby doing in the great state o' Maine? I don't have much time to write—they're about to send us out again—so I'll keep it short and

sweet. (At least I hope you'll think it's sweet). But I can't restrain myself any longer.

Will you marry me? (cue begging and pleading eyes here)

Please say yes by return mail and give this flyboy a reason to carry on.

Yours always,
Chet C.

CHAPTER 4

Sophie and Madison came to read over my shoulder. "That's so romantic." Sophie's eyes were wide with excitement. "Do you think she said yes?"

"I have no idea." I flipped the page over, but it was blank. Then I felt around in the pockets. No envelope or additional pages. "If it was Florence's letter, then no. She married Alan Ricci's grandfather."

Madison was scrolling on her phone. "As I thought. There were two more Bailey daughters, Doris and Gloria. According to the family history on the lighthouse site, Florence was the middle daughter, with Doris a year older and Gloria a year younger. Their brother Roger was two years older than Doris."

"So it could have belonged to any of them," I said. They were all in their late teens or early twenties in 1953.

"We could ask Florence," Sophie pointed out. "She would know."

Sophie was right, but something was holding me back. I folded the page and tucked it back into the trunk. "What if it was Florence's letter and Chet died in battle or something? I'd hate to open old wounds."

Light footsteps ran up the stairs and a moment later, Alice popped into the room, a big smile on her face. Her shiny dark hair, so like her mom's, swung in a long po-nytail. "Hi," she said. "Nonna used to live here."

I rose to my feet, still holding the apron. "So I heard. It's a great place to live, isn't it?"

Alice was spinning around, staring at everything. "It sure is." She looked toward the stairs, where a slower set of footsteps could be heard. "She's coming up to show me her bedroom."

A moment later, Florence appeared. She put a hand to her chest, catching her breath. "This sure is a blast from the past."

Alice and the rest of us laughed at her use of the slang phrase. "Was this your room?"

Florence shook her head. "No, my sisters and I shared the big room." Her gaze roamed around the storage room, then landed on the apron I was holding. "My apron."

I handed it to her, my pulse leaping up a notch. Maybe the letter *had* been hers.

But she didn't mention that or Chet. Instead she ran a finger over the embroidery on the apron front. "I did this myself, one winter. When we were snowed in, we did a lot of sewing."

"Nothing much has changed, then," I said with a roll of my eyes. "That's what Grammie and I do, too."

She pushed it back toward me. "Why don't you hold on to it, for the museum. Anne was saying you wanted to do exhibits showing daily life in the lighthouse. And nothing says daily life more than an apron."

I took the apron. "Are you sure? We'd love to keep it, but . . ."

"I'm positive." A sad expression crossed her fea-tures. "That was such a difficult time, that year we left. My brother had been wounded in action in Korea, and everything was such a mess. My poor mother. She could barely function."

And maybe something went wrong with Chet, too? But this wasn't the time or place to ask. Then Alice pulled on her great-grandmother's hand and the moment passed. "Let's go into your bedroom, Nonna. Then I want to go up in the lighthouse."

Florence looked at us with a laugh. "These young ones. Keep me on my toes."

We decided that now was a good time for a break and tagged along on the tour. Connor and Alan joined us, and we went through the house as a group. Florence shared little anecdotes about her childhood, Alice and Connor listening with wide-eyed fascination.

The family had kept chickens and it was her job to feed them. "I was about your size," she told Alice while we walked across the grass to the lighthouse, part two of the tour. "And I was so afraid of those hens when they came rushing at me. They'd peck my toes if I wasn't careful." Alice danced away as though imaginary chickens were attacking her.

"Did you go sailing?" Connor asked. "Like us?"

"I certainly did," Florence told him. "In fact, we used to haul lobster traps with our little dinghy. Rules weren't so strict then. We ate lots of lobster and clams."

"Cool," Connor said. "Can we haul traps from our sailboat, Dad?" He slipped his hand into his father's larger one.

"A sailboat's not the best boat for that," Alan said. "But we can work on getting you a student license." Students were allowed to run a limited number of traps.

"I want one, too," Alice said. She slapped her brother's shoulder. "Tag. You're it." The two of them tore off toward the lighthouse, screaming.

Walking beside me, Bella rolled her eyes and muttered something. I thought she said, "Always the hero." She turned to me with a bright, fake smile. "Want to go to the yacht club for a drink later? I'm meeting Lance."

Despite the snark a moment ago, her voice dipped in volume when she said her date's name. I glanced toward Alan, who was laughing with Grammie and Florence. Interesting.

"Sounds good," I said. "Let me see if Ian wants to go." We'd tentatively planned to hang out tonight after volunteer duties. Ian and Jake had finished washing for the night and were now back on the ground.

While Bella went into the lighthouse, I walked over to where they were packing up equipment. "How'd it go?"

Ian squinted up at the gleaming white tower. "Pretty good. We'll prep the other side tomorrow, then start painting the day after. You find anything good inside?"

I thought of the letter, but only said, "We found one of Florence's old aprons and she basically gave it to us for the museum."

His heartwarming grin broke across his face. "That's the way to your heart, for sure."

The gang had reached the upper room of the lighthouse and were now spilling out onto the circular deck. Sophie waved at Jake, her long hair hanging down like Rapunzel. "Hey, sweet prince. I'm waiting for you." Jake threw down a tool and bolted toward the tower to join her.

Ian pointed. "Going up?"

My belly immediately clenched with dread. Heights were not my thing, and the lighthouse had a dizzying spiral staircase built of open metalwork.

He stepped closer, his delicious scent of clean

cotton, spicy aftershave, and healthy male engulfing me. "I'll be right behind you. I won't let you fall."

My phobia wasn't about falling, exactly. More like my primitive reptile brain wouldn't let me climb when I could see the ground below. I was fine on normal stairs. I licked my lips. "I'll try." I hated to be held captive to this or any fear.

I kept my gaze firmly straight ahead as we climbed, step after step, Ian warm at my back. Right there in case I slipped. My heart hammered in relief when we reached the top landing and entered the optic room, where the light rotated day and night through a Fresnel lens. Such a simple mechanism, but vital for travelers. Each lighthouse had its own pattern of flashes that informed mariners where they were on the coast.

Florence and her great-grandchildren were looking out at the wide blue water. "During World War Two," she said, "my daddy and I used to watch for German U-boats out there." Connor and Alice appeared fascinated, staring at the water as though expecting a submarine to surface.

By the time Florence was an adult, she had lived through two wars back-to-back. This realization made me even more reluctant to bring up the letter. What kinds of scars did those experiences leave?

"My father told me German spies landed up the coast," Grammie said.

"Real spies?" Connor yelped. "Wow."

As they chatted about World War II Maine, Ian pulled me back against his chest and kissed the top of my hair. "What are you doing later, babe?" he asked, arms wrapped around me.

"Going to the yacht club for a drink. And after that"—I smiled up at him—"maybe you have something in mind."

He kissed me on the tip of my nose. "Oh yeah. I most certainly do."

The yacht club was on the north side of the harbor, at the end of a street lined with lovely old homes. The club building was simple, a rambling wooden structure built in 1911, with a hip roof and wide verandas overlooking the docks.

I slid into a parking space, noticing that the lot was only half-full. Since the club was members only, the bar and limited restaurant didn't get traffic like the local restaurants did. Tonight we were Madison's guests, since her parents were members.

Ian's truck rumbled down the drive and pulled in right beside me. We met next to my car for a long kiss and snuggle, and then, his arm around my shoulders, we strolled toward the club. Freshly showered, he smelled extra delicious after a detour home to his apartment over the garage at his parents' bed-and-breakfast.

Headlights announced the arrival of Madison and Bella in the Mini, followed by Jake's truck. Ian and I lingered on the veranda by the main entrance, waiting for them to join us. My gaze fell on a poster announcing sunset cruises on the schooner *Lucy Ann*.

"Oh, I want to go on one of those," I said, imagining the romance of sipping wine while big white sails billowed overhead, carrying us past islands in the bay. How relaxing and restorative, just what I needed right now.

Ian peered over my shoulder at the poster. "I'll buy us tickets, then."

"Tickets to what?" Jake asked as he and Sophie trod up the wide stairs. After taking in the poster, he turned to his fiancée. "Want to go on a cruise?"

Sophie laughed, rubbing her hands up and down her

arms. She was wearing short sleeves and the evening air had a bite. "Only if we can sail right out of *here*."

Jake's brows rose at her shrill tone, so unusual for my placid-natured friend. I stepped in. "Talk to your mother tonight?" Warm enough in my knit top and jeans, I handed her my cardigan. Vintage pink cashmere adorned with crystal buttons.

"Just got off a call with her." Sophie arranged the sweater around her shoulders with a smile of thanks. "I promised I'd check this place out tonight. Hopefully that will keep her at bay."

"We can do that," I said, waving as Madison and Bella came across the parking lot. They'd also gone home to change, and both wore pretty tops with jeans and sandals.

"Hey, Madison," I said as they climbed the steps. "Is Anton coming?" She had been seeing the chief of police for several months now, a record for my best friend, who had dated way too many frogs—guys who looked good on dating apps, but in real life, not so much.

She shook her head, making turquoise bead earrings swing. "He's on duty tonight." She pouted briefly before breaking into a grin. "But we're meeting for breakfast at the Bean." The anticipation in her voice told me that all was well with the pair.

"The best place in town," Sophie quipped about her restaurant.

We trooped inside, entering a wood-paneled foyer lined with cases of trophies and photographs from days of old. Crossed oars guarded the archway into the front dining room. Wide, worn boards creaked as we passed under the arch.

Except for a party of four, the dining room was empty, with most of the action out on the lighted deck, where a guitarist played. Kyle Quimby, Bella's neighbor, was behind the bar, which wasn't that unusual around here, where many people had two—or more—jobs. He nodded a greeting, and the lone woman sitting on a stool turned to look. Gretchen, from the dentist's office. She almost smiled at me, but when she noticed Bella, she turned abruptly and stared into her draft beer.

Down a few seats, an older man in a yachting cap was standing at the bar, one foot up on the rail. Ian clapped him on the shoulder. "Captain Greg. How's it going?"

Captain Greg chuckled. "Still vertical, last I checked." He glanced up and down his own body as if making sure he was upright, then chuckled again.

Madison was signing our names in the log on the bar. "Go ahead and order," she said. After reading the blackboard, I chose a drink special called a Blueberry Cove, made with gin, Lillet Blanc, and Prosecco.

"Hey, did I tell you?" Captain Greg asked Ian. "Old Navy buddy of mine said he has a foghorn motor we should look at." Ian and Jake had been restoring some of the old lighthouse equipment.

"Awesome," Ian said. "How much is he asking? Do you know?"

Captain Greg made a scoffing sound. "He doesn't want a dime for it." He picked up his beer mug and took a healthy swig. "Says he's honored to return it to its rightful home." Captain Greg's friend wasn't the only generous one. Once word got out about the museum, items that once belonged to this lighthouse were returning from attics, garages, and barns.

A door to the deck opened and a tall man with blond hair entered, dressed in shorts, boat shoes, and a faded red sweatshirt. At first I thought it was Lance Pedersen, but then his features slotted into place and I recognized his brother Peter, my dentist.

"Hey, Peter, how was it?" Kyle didn't pause as he poured wine and dispensed beer for our group.

"Not bad until the wind died," Peter said with a laugh. "I had to ghost into shore." "Ghosting" referred to techniques used in light winds to keep a boat moving.

Gretchen slid off her stool but instead of going to stand beside her boss, she made a wide berth around us all and headed out of the room, probably toward the restroom. I didn't blame her. Who wanted to run into their employer after hours, especially while drinking? I put a hand to my cheek, thinking about the discomfort I'd noticed while eating tonight. My new filling wasn't quite right. But now wasn't the time or place to mention it. Maybe it would get better after I chewed some more.

"You didn't use the motor?" Kyle muddled blueberries in a shaker for my drink. I loved the word "muddle."

Peter leaned on the bar, propping himself with both hands. "I challenge myself not to. But if I thought I was going to spend the night out there, I would probably break down and fire it up."

Kyle poured gin, Lillet, and syrup into the shaker, then added ice. Seeing me watching, he grinned while making some fancy moves with the shaker. "Tastes better that way," he said, pouring the mixture into a tall glass. He filled it with Prosecco, added a few blueberries, then slid it across the bar. "Try it."

I lifted the glass to my lips. Sweet, light, and frothy. "Yum. I love it."

He gave me a thumbs-up. "That recipe was developed by Sara Bond, a good friend of mine and a fantastic bartender. I told her I wanted a signature drink for the club."

"It's perfect. Tell her I said so." I turned to Ian. "Ready?"

Carrying our drinks, we left the bar in a group and headed for the deck doors. Sophie fell into step beside me. "I really don't think this place is right for my reception." She wrinkled her nose. "It's too rustic."

"I see what you mean." The space was reminiscent of a summer camp, attractive in its own right but more functional than fancy.

Ian opened the French door for us and we filed past. Derek Quimby, the mechanic, was on his way in, holding an empty beer mug. "Hey, Bella," he said, shifting from foot to foot. "I've got your part coming. Should be here tomorrow. Or the next day."

"Great, Derek," she said, rolling her eyes at the delay. "I hope it wasn't expensive."

"Not too bad," he said. "I know where to get good discounts." He stepped aside. "Let me get out of your way."

"We're looking for Lance Pedersen," Bella said. "Have you seen him?"

Derek scowled, jerking a thumb over his shoulder. "Unfortunately, yes. He's sitting in the back corner of the deck." Hunching his shoulders, he made his way past us and inside. Interesting. Did he not like Lance or was he yet another male enamored of Bella?

Bella was in front so we let her lead on. She stopped dead in front of me and I bumped into her, almost spilling my precious drink. "I do not believe this," she said in a low and deadly tone.

Sophie, whose view wasn't blocked, grabbed my arm. "Uh-oh."

Bella charged forward again, practically running

toward a table at the far end of the deck. I squinted at the occupants sitting there, a man and a woman, their faces lit only by a flickering battery candle. The woman had her arm wrapped around the man's neck.

"Nice," Bella was saying, loud enough that the whole deck could hear. People stopped chatting to listen and even the guy on the guitar gave it a rest. "Really nice. Is this what you wanted to talk about tonight?"

The man jumped to his feet and I saw it was Lance Pedersen. He put up both hands. "Bella. It's not what you think."

The woman smiled up at Bella with a sly, catlike smirk. "I wouldn't be so sure, Lance. We have no idea what Bella is thinking."

Moving closer, I recognized Donna Dube, police department dispatcher and sailing instructor. The latter must be how she knew Lance. The question is, how *well* did she know him? They had looked pretty cozy.

"You got that right," Bella said. In a sudden move, she flung the contents of her wineglass at Lance, which hit him square in the face.

CHAPTER 5

What did you do that for?" A spluttering Lance wiped white wine off his face with the back of his hand. But Bella didn't answer. She spun on her heel and bolted back into the building.

"Let me help you with that, honey." Donna dabbed at Lance's skin with a napkin.

"I don't get it," he said, plunking back into his seat. "Why is she angry? I had no idea she was so volatile." Donna made soothing noises.

Oh yes, Bella had a temper, rarely seen but volcanic. I turned to Madison and Sophie. "We need to go after her." With an apologetic smile at Ian, I reversed my route and hurried back inside, followed by my friends.

"She went that way," Kyle said, pointing toward the ladies' room. Captain Greg and Peter looked up in curiosity then returned to their discussion. Gretchen hadn't returned to her stool and her drink sat at her place still half full.

A brief worry about her flitted through my mind but was pushed aside by my more urgent mission. The restrooms were down a short corridor between the dining room and a function room. I pushed open the swinging door. "Bella?"

"I'm in here," came the muffled response. When

we squeezed inside, we saw her standing at the sink, hands propped on the edge. "I can't believe I did that." In the mirror, her reflection was wide-eyed, almost haunted. Her olive skin was washed out and pale in the bathroom's harsh light.

"You think it was all innocent?" Madison asked, skepticism heavy in her voice.

Bella shook her head. "No, I don't. But I'm mad at myself for losing my temper." She pushed back her hair with a trembling hand. "It was like a flashback to the situation with Alan."

"Totally understandable," I said. Seeing Lance with another woman was like a reprise of Alan's betrayal. And if Lance knew about Bella's traumatic experience, his behavior was even more despicable.

Sophie's face twisted in distress. "I thought you two were great together." Her fingers went to her diamond engagement ring, turning it around on her finger, over and over. Tenderhearted Sophie, so much in love, wanted to see happy endings for everyone.

"Me too," Bella said with emphasis. "We were supposed to go away after Labor Day. He said he was booking rooms at the Bar Harbor Inn and Spa." She sighed. "I was so looking forward to a spa vacation." Tears pooled in her eyes and began to spill over. "And I was starting to care for him. Darn it, why do I always fall for the bad boys? What's wrong with me?"

Madison plucked tissues out of a box and pressed them into Bella's hand. "Not a thing. It isn't us, it's them." Her lips curved in a wry smile. "As they often tell us."

"Madison is right," Sophie said. "You're a wonderful, beautiful woman, Bella. Any man would be lucky to have you."

"You'll find the right person," I said with optimism.

"Someone who will never, ever cheat on you." The only upside of this situation was that it might reinforce her hesitation about giving Alan another chance. Once burned and all that.

"Aw, you guys are so great." With a sniff, Bella wiped her eyes, then peered at her reflection. "Gosh, I look horrible. Let me fix my face and then we'll go have our drinks." Her glance fell on the empty wineglass sitting on the counter. "After I get a refill."

"What if, um, *he's* still out there?" Sophie's brow creased in concern.

Bella blew out air in a rude noise. "I'm over it." She fished a lipstick out of the tiny handbag slung around her shoulders. "He can take a good look at what he just lost." She began to spread a dark, creamy red on her lips, using the assured movements of a woman applying war paint. Poor Lance. He was going to be toast by the time she got through with him.

But Lance and Donna were gone, I discovered when we joined Ian and Jake at a large table near the deck rail. The guitarist was wailing away, giving his nasal rendition of R.E.M.'s "Everybody Hurts."

"Poor choice, buddy," I muttered, sliding into an empty chair beside Ian. "What happened after we left?" I whispered to him, seeing that Bella was chatting happily with Jake and Sophie about the wedding. On my other side, Madison leaned closer to hear.

Ian curled his top lip. "After he got cleaned up, they decided to scoot. I think he wanted to stay but Donna practically pushed him out of here." He tipped his chin toward their table, where two glasses still sat. "I don't even think they finished their drinks."

"That *is* a hasty retreat," Madison said. She looked at my glass. "How is the Blueberry Cove?"

"Delicious," I said. I'd been drinking it slowly, savoring each sip, since I didn't usually drink gin on a weeknight. Or on the weekend, either. One was good; two, a recipe for a headache.

Kyle emerged from the building, holding a tray under one arm. He began to move about the deck clearing empties and checking if anyone wanted something else. Most people gave headshakes of refusal and the place began to thin out, maybe because the singer was driving them away. He had now segued into "Against the Wind," and I was tempted to make a request—that he call it a night.

The bartender stopped by the table, standing between Ian and me. "Anyone want a refill?" We all looked at one another. No one wanted another drink.

"We're good," Ian said. "About ready to head out."

But Kyle lingered, his gaze on the empty table where Lance and Donna had been sitting. A bitter expression crossed his face. "Good old Lance. He hasn't changed a bit." His eyes shifted to Bella, who was laughing at something Madison said. "Still an idiot."

Tell us how you really feel. I finished the Blueberry Cove, sliding the tart blueberries at the bottom of the glass into my mouth. I sympathized with him, though. It must be tough to watch all the adulation and love Lance received when it should have come Kyle's way as well. If he hadn't blown it by getting kicked off the sailing team.

"I was going to ask how it was seeing your old sailing partner," Ian said lightly. "But I guess it's a sore subject."

With a shrug, Kyle picked up Ian's empty beer glass. "All water over the dam. *I'm* fine but I hate to see him tromping on people's feelings. Not cool, you know?"

"I get it," Ian said. "But what can you do?"

Kyle muttered something as he lifted the laden tray. "Have a good night, folks."

"Ready?" Ian asked, putting a hand on my knee. "I'll meet you at the house." Our plan was to hang out at my place. The summer had been so busy, time together was rare—and cherished.

After saying good night to everyone, we headed out, Ian following Beverly in his truck. The farm was a mile or so from the center of town, and soon we were pulling up the drive and parking beside the barn. Footsteps crunching on gravel, we strolled toward the sweet little Cape Cod that had been in my family for almost two hundred years. I'd spent my childhood here, and after a decade living in Rhode Island and Portland, Maine, I was back.

"Want to sit on the porch?" I suggested. One of my favorite spots was the hanging swing on the back porch overlooking Grammie's flower gardens. As we crossed the footpath through the flower beds, a patch of daylilies rustled. With a meow, Quincy came running toward me. "Hey, Quince." I scooped him up for a snuggle. "Were you waiting for me?"

Ian settled on the swing, and after handing him the cat, I went inside to grab ice water and a couple of those chocolate chip cookies. As I was popping the top on the plastic container, Grammie came into the kitchen, dressed in a robe.

"Did you have a nice time at the club?" she asked, reaching for the teakettle. She liked to drink herbal tea before bed.

"Pretty good," I said. "Except for a little drama." Mindful of Ian waiting, I only gave her the highlights about the scene with Lance and Bella.

Grammie tutted as she opened a tea bag and placed it in a mug. "I'm sorry to hear that about Lance. But better she find out now than down the road." Unspoken was the word "again." "She needs someone nice. Maybe not as flashy, but with a good and loyal heart."

I kissed her on the cheek. "You mean like Papa?" My grandfather had been a total peach. Unfortunately, we'd lost him last winter, his illness precipitating my move home. "He's my gold standard."

"I was a very lucky woman," Grammie said. "Don't think I didn't realize that. But when emotions get involved, good judgment often goes out the window."

"Papa was lucky, too," I said, placing the plate of cookies on a tray. "And he knew it." I added two tall glasses of well water.

Grammie smiled. "See you in the morning, sweetie." The kettle whistled and she poured steaming water into her mug.

Ian, Quincy, and I sat on the swing, gently rocking back and forth, listening to the sound of crickets in the grass. A hazy half-moon hung in the sky.

"I bought us tickets for the schooner sunset cruise," Ian said. "We're going later this week."

"You did?" I turned to him, upsetting our rhythm for a moment. With a laugh I used my foot to straighten us out. "What a nice surprise."

His eyes twinkled. "But wait, there's more." After a brief hesitation to torture me, he said, "I bought a ticket for Anne, too. I thought she'd enjoy it." Another pause. "I hope you don't mind."

"Of course not." I threw my arms around him. "That is so thoughtful. Thank you." While some women might resent bringing their grandmother along on a date, I was thrilled.

She needed a treat as much as I did, if not more. "I can't wait to tell her." As I planted a fervent kiss of gratitude on his lips, I reflected that Grammie wasn't the only one who'd found a good man.

My ringing cell phone woke me way too early the next morning. Outside the window, the birds were going nuts and the sky still had the gray tint of dawn. Quincy opened one eye, glaring at me as though to say, *Aren't you going to get that?*

I reached for my phone, which was on the nightstand. My fingers fumbled and it fell to the floor with a clunk. Facedown, of course. Flipping over on my stomach, I stretched my hand out and managed to pick it up.

Bella. She never, ever called me this time of day. My thoughts immediately went to the kids. And Florence. Oh, how I hoped something wasn't wrong with her. At her age, you never knew. "Hello?" I said, fear squeezing my chest. "Is everything all right?"

Bella gave a sob. "Iris. It's so awful. You must help me."

I sat upright, the movement shifting Quincy, who gave a mew of discontent. "What is it?"

The answer was a garbled word that sounded like *Lance.* That couldn't be right. Even if she were heartbroken, she wouldn't wake me up to talk about it.

"Lance," she said again. "He's dead."

"What?" My voice rose to a shriek. Quincy jumped off the bed and bolted. "What are you talking about?"

The sobbing returned, softer this time. "He's *dead.* Hit with my loaner car. The Beast."

CHAPTER 6

My mind wasn't working correctly. What did she mean, the *Beast* hit Lance? That was an odd way to put it, since someone had obviously been at the wheel. Cold sweat trickled down my spine. Had it been Bella? Was she calling me to confess?

"Bella," I said, forcing calmness into my voice. "Please, tell me what happened."

In between sobs, she stuttered out the story. Someone had stolen the Beast from her driveway and had hit Lance with it while he was taking an early morning run. He'd been on a loop that led up Bella's street and along the top of the hill, where there were very few houses but spectacular ocean views. Then the driver had abandoned the Jeep and run away.

"How do you know all this?" I asked. "Did the police tell you?"

"No, I haven't talked to them yet." She swallowed audibly. "Alan called me. He came across . . . him." Her teeth began to chatter.

I pictured the scene with a shudder of revulsion. And why had Alan been driving around so early in the morning, only to happen on the scene of a crime? I hopped out of bed. "Don't move. Don't talk to anyone else. I'm coming over." I flew to my closet and chose the first dress I saw and riffled through my bureau for underclothes. Sandals went on my feet, and a quick face wash and a tug of the comb through my hair was the extent of my grooming.

Grammie opened her bedroom door as I left my bedroom. "Iris? Is something wrong?" She was usually the first one up in the morning.

My sandal heels squeaked when I slid to a halt. "Yes, something terrible." I told her what I knew, which wasn't much. "I'm going to Bella's. She needs my support." I lurched into action. "Call you later."

Halfway down the stairs, I heard her shout, "Call Cookie." Catherine Abernathy, a local attorney. "Cookie" was her nickname, short for "tough cookie." Good idea, although I hoped Bella wouldn't need a lawyer. Why would she? She hadn't been driving.

But who had? And why had they used the Beast, of all vehicles, especially since it had already been loaned out to Bella? A chill raised the hair on my arms. Was someone trying to *frame* Bella?

I didn't stop in the kitchen to make coffee, which for anyone who knows me is a definite indication of my distress. I needed my coffee in the morning or else I didn't even feel human. Instead, I grabbed my handbag and raced out the back door, a forlorn Quincy watching me go. "Grammie will feed you," I assured him.

Beverly started right up, and within moments I was on the main road heading into town. The sun was only now nudging the horizon, creating streaks of orange across the sky. It was another beautiful day, but to me it felt like a waking nightmare.

Lance is dead. My belly jolted every time the thought crossed my mind. I couldn't believe it. Only last night he was so vibrant and alive, if acting like a royal jerk.

I slowed when I got into downtown, mindful of the speed limit and possible pedestrians out and about. Lights were on in the Belgian Bean as Sophie prepared to open at seven. I turned up Bella's street, passing quiet morning houses.

No cars were in Bella's driveway, which probably meant the police hadn't come to question her yet. I pulled in and shut off the engine, then gathered my handbag. To be thoughtful of neighbors, I shut the car door softly and hurried toward the side door, which led into Bella's kitchen.

"Iris," a soft voice called. "What's going on?"

I whirled around to see Kyle standing near the hedge, scratching at his unshaven chin. He was barefoot, dressed in shorts and a ragged T-shirt. Before I could frame an answer I wanted to give, he said, "I heard sirens earlier. And I see the Beast is gone. Is Bella okay?"

Not really, but of course I didn't say that. "She's fine. What are you doing up so early?"

He shrugged. "Sometimes I can't sleep. Even when I go to bed late, after closing the bar." The dark circles under his eyes and his general air of fatigue bolstered his claim.

I gestured toward the back door of the house. "Hate to be rude, but I've got to go." Without giving him a chance to ask more questions, I continued up the drive to the entrance, where I let myself in.

"Bella?" I crossed the mudroom and entered the kitchen, beautifully restored in the bungalow style, with tall cabinets and hanging Art Deco light fixtures over the island.

"I'm right here." Bella appeared in the doorway to the dining room. "Want coffee?" Without waiting for an answer, she went to the coffee maker and filled a mug for me. Her face was pale and her eyes red-rimmed, but the panic and upset I'd witnessed during our call were gone. It was as though she were resigned to whatever came next. "I'm so grateful the kids aren't home. But I'm certainly not looking forward to telling them about this. They both liked Lance."

"I don't blame you," I said, dropping my handbag to the floor and then perching on the next stool. "It's absolutely horrible." I glanced around, realizing something was missing. "Where's Pello?" Bella's Great Pyrenees would normally have come to greet me, slobbering tongue and all.

"He's at the resort." Bella sniffed, then reached for a tissue. "The kids wanted him and Alan didn't object, even if he did have to pay extra."

Another vote in Alan's favor, I reluctantly conceded. But the dog's absence explained why the thief had been able to steal the Jeep. I said as much.

"You're right," Bella said. "Normally Pello would have barked his head off if someone came into the yard." She bit her bottom lip, tears filling her eyes. "I just can't believe Lance is gone. He was so full of life, with so much to look forward to." Her mouth twisted in a rueful grimace. "Even if not with me."

A note of warning chimed in my mind. After the very public fight last night and the theft of her rental vehicle, Bella was going to be *the* prime suspect. "Bella, you need to call Grammie's attorney, Cookie Abernathy. Like right now. This minute." I slapped the counter in emphasis.

Bella's brows rose. "An attorney? Why? I didn't do anything. I haven't left the house since I got home last night."

"I know," I said, hoping I could get her to take this

seriously. "But someone used a car that you had access to and killed someone."

"But surely it was an accident? Someone didn't see him in the dark, then got scared and ran off." She gave a sharp nod, as if this was the only scenario that made sense.

I inhaled deeply, hoping I could get her to understand the jeopardy she was in. "That may be true. But Bella, I hate to say this: they are going to think it was you behind the wheel. The Beast was in your possession—at least until whoever hit Lance took it."

Frowning, she put a hand on her chest. "Me? Why would I go out driving around so early in the morning?"

I'd already thought of a reason. "To meet Alan, maybe? Why was he on that road?" Again I thought how strange that he'd happened along and found the man Bella was dating. Had been dating, I amended.

Bella shrugged. "Maybe Alan planned to stop and look at the sunrise? A lot of people do that." She was right, since there was a spectacular vista of the bay and islands from up there. After decades of people congregating in that spot, the town had given up and made it an official overlook, with a trash can and rocks lining the parking area.

"Please, Bella," I said, pleading in my voice. "Call Cookie. It's better to have an attorney and not need one than the reverse."

She huffed a little but picked up her phone. "All right. Give me the number."

I scrolled through my contacts and found the number, then read it aloud. While she placed the call, I focused on drinking my coffee. The first surge of adrenaline had ebbed, leaving me groggy.

Bella got voice mail, as to be expected this early, but

left a message. "I might be done with the police by the time she gets that," she said after disconnecting.

"No, she'll call back—" My smile was a touch smug when Bella's phone rang, interrupting me. "She's really good." Cookie had helped Grammie when she'd been a suspect in a murder last spring.

After hanging up, Bella said, "She said to call if the police get ready to question me." Her expression was rueful. "And not to say anything until she gets there. You were right, Iris, thank you."

"What are friends for?" Making attorney referrals, apparently. Hopefully they would figure out who had been driving soon and Bella would be off the hook. Then I had a thought. "Where do you suppose the driver went?"

"They could have gone anywhere," Bella said. "The hillside is covered with trails, some official and some just cut-through. The kids and I walk in there all the time."

I brought up a map of the area on my phone. She was right, a maze of official walking paths had been created in the undeveloped area, with egress from a couple of residential streets and the lane on top of the hill. I pictured the driver hitting Lance with the Beast, realizing he was dead, and then escaping through the woods. To the casual observer, he or she would have probably looked like an early morning walker. If anyone had been awake and saw the driver, that is.

My heart gave a painful lurch as a police SUV, blue and white lights flashing, pulled into the drive beside Beverly. Anton, the police chief, and Officer Rhonda Davis climbed out. The fact that the chief was here told me that they were looking seriously at Bella as a suspect. Otherwise he would have sent two patrol officers.

Bella appeared frozen in place at the island so I went

to answer their knock. "Iris," Anton said, squaring his bulky shoulders. "Is Bella here?" He was a good cop, dedicated and fair. But the uneasy expression in his dark eyes told me that he wasn't enjoying his job right now. Bella was his friend, too.

"She is. In the kitchen." Holding the door wide, I stood back to let them in.

"What brought *you* here this morning?" Rhonda asked as she walked past, her heavy boots clomping on the Italian tile.

I didn't take offense. Under the circumstances, they had to ask. "Moral support," I said. "Bella called me."

Anton's eyes met mine, an assessing stare. "So you know."

"Only a little," I replied. "I know that Lance Pedersen was killed in a hit-and-run this morning. And the driver is missing." Although I liked and trusted Anton, had known him since high school, my heart began to race. It was the same feeling you get when a cruiser tails you on the road—times ten.

Bella stood by the island, one hand clutching her white robe at the neck. "I can't talk to you," she blurted. "My attorney said so." No one ever said Bella wasn't a fast learner.

"Okay," Anton said slowly. "Right now there is only one thing I want to confirm." Hope flared in Bella's eyes, then faded when he added, "Before we question you at the station."

"What is it?" she asked, her voice hoarse. She backed up to the island as if to lean on it for support.

Anton nodded at Rhonda, who pulled out her notes and read, "Were you in possession of a 1999 Jeep Cherokee, Maine plate number—" She read off the plate digits.

Bright spots flared in Bella's cheeks. "I am, I mean,

I *was*. I borrowed it from Quimby's Garage. There's a sticker in the window saying so, as you must know. Someone stole—"

I made a chopping motion with my hand. "Bella," I barked. "Wait for Cookie."

She put a hand to her mouth as though to stop the flow of words. "Sorry. Yes, I will." She glared at Anton and Rhonda. "That's it. No more questions." The proud, imperious native of Milan, Italy, was back, in spades. "I assume you will let me dress before you take me away?"

"Please do," Anton said wryly. "But make it quick, okay?"

"Iris, I have a favor to ask," Bella said. "Will you go out to the resort and take the children to their sailing lessons? Since Alan and I are going to be busy for a while." She looked at Anton. "I assume Alan is being questioned as well?"

He answered with a nod.

"Of course I'll do that," I said, although the idea of seeing the children and Florence right now made wince. What was I going to tell them? I certainly didn't want to be the one who broke the news about Lance's death or the fact that Bella was being questioned.

"The lessons start at eight," Bella said, glancing at the stove's digital display. "So maybe head out now?"

I swallowed the rest of my coffee and picked up my bag. "I sure will." I gave her a quick hug. "Hang in there. And keep me posted."

Her body was trembling, betraying how nervous she was. "I'll call you as soon as I can."

Before pulling out of Bella's drive, I called Grammie on my cell. After telling her about the arrival of the police, I said, "I might be late getting to the store.

I'm going to take Alice and Connor to the yacht club for their sailing lessons." I couldn't hold back a gut-wrenching sigh. "I'm so worried about Bella."

"Have faith," Grammie said, her voice comforting. "You and I know she had nothing to do with Lance's death."

"Oh, and Cookie *is* going to represent her, so that's good." It wasn't that I didn't trust our local force. But in Maine, suspicious deaths fell under the jurisdiction of the state police. Right now the evidence pointed to Bella, and my worry was that the state detective wouldn't look any further.

I inhaled a deep breath, trying to release my troubled emotions. "Anyway, I'll see you at the store later this morning." My belly chose that moment to rumble, reminding me I hadn't eaten breakfast. "Can you please bring me something to eat? I'm starving."

"I certainly will," she promised. "See you then."

We disconnected, and after firing off update texts to Madison and Sophie, including telling them I would be on the road for a while, I set off for the resort. The hotel was located about five miles north of town, so I cut through the back streets to the state route. As I passed by Quimby's Garage, I wondered if Derek knew that his loaner vehicle had been involved in a hit-and-run.

One thing I hadn't asked Bella was about the Jeep's keys. Had she left them inside the Beast overnight? Even though she lived in a low-crime area, I doubted that. We might leave our cars unlocked in Blueberry Cove, but we didn't generally leave our keys in the ignition. Why make it easy for a curious teenager to take a joyride? That was the typical level of crime around here—Bella would never have expected *this*.

My assumption about the keys begged the question. How had someone managed to steal the Beast? How did they get a key? Or was it hot-wired? A 1999 vehicle was probably old enough to make that possible.

This time of day, Route 1 was quiet, mostly delivery trucks and a few people commuting to work. Most of the businesses were shuttered, antiques stores and restaurants and tourist traps. Dunkin' Donuts was hopping, though, and on impulse I pulled into the drive-through for another coffee and a Boston Kreme. This raised donut delight was filled with custard and topped with chocolate frosting, and no, you did not want to know the calorie count. They were wicked good, as Mainers say, a decent nod to the regional dessert, Boston Cream Pie.

The resort entrance loomed up on the right, two stone pillars and a giant sign. I dabbed the last of the cream off my mouth and turned into the winding drive. This led between rolling lawns landscaped with clumps of slim birches and flower beds. Around the last curve, the main building came into view, white four-story wings flanking the original section built in 1902.

I found a space in visitor parking after realizing I didn't know the suite number. And I certainly wasn't going to call Bella right now and ask. As I walked toward the main entrance, my phone chirped with an announcement. Someone had sent a text.

Oh good, maybe Bella had remembered the oversight about the room number. But when I stopped to read it, I saw it was from Alan.

They arrested Bella.

CHAPTER 7

I stopped dead under the front entrance canopy, staring at the text and trying to absorb its message. *Bella. Arrested.* How could that be? When I'd left her house fifteen or twenty minutes ago, they were only going to question her.

Ignoring the curious glances from guests exiting through the automatic doors, I dialed Alan. He answered immediately. "I really can't talk," he said. In the background, I heard voices and the bustle of activity. I guessed he was at the police station.

"I won't keep you," I said. "But please, tell me what's going on."

"Hold on." A door squawked and footsteps echoed in a hollow-sounding room. The men's room? "The state police arrested Bella at the house. I was down here at the station for questioning when they brought her in. She barely had a chance to tell me to contact you." He drew in a shuddering breath. "Oh, Iris. It's awful." His voice broke on the last word.

In the shop, I'd glimpsed the man behind the polished façade, and now here he was again, the real Alan. I threw him a lifeline. "Has Cookie Abernathy gotten there yet? She'll straighten out this mess."

"I haven't seen her." He inhaled again. "Bella said you were going to pick up the kids and take them to sailing."

"Yes." I glanced up at four stories of pristine white clapboard and blank windows. "I'm at the resort, about ready to go inside."

"Tell my grandmother what's going on, okay? But not in front of the kids. I want to talk to them myself."

"I will," I promised. "And while I have you, what's the room number?" He gave it to me. "Check in with me later, please." My voice was cracking now. "I'll do anything to help Bella."

"You're a good friend, Iris," Alan said. "And at times like these, she needs all the friends she can get." He had that right. Being accused of a crime—guilty or not—quickly revealed who was a true friend and who wasn't.

After we disconnected, I sent status updates via text to Grammie, Madison, and Sophie while a curious parking valet watched from behind his podium. Throwing him a distracted smile, I walked past him into the spacious lobby.

There, I pointed myself toward the bank of elevators at the rear, noting that every inch of the Sunrise Resort radiated elegant, gracious living. No wonder it was so popular—and pricy. Classical music played over the sound system, attractive employees smiled at me from behind the marble-and-ebony reception desk, and a central fountain misted glittering droplets into balsam-scented air.

Meanwhile one of my best friends was downtown, being booked by the police.

The juxtaposition was jarring, and I shook my head to clear it as I pressed the UP button. The elevator doors slid open with a soft *ding*, and I was on my way upstairs.

Room 336 was down the corridor a distance, located on the side with an ocean view. *Nice.* Those rooms were much more expensive. I knocked on the door, listening for sounds of life inside. Faint sounds from a television radiated through the thick door, so I knocked a little louder. This time a familiar bark sounded. Pello. After a moment, the locks rattled and the door opened to reveal Florence, wearing a loose floral housedress and slippers. Pello tried to push past her knees but she held him back. "Oh, hello, Iris. I was expecting Bella." She gave a little laugh. "I'm not sure where Alan is. Maybe an early golf game?"

I peeked inside the suite, spotting Alice and Connor seated at the island, their gaze fixed on a television in the living area. "Bella asked me to take the kids to their sailing lessons. Can we talk for a moment? Somewhere private?"

Alarm crossed her face but she didn't question my request. Stepping back, she said, "Come on in. Want coffee?"

I really didn't, not after the large one from Dunkin Donuts, but I said yes to be polite. After greeting Pello with a pat, I said hello to the children, who barely looked away from the television show or their bowls of cereal to say hello back. Once Florence filled a mug for me, we stepped out onto a balcony overlooking the swimming pool and gardens, and beyond those, the ocean.

Setting my mug on a side table, I said, "Florence, I've got some bad news." Her body tensed but again she didn't say anything. The result of a long life full of all kind of news? Probably. "Early this morning, someone hit a man named Lance Pedersen with their vehicle."

"The Olympian?" Florence asked. "What a shame."

I shouldn't have been surprised that she'd heard of Lance. He was—had been—a household name after competing in the Olympics. "There's more." I sipped the coffee to moisten my throat. "Bella's loaner car from the garage was stolen this morning, too. And the driver hit Lance with it."

Now she gasped. "That's awful. Who was it? I hope it wasn't a teenager going for a joyride. Something like this could ruin their life."

You got that right. For a few seconds, I struggled how to frame the bad news. I finally realized there wasn't a good way to say it. "The police think Bella did it. She's been arrested."

Florence sat heavily in a wicker chair, confusion creasing her face. "Bella? Arrested? I can't get my mind around it."

"Me neither," I said. "Of course she didn't do it. But she had a connection with Lance—" Why had I said that to Alan's grandmother, of all people?

"A connection?" She looked up at me with wary eyes. "What do you mean?"

I slumped against the railing. "She went on a few dates with him, that's all. And why not? She's a divorced woman." I didn't mention the argument at the yacht club, nor did I plan to.

Florence ran a hand over her housedress to smooth it. "It's to be expected, of course. Bella is lovely. I told Alan—" To my chagrin, she stopped there and changed the subject. "So what is happening right now? Do you know?"

"Bella is down at the police station with Alan. He's the one who called and gave me the news. He also said that he wants to be the one to tell the kids." I waited until she nodded in agreement, then told her that Bella had hired Cookie Abernathy, a defense attorney. I thought about telling her that Alan had found the body, but I'd let him handle that revelation. She had enough to think about right now. "So now we wait and see," I concluded. "About Bella getting bail, et cetera. They'll be scheduling a hearing soon."

She pursed her lips, brow furrowed. "You sound like you have experience in this kind of matter."

Oh, did I ever. "It's a long story, but yes I do, unfortunately. My grandmother was falsely accused of murder last spring." I attempted a smile. "But as you can see, she's still walking around, a free woman. Cookie Abernathy was her attorney, too." I didn't tell her about the investigation my friends and I had launched to clear Grammie. Or that now we'd be doing the same for Bella. Oh yes, we would be.

"I want to meet this Cookie," Florence said. A fierce expression flashed in her eyes. "And if there is anything I can do to help Bella, let me know." She shook her head. "The day the divorce papers came through, I almost disowned Alan. What a fool he was, to destroy his beautiful family. He told me the other day that he wants to make amends. But it's probably too little, too late."

I had to agree. But, thankful that Bella had Florence's support, I didn't share my thoughts about Bella's ex-husband.

Alice looked up from her cereal bowl when we walked back inside. "Where's Mom? She was supposed to come get us this morning."

Connor slid off his chair and carried his empty bowl to the sink. "Yeah. It's almost time for our sailing lessons."

Florence and I exchanged glances. "Your mom is busy this morning," Florence said. "She sent Iris to give you a ride."

"Aww," Connor said, his mouth twisting in disappointment. "I want to see Mom."

"You will soon," I said, praying that I was telling the truth. "And guess what? I'm giving you a ride in Beverly." Both children had expressed admiration of my vintage auto in the past.

Connor perked up. "We're riding in Beverly?"

"I call shotgun," Alice said, dumping her own bowl in the sink and running toward the bedrooms.

"That's not fair. I was going to call it." Connor dashed after his sister, and the two bumped shoulders as they fought to get through a doorway first.

Florence shook her head. "Oh, for a fraction of that energy." She opened the fridge and pulled out water bottles, fruit, and individual yogurts, then packed them into lunch boxes. "They need to take their windbreakers and fleeces, in case it's cold on the water." She pointed to a coat closet, and I retrieved the garments.

The pair soon returned, teeth brushed and hair combed and carrying backpacks. After packing their outerwear into the packs, they snatched the lunch boxes off the counter and gave Florence kisses.

"Be good today," Florence said. "Listen to Iris and your instructors."

"We will," they chorused, little faces somber. "Goodbye, GG." Their nickname for great-grandmother. "Bye, Pello."

I opened the door, managing to keep the dog from following us. "Come on, guys, let's go."

Once outside the suite, the serious demeanor dropped and both raced down the corridor toward the elevators, backpacks bobbing. I plodded along behind them, wishing I had some of their youthful vitality as well.

Thankfully, they waited for me at the elevators, and with much commentary, we descended to the main floor. Everything was an adventure to these two and I liked that. We skipped and danced out to Beverly, where I broke the news to Connor that at age ten, he wasn't allowed to ride in the front seat. Alice had barely made the cutoff at twelve.

Without too many grumbles, I got them settled in and we set off for the yacht club. Golf carts now dotted the greens and the first sailboats were coasting across the bay, the waves crested with whitecaps. Another beautiful summer morning in Maine.

I turned on the radio, thinking to hear some music, only to be greeted by a newscast. "Olympian Lance Pedersen has d—" I quickly switched the radio off. Of course this was going to be all over the media. Lance was a sports celebrity.

Big ears in back said, "Lance is my teacher. I'm going to be in the Olympics, too."

Alice turned to look at her brother. "Me too. And I'm going to get there first, since I'm older."

Sibling rivalry at its best. Should I intervene? Before I could decide, Connor piped up. "So? I'm gonna learn from your mistakes."

His sister turned around with a huff, crossing her arms, and I hid a smile. Connor might be younger, but he could take care of himself.

The yacht club parking lot was pretty full, with parents dropping off children and members arriving to take boats out for the day. Deciding I needed to escort them inside, I found a parking spot down near the docks. After they gathered their packs and lunch boxes, we walked along the waterfront boardwalk to the building.

With every step, my anxiety grew. It was inevitable that the news about Lance's death would spread like wildfire through the club—and that Bella was the prime suspect involved. Maybe Alice and Connor should avoid the club for a while.

But then a little boy on the porch waved and shouted their names, echoed by several other children. Alice and Connor both sped up to join their friends, leaving me to hurry behind them.

The first adult I spotted was Kyle Quimby, knee-deep in young 'uns. He picked up the whistle he wore around his neck. "When you hear me blow this, it's time to line up and go down to the docks." He pointed at Alice and Connor. "Stash your packs and lunch but bring your windbreakers. It's pretty breezy today."

"I take it that you're teaching today," I said to Kyle.

He ran a hand through his curly locks. "Yeah, me and Donna." He had dark circles under his eyes, and his complexion had a greenish tinge. "We're going to do our best to keep things normal for the kids."

A little boy tugged at Kyle's shorts. "Where's Lance? Isn't he coming?"

Kyle gave him a closed-mouth smile. "I'm afraid not, Billy. I'm your instructor today. I used to sail with Lance, so I know my stuff."

"Oh, okay." Billy seemed to accept that, and he turned away to shout something at one of his friends.

Donna emerged from the building, handing Kyle coffee in a paper cup. She looked equally tired and upset, although she smiled when she saw me. Then her glance fell on Alice and Connor headed our way, and the smile dropped from her face.

Of course Donna knew about Bella's arrest. She worked for the police department. They rotated shifts, so she must be on nights.

"She didn't do it," I blurted. Kyle and Donna stared at me but I couldn't read the expressions in their eyes. Then Alice and Connor reached us and the moment was lost.

"Are you going to watch us sail?" Connor asked me. "Mom usually does."

"She goes down to the docks and waves to us when we cast off," Alice added. "She doesn't leave until we are out of sight."

Who would ever have the heart to deny them, especially right now? "I'd love to watch you sail," I said. "I used to take lessons when I was your age. Probably in those same boats." The club used JC 9s and 420s, classic sailing dinghies.

"How long ago was that?" Connor asked, studying me with dubious eyes.

"The Stone Age," I quipped, making Kyle laugh. "Seriously, your mother and I are about the same age."

"She's thirty-five," Alice said with a sigh. "So old."

Now all the adults laughed. "I'd better start getting these kids in line," Kyle said.

Donna gulped down her coffee. "Meet you down at the docks? I need to hit the head before we go out." "Head" was boating lingo for restroom.

I leaned against the porch rail and watched as Kyle herded the youngsters into lines, had them put on life jackets, and then marched them down to the docks. He did great, firm enough so they listened, but good-humored and kind, too.

My babysitting duties thus completed, I decided to stop by the restroom myself before leaving the club. This time of the morning, the building was basically deserted, except for the staff clattering around in the kitchen, preparing for lunch.

I pushed open the ladies' room door, then halted in the doorway.

Donna Dube stood at the sink, shoulders hunched as she cried loud, heart-wrenching sobs.

Chapter 8

"Sorry." I took a step backward, not wanting to intrude on a private moment.

Her head went up, red-rimmed eyes meeting mine in the mirror. "It's okay." She reached for tissues and snagged several. "I'm just upset about Lance."

Encouraged, I walked into the room, allowing the door to swing shut behind me. "I don't blame you. The whole thing is horrific."

"It sure is. I can't believe someone would do such a thing." Her vicious tone said she would gladly draw and quarter that person.

"Maybe it was an accident," I said, hoping to help her calm down. Donna had to know Bella was a suspect. Even if she wasn't on duty this morning, surely one of the other officers would have given her an update. "The driver might not have seen him in the dark. The sun wasn't really up yet."

"Ha, right." Her eyes narrowed. "Already thinking of defense strategies for your friend?" So she did know about Bella's arrest. "Good luck with that."

Denials rushed to my lips but I managed to choke them back. Anything I said—to anyone—would spread through town like wildfire. And I couldn't take the chance of hurting Bella's case, even by accident.

Donna balled up the tissues and tossed them toward the trash can, missing by inches. "I knew she was jealous. Ha, who didn't, after she threw a drink in his face? But I never thought she'd go *this* far. She went out with him, what, a half-dozen times, maybe? But Lance and I had a history." Reaching down, she picked up the used tissues and threw them away.

"A history?" I echoed. This was news to me. Lance was from Blueberry Cove, but I didn't know Donna's backstory. She was almost a decade older than me and we really hadn't crossed paths often until now.

"Yeah, we sure did." Donna turned on the taps and began washing her hands. I moved closer so I could hear over the running water. "We were serious about fifteen years ago," she continued, "before Lance started sailing around the world." Her mouth sagged into a frown. "We tried to keep a long-distance relationship going but it was just too hard." She turned the water off with firm movements and reached for paper towels. "But this summer we reconnected, and things were back on track until—until your friend ran him down." She crumpled the towels forcefully, as if they were someone she despised, then smashed them into the bin.

I moved aside fast when she barreled toward the door. Donna Dube was angry and grieving and I certainly didn't want to get in her way.

While walking through the main room a few minutes later, I saw Captain Greg sitting at a table, reading a newspaper. When he glanced up with a nod, I detoured over to his table. "How are you?" I asked.

"It's a pretty sad day around here," he said, smoothing the paper with the heel of his hand. "Big loss."

"Yes, it is." Without invitation, I pulled back a chair and perched on the edge of the seat. We sat in silence for a minute, neither of us wanting to get into it. Then I thought of another topic. Maybe I could learn more about the love letter we found in the lighthouse. "Captain Greg, I understand that you're a Korean War vet."

He lifted his mug and slurped. "I sure am. Discharged with honor after getting wounded in battle." His tone was matter-of-fact, belying the suffering and trauma he must have experienced as a wounded combat veteran.

"Thank you for your service," I said. "I'm really grateful for your sacrifices."

His whiskery cheeks pinked. "No need to say that. I did my duty, that's all." He pursed his lips. "And I least I made it home. A lot of my buddies didn't."

I took a breath and asked, "Did you know a soldier from Blueberry Cove named Chet, last name beginning with *C*?" When he frowned, seeming puzzled, I added, "I came across him while doing historical research." Which was true. "But I don't know his last name or any details about his service. The . . . document . . . didn't say."

"I knew a Chester Chapman," he said after a moment of silence. "We called him Chet. A little younger than me. Flyboy. After his plane was shot down, he was taken prisoner. In fifty-three, I think. That's all I know."

My heart sank. So many men hadn't made it home after the war. Was Florence's beau one of them? That was probably why she had married Alan's grandfather. Chet had died—or remained missing in action.

"Do you know when that was, exactly?" I asked. "The date he was captured?" If Chester Chapman had written the letter, his captivity had to occur after the date of the letter. That was one fact we could verify.

Captain Greg shook his head. "I don't. You have to

understand, I was out West for quite a while, recuperating in the hospital. A lot got by me." Disappointment must have shown on my face, because he added, "I can ask around, if you want. One of my buddies, Stan Perkins, keeps up with everybody." He grimaced. "Of course, there are fewer of us around all the time. Reunions are getting smaller every year."

So if Chet had survived the prison camp, he might have already died of old age or another cause. Chances were very slim that we could find him alive. But the stubborn part of me wasn't ready to give up.

"Could you do that, Captain Greg?" I asked. "I would really appreciate it."

He smiled. "I'd be glad to, Iris. Not many people are interested in us old fogies anymore. The Korean War seems like ancient history, especially to young folks like you."

"Thanks, Captain Greg." As I continued on my way, I reflected on the truth of his comments. Although World War II still seemed to command a lot of interest, the Korean War was barely ever mentioned.

In the entrance area, I paused to study the display cases. Behind the trophies, photographs of Lance were featured prominently, along with news articles about his Olympic victories. Older photos showed him as a beginning sailor and then as an instructor. I easily recognized Donna Dube in a class photograph from fifteen years ago. She and Lance stood behind a group of children and teens, all wearing wide grins and life jackets.

The front door opened and Kyle entered. "Hey, Iris. Sticking around to watch the class?"

"That sounds like fun," I said. "Unfortunately, I have to go to the shop." My phone had just pinged, reminding me of a scheduled interview. The advertisement in the *Herald* had already produced several applicants.

He came and stood beside me. "Good old Lance," he said. "Blueberry Cove's favorite son."

I couldn't tell if he was being sincere or sarcastic. "It's a loss for sure," I said, equally neutral. "Poor Donna is really upset." That was bait, placed to see if he'd take it.

And he did. "Oh, Donna," he scoffed. "She honestly thought Lance would go along with her do-over."

"Do-over?" I asked. "You mean their relationship? She told me they used to be involved." I pointed at the group photograph. "Back then."

"Yep," he said. "They were hot and heavy for a while." He shook his head. "But she never understood something about Lance. He was only ever out for himself." He moved away with a flap of his hand. "Duty calls. See you later."

My gaze fell on a photo of Lance and Kyle, fresh from their first Olympic race, then another of Lance and Kyle's replacement. Was Kyle right about Lance and Donna? Or had his own bitter experience colored his opinion?

CHAPTER 9

After waving goodbye to Alice and Connor, who were sitting on the docks listening to Donna, I hopped into Beverly and drove to the shop. As always, when driving past the building, I slowed to admire our window display, trying to see it as customers would. Right now it contained a model lighthouse and a family enjoying a picnic, all wearing aprons, of course. On Labor Day weekend, we would put up a back-to-school display.

In the back alley where we parked, I discovered that somehow I had arrived before Grammie. Checking the time, I saw it was only a little after nine, and we opened at ten. I felt like I'd worked a full day already.

Dragging myself out of the car, I unlocked the back door and went inside. How was I going to make it through the day ahead? Worry about Bella's situation gnawed, plus I was especially worried about her children. So far, we'd been able to keep the truth from them, but that wouldn't last long. And we were only at the beginning of the ordeal. A trial could be months away, if things went that far. What if she was denied bail? What if she was found guilty? Innocent people went to jail sometimes, didn't they?

We couldn't allow any of this to happen. With an

effort, I inhaled a deep and hopefully calming breath, calling to mind some of Grammie's hard-won wisdom. *One thing at a time. First things first.*

Right now, the first thing I needed to do was make a pot of coffee. In the side room, we'd set up a small snack area with a mini-fridge, a microwave, and a commercial Bunn coffee maker like the one we had at home. I loved the way it made piping hot and delicious java in two minutes flat.

While the coffee brewed, I started the shop computer and logged into the point-of-sale system. I loved the ability the software gave us to track sales, to see what was hot and what was not, and to analyze trends. Our kitchen category, which included cute dish towels and oven mitts, was taking off. We needed to look for more fall- and winter-themed items before the cold weather set in. People loved the cozy ritual of holiday baking.

I heard the back door open, followed by Grammie's voice as she ushered Quincy inside. "Hold your horses, young man. You'll get your snack when I'm ready." Over the past week, he had started a new morning ritual. He absolutely had to nibble on salmon treats while we drank coffee and got ready to open. Quincy was funny that way, as set in his ways as any human.

"Morning," I called as they made their way into the front room. Grammie set her tote behind the cash register, then placed a plastic container of something baked next to the coffeepot. "Ooh, what did you bring?" I reached down and patted Quincy. "Good morning, buddy." He rubbed against my ankles, purring.

"I couldn't sleep after you left, so I made a batch of applesauce cake." She popped the top, releasing a mouthwatering aroma of cinnamon, sugar, and nutmeg. "I know you like it for breakfast."

I thought ruefully of the Boston Kreme donut I'd gobbled earlier. But I always had room for applesauce cake, made from an old Betty Crocker cookbook that had belonged to Grammie's mother. So I didn't object when she placed a healthy slab onto a paper plate and handed it to me, along with a fork.

"We have a potential employee coming in for an interview this morning," I said after swallowing the first big bite of cake. "A Cathy King. Do you know her?"

Grammie shook her head. "Doesn't ring a bell." She opened the package of cat treats, which drew Quincy like a magnet. She doled out exactly six into a little dish and he began to crunch. We had to limit the addictive morsels or else he would eat them all day long.

"Well, we'll both meet her for the first time, then." I carved off another bite. "I figure I can do the interview in the side room while you wait on customers." We'd had a sliding door installed to close off that room during classes, which we hadn't started yet. On the agenda for fall, too, once things slowed down. *If* they ever slowed down.

After I finished the cake, Grammie asked, "So what is the latest with Bella?" She was so thoughtful that way, not wanting to upset me while I was eating.

"I don't know anything more than I told you earlier," I said, anxiety knotting my stomach again. "I hope Alan gives us an update soon."

"Me too." Grammie sighed. "The whole thing is so ridiculous. How could anyone think that *Bella* would run a man down?"

"The state police do," I said grimly. "Oh, let me tell you about my run-ins with Donna Dube and Kyle Quimby at the yacht club."

Someone rapped on the shop door and we turned to

look. Madison peered through the window, waving at us. Glad to see her, Quincy and I hurried to let her in. "You're just in time," I said. "I was giving Grammie the update from the yacht club."

"Bella's arrest is already all over the news." Snuggling Quincy in her arms, Madison stayed on my heels as we crossed the shop. "I have a feeling it's going to turn into a feeding frenzy." With Madison's background in marketing, she had a good nose for what might attract media attention.

"Me too," I said glumly. "I had to turn off the radio in the car because Alice and Connor were listening. They have no idea that their mother was arrested."

Grammie winced. "Those poor children." She clasped her hands together, practically wringing them in her distress. "How can we protect them? They could be scarred for life by this."

"Figure out who killed Lance," Madison said crisply. "And fast." Her gaze fell on the container of cake. "Is that applesauce cake? Yum." After setting Quincy down, she washed her hands and served herself a piece. Around a mouthful, she asked, "So what's the update from the yacht club?"

I gave them the blow-by-blow regarding my conversations with Donna and Kyle while they drank coffee, ate cake, and listened intently.

"Sounds like we have a couple of suspects," Madison said. "Not that I'm jumping to conclusions." She topped off her mug with coffee.

"I agree about Kyle," I said. "He definitely resents Lance. And who can blame him? But what would Donna's motive be?"

Madison lifted one shoulder in a shrug. "Maybe Lance lowered the boom, told her that he wasn't going to get back with her." Her mouth turned down in a frown. "It's entirely possible Bella misread the situation with Donna. Not that I'll ever say that to her."

I thought back to the previous night, when Lance had said, "It isn't what it looks like." Everyone caught red-handed said that, as if it were scripted in the cheating partner handbook. But what if he had been telling the truth? Donna had implied that she and Lance were together, but maybe she'd been the liar in this case.

"Is it possible whoever stole the Beast hit Lance by accident?" Grammie asked. "The sun wasn't fully up yet, so maybe they didn't see him."

Madison pressed her lips together and shook her head. "According to what Anton told me—and it wasn't much—they have reason to believe he was hit on purpose."

A chill fell over the room at her words. I admittedly didn't know much about forensics, but I could guess the reasons for this conclusion. A lack of skid marks showing the driver had tried to stop. Where Lance was on the road when he was hit. The speed the driver was traveling. Cars were forced to amble along that lane due to its numerous potholes and rough surface. Under normal conditions, a runner would have plenty of time to get out of the way.

Grammie opened the mini-dishwasher and placed her mug inside, then added Madison's. "On a more pleasant topic, will you be able to join us at the lighthouse tonight, Madison? We made a great start last night, and I want to keep the momentum going."

"I'll be there." Madison's dark eyes gleamed with determination. "And after we finish our work, we're going to figure out how to get Bella off the hook."

Grammie's features sagged with worry. "I sure hope so, honey."

"I *know* so," Madison declared, giving us each a

hug. "And now I've got to fly. Client meeting. See you tonight."

She strode out of the shop, leaving spicy perfume and positive energy in her wake. I was so grateful to have her on our crime-solving team. Not that we'd ever planned on having such a team in place, but desperate times called for desperate measures.

Grammie turned the store sign to OPEN, and customers began to drift in. At ten fifteen on the dot, a short, slender woman bustled through the door. Judging by the suit she was wearing and the clipboard under her arm, I guessed she was Cathy King.

The woman glanced around the shop before noticing me behind the counter. She thrust out a hand as she approached. "I'm Cathy King. Here for an interview with Iris Buckley?"

"I'm Iris," I said, shaking her hand. "And this is my grandmother, Anne Buckley." Helping a customer nearby, Grammie nodded a greeting. I ushered Cathy toward the side room. "Would you like a coffee?"

"I'd love one, although I just ate breakfast at the Belgian Bean. Have you been there? It's awesome." On and on she chattered as she followed me into the side room, while I closed the sliding doors, and over my suggestion that she sit at the table.

"Coffee?" I asked again, holding up the pot.

"Oh yes. Sorry." She wiggled around on her chair. "When I get nervous, I talk a lot." She giggled. "Well, actually, not only then. I love people." I couldn't help thinking that her grin was a trifle manic.

"That's a very good trait." I brought her a mug, along with sugar packets and the container of half-and-half. While she doctored her mug, I flipped through a folder and found the interview questions. I'd been interviewed myself many times and now it was my turn to sit on the other side of the desk, so to speak. While planning the interviews, I'd made a point of not including questions I hated. *Where do you see yourself in five years? What are your greatest strengths and weaknesses?*

I picked up a pen, ready to take notes. "Tell me about your retail experience."

Cathy laughed. "Oh, I have tons." And so it began. For a solid twenty minutes, she spewed details regarding her various jobs. Many details. Details I didn't need, like the day of the week she started working at a place. The day of the week she left. How many weeks it took her to get another job.

At first my desire not to be rude prevented me from interrupting. But as the minutes ticked by, I realized I needed to regain control of the interview. "Cathy," I said. When she continued to talk, I said her name again, much louder. "CATHY."

Silence. Then an uneasy giggle. "Oops, I'm so sorry. Did I do it again?"

This wasn't going to work. Grammie and I preferred to let customers lead conversations, not overwhelm them with our words. "I have a few more questions. Please just give me the overview, okay?" Chastened, she agreed, and I rushed through the rest of the interview.

Then I showed her out with a limp promise to "be in touch." After I closed the door behind her, I leaned back against it with a huge sigh, thankful that the store was empty at the moment.

"Didn't go well, huh?" Grammie asked. She was straightening sheets in one of the displays. "I could hear her nattering away from in here. With the doors closed."

"I didn't even get a chance to ask her about her sewing skill," I said. Maybe she'd be quiet while stitching.

"She's a nice person but . . ." I felt awful. How did people do this all the time? I couldn't stand rejecting someone even when it was the right thing to do.

"She's not the right fit, Iris," Grammie said. "No point in hiring someone if you know going in that it won't work." She shrugged. "We'll get there."

Standing aside to let a swarm of eager customers enter the store, I sure hoped she was right. We were becoming victims of our own success.

That evening was almost a reprise of the previous night—except for one awful omission. Bella. She was still in jail, held until the bail hearing scheduled for tomorrow. We all planned to attend, with Madison threatening a demonstration if she was denied bail. I sincerely prayed that they would agree to release her, since I wasn't convinced that a protest would sway the judge.

Sophie and I were tasked with finishing the storage room, which was still a jumble of boxes and belongings. Madison and Grammie were continuing work in the keeper's office, since the college student was starting the digitizing project the next day, and Ian and Jake were pressure washing the tower. We'd brought Quincy with us tonight, and he was supervising Sophie and me.

"I got a lead on that letter I found," I told Sophie as we lugged boxes of old books from one room to the next. "Captain Greg knew a pilot from Blueberry Cove named Chester Chapman, who went by Chet."

Sophie set a heavy box down with a grunt. "That fits, since he signed the letter Chet C., right? So what's the next step?"

"Captain Greg is going to talk to one of his friends." I pushed boxes into place using my foot. "He told me that Chet's plane went down and he was captured by the enemy. He doesn't know if he survived and made it home."

"I can't even imagine." Sophie shook her head. "That must have been so intense, finding out that the man you loved was a prisoner of war." She made a scoffing sound. "And here I am, fretting over a wedding venue. At least I have Jake here with me, whole and healthy."

"It certainly makes you think." Resting my hands on my hips, I surveyed the room. "We're just about done here." What we didn't want to keep for the lighthouse museum was going to be picked up by the local historical society. They'd decide what to hold on to for their own archives and dispose of the rest. Nothing was especially valuable, unless you counted nostalgic and historic worth.

"So," Sophie said. "The latest on my mom. She agreed that the yacht club was a no-go. But now she's pushing me to check out the Sunrise Resort. She looked at their website and decided she loves it."

"It's pretty nice," I said. "I was impressed."

Sophie screwed up her features. "I hope it's not *too* fancy, though. And I'm sure it costs a fortune." She laughed. "Here I go again. Who cares where we get married?" She held up her hand, the diamond on her finger sparkling. "I'm going to be Mrs. Jake Adams."

"You sure are." I threw my arms around her and we both jumped up and down, squealing. Sophie and Jake made such a great couple, a real inspiration to the rest of us. Maybe someday with Ian—with a mental chopping motion, I cut off that train of thought. We'd decided to take it slow and enjoy the journey, and by jiminy, I was going to do that this time. No more head-over-heels Iris. Been there, still had the scars.

* * *

We ate dinner on a picnic table overlooking the water. Ian and Jake were still working, racing against the setting sun to finish washing the tower. A leashed Quincy ate from his dish on the grass behind me.

"I love this potato salad," Madison said, scooping out another spoonful. "What did you put in it, Anne?"

"Dill relish and a squirt of spicy mustard," Grammie said. "Saves it from being too bland." She passed me a container. "Another slice of ham, Iris?"

"Don't mind if I do." I speared a piece and added it to my plate. My new filling was still bothering me. I should call the dentist, but they probably weren't seeing anyone right now due to Lance's death.

Sophie forked up a tomato wedge. "Is this from your garden? There's nothing on earth like fresh garden tomatoes."

"It is," Grammie said. A green salad with lettuce, cucumbers, and tomatoes from our garden rounded out the meal. "The tomato plants went bonkers this year, so I'm going to have to start canning."

"I'll buy some for the Bean," Sophie said, sounding excited. "I'll do a summer salad with waffle croutons."

"You can have all you want," Grammie said with a laugh. She always planted a huge garden so she could freeze and can the excess. But this year, being so busy with the shop, I could tell her enthusiasm for gardening was waning.

Which reminded me of something. "By the way, Ian bought you a ticket for a sunset cruise, Grammie. You're coming with us." I pointed toward the water, where the *Lucy Ann* was coasting by, big sails catching the sunset glow.

She turned to look at the schooner, her face brightening. "Oh, Iris, that's wonderful. I can't wait."

"You have a good man there," Madison said. "A real keeper."

I grinned. "I know. And speaking of keepers, how are you and Anton doing?"

Madison dropped her gaze, a secretive smile curving her lips. "We're good. He's going to come by later, once he gets off his shift. He's been so busy with the . . ." Her voice trailed off, and just like that, the elephant in the room walked over and sat on the picnic table.

Bella. Who was sitting in a jail cell while we enjoyed a lovely dinner on the cliffs near the lighthouse. Frustrated, I said, "What can we *do*?"

"First, we're going to get the lay of the land." Madison swiveled around and pulled a folded paper out of her tote. As she opened it up, I saw it was a detailed map of Blueberry Cove. We moved our dishes aside to make room, using the serving bowls and platters to hold down the map.

"Hold on," I said, seeing Ian and Jake coming across the grass. "They'll want to be in on this."

After the guys washed up in the cottage and filled plates with food, Madison began. "The Beast was stolen here." She pulled out a thin marker and made a big X on the approximate location of Bella's house on Hillside Avenue. Then she made another on the unnamed lane that ran along the top of the hill, less than a mile away. "And Lance was hit about here."

Ian's brow creased. "Isn't the speed limit, like, fifteen up there?"

"It is," Madison said. "But I have it on good authority that the driver was speeding."

"So they did it on *purpose*?" Jake's expression was disgusted. "Man, I can't believe it."

"Yeah, that's the theory," I said. "That's why Bella will probably face murder charges."

A silence fell over our little group, the only sounds the shushing of waves on the rocks and a lone seagull squawking in outrage overhead.

"I hear you, buddy," I said to the gull. "Okay, back to work." I put my finger on a spot up the street from Bella's. "The Pedersen home and dentist office." Madison marked it. Then I traced dotted lines crossing the neighborhood. "Those are the trails Bella told me about. She thinks someone ditched the car and ran down one of them to get away."

"Makes sense." Madison tapped her pen on the table. "Where do the other players live?"

"Other players?" Ian asked. "You have suspects already?"

"A whole list," Sophie said. "The Blueberry Cove crime team has been on the case."

I pointed out Kyle's home, right next door to Bella. "I don't know where Donna lives." I touched the Pedersen's home again. "And Lance's brother lives there." It was a huge house, certainly big enough for two adult sons to co-exist with their parents.

Kyle certainly lived in a good spot to sneak over and steal the Beast. But would he do that, knowing that Bella might be blamed? I couldn't quite wrap my mind around that. He may have had a problem with Lance but he seemed to be a good guy otherwise.

Sophie picked up her phone and began to search. "Aha," she said after a minute. "Donna Dube lives at forty-six Elm." The cross streets on the hill were named after trees.

"How did you find that?" Grammie asked. "I suppose I shouldn't be, but I'm shocked."

"There's a search site that lists street addresses,"

Sophie said. She tapped the phone again. "Look, here are my results." She showed her phone to Grammie. "It doesn't have all the places I lived, but most of them."

"Let me see," Jake said. "Wow. Stalkers could use this."

"And have," I said dryly.

"Donna could have done it," Madison said. She ran the marker along Elm Street, which extended between Hillside and Lake Street. "It would have been easy for her to go down this path"—she traced above the map with the marker—"and pop out here on Lake, then walk home."

I thought about Donna as a suspect. Maybe Kyle was right, and Lance hadn't wanted to rekindle his romance with her. So she'd stolen the Beast and run him down—and pinned the murder on Bella in the process. Maybe her tears today hadn't been out of sorrow, but guilt and fear instead.

Gosh, investigating a murder sure meant thinking the worst of people.

Grammie stood up to take a closer look at the map. "Any of the suspects could have easily stolen the Beast and chased Lance down. They all live close to Bella."

"Correct," Madison said, drawing a circle on the map around Bella's home. "Within a few-blocks radius."

"We'll have to share this information with Cookie," I said. "All we need to do is cast doubt on the police's case, right?" Although I'd prefer to have Bella totally cleared, rather than found not guilty, which would mean they didn't have enough proof for a guilty verdict.

"What about DNA evidence?" Ian asked. "Maybe they'll find the killer's."

Madison's brow furrowed. "And about a million other people's. I've driven that Jeep and so have my parents."

"Everyone in town has driven that thing," Grammie said. "Even me, back when Joe was alive. We needed the second vehicle while my Saab was in the shop."

Our attention was caught by a black pickup truck with fancy silver wheels trundling up the road toward the lighthouse. "Your ride is here." Sophie elbowed Madison with a grin.

Madison turned to look, lighting up at the sight of Anton at the wheel. He parked and swung out of the cab, buff, built, and pretty darn good-looking. He was out of uniform, dressed in a T-shirt, khaki shorts, and Top-Siders.

"We'd better put this away." Madison capped the marker, tossed it into her tote, and then folded the map.

Grammie frowned. "He doesn't know we're investigating?" In the past, Anton had been surprisingly good about our involvement, and we'd been really careful not to step on police toes. We were more like an auxiliary unit, sharing everything we learned with the department.

"Let's just say Bella's arrest is a bone of contention," Madison said. "I'm trying to separate our relationship from the investigation, but it's hard."

Anton's expression grew wary as he approached us. No doubt the fact we were all quiet aroused his suspicions. That was so not like us.

"Hey," he said. "How's it going?" He pecked Madison on the lips. "Ready, babe?"

"Just about," Madison said, crossing her arms. "Hold on a minute."

Amused trepidation skated across Anton's face. "Uh-oh. What'd I do now?"

Madison took a deep breath. "I wasn't going to say anything, but I changed my mind. Since we're all here."

Anton's gaze skittered from face to face. His shoulder slumped. "This is about Bella, right?"

"Of course," I said, deciding to take the heat off Madison. "We're in shock that she was arrested."

"A number of people could have stolen the Beast," Grammie put in. "A Jeep of that vintage is easily hotwired, not to mention the number of keys that could be floating around."

Anton's brows rose. "What do you know about hotwiring, Anne?"

Grammie shrugged modestly. "I've done it to my own Jeep." She put up a hand. "Don't ask." I remembered the incident. Something about the keys falling out of Papa's pocket during a fishing trip. While he was in the middle of a lake.

"Not to mention, the DNA evidence must be a total mess," added Sophie. "Tons of people have borrowed that car."

Anton rubbed his chin. "You're all making very good points." He paused. "Ones I raised myself."

"So why did they arrest her?" Madison's eyes flashed as she stomped her foot. "She's the mother of two young children and a small business owner. She has a lot to lose."

Anton's broad shoulders sagged. "I'm well aware of that, Mads. But it wasn't up to me." He sighed. "An eyewitness came forward. A neighbor saw Bella behind the wheel."

CHAPTER 10

We all squawked protests of shock, dismay, and disbelief. "They must be lying," Madison said. "Who was it?" Anton shook his head. He wasn't going to tell us the witness's identity. But Cookie Abernathy would find out; they had to tell the defense attorney.

"It must be a mistake," I said. How clearly had the witness seen Bella's face? "It was still dark out, right?"

"Pretty much," Anton said. "The sun wasn't quite up." He rearranged his features in what he probably hoped was a reassuring expression. "They believed they had enough to arrest her, but it's a long journey from an arrest to an actual conviction. The case might fall apart before then. And she does have a very good attorney."

Madison snorted. "Good thing your state police colleagues can't hear you right now. You're basically giving them a vote of no confidence."

Anton made a zipping motion across his mouth. "Then I'd better shut up." He glanced at his phone. "We'd better get a move on if we want to make the movie." His confidence wavered for a second. "If you still want to go, that is."

"Yes, I want to go." Madison sounded as if saying

no was a ridiculous option. She picked up her tote and slung the strap over her shoulder. "I'll see you all tomorrow, at the bail hearing."

We called goodbyes as the pair walked away, so close that their shoulders almost bumped. "Seems to me that Anton wants us to investigate," Grammie said once they were out of earshot.

"I'm taking his doubts as permission," I said. "Bella is not going to jail. Not on my watch."

A line of television trucks with antennas was the first clue that Bella's bail hearing was big news. Newscasters stood beside the trucks, opining into microphones about Lance's death, while cameramen filmed.

"Citizens are out in force today," one heavily made-up woman intoned, the sea breeze barely ruffling her blonde flip. Her gaze fell on Grammie and me as we hurried past, eager to get inside before the place filled up. "Good morning," she called. "Bella Ricci. Is she guilty?"

I put my hand up to block my face, shook my head, and kept going. Although I longed to shout, *She's innocent*, the last thing I wanted was to become a sound bite.

Frustrated, the newscaster turned to another person and asked the same question, with the same result. *You're in Maine, lady*, I wanted to say. *We're not going to blab to reporters*. This was one instance where our famed reticence came in handy.

Even with our own. Lars Lavely, reporter for the *Blueberry Cove Herald*, popped up beside me. Lars and I have a *complicated* relationship. I have to stay on his good side so he'll promote Ruffles & Bows while simultaneously fending off his ferret-like reporting techniques. Ferrets have a nice little trick called "latching on," and so does Lars.

"Hey, Iris," he said, keeping pace. "Got anything for me?"

"Afraid not, Lars," I said. "No comment."

He feigned shock and disapproval. "That's lame, Iris. Isn't Bella one of your good friends? Does this mean you think she's *guilty*?"

I clenched my teeth to hold back a sharp retort, exactly what he was hoping to get from me. "No comment," I said again. When he looked past me to Grammie, I added, "And she's not talking, either." Taking Grammie's arm, I put on a burst of speed to position us in front of Lars.

In the foyer, we funneled through security, barely making the cutoff before additional spectators were denied entry. Behind us, Lars flashed his press credentials even though everyone knew him. "Special dispensation," he said. "I'm the only member of the fourth estate allowed today." Maine allowed judges to decide upon press presence in the courtroom and this was quite a coup for Lars, considering all the networks and bigger newspapers barred from attending. He'd probably be able to sell his stories nationally.

The deputy waved him through with a thumbs-up. "Good for you, Lars."

Inside the courtroom doors, I paused, searching the bank of seats for Sophie and Madison. A text blurted on my phone. *In the balcony.* I looked up to see my friends hanging over the rail and waving. I waved back, and then Grammie and I pushed against the throng to get to the balcony stairs.

Sidling through tight-packed bodies, I picked up on the palpable excitement and anticipation in the air.

Was this what attending a hanging had been like in the olden days? I'd always thought public executions were ghoulish, and this felt similar. Especially since the fate of someone I cared about was on the line.

Bam. A woman not looking where she was going bumped right into me. "Sorry," I said with a laugh, although it wasn't my fault.

It was Gretchen Stolte, the cranky dental hygienist. "No, I'm sorry," she said. She seemed jittery, her gaze bouncing around. "Wow, what a mob scene."

"Exactly what I thought," I admitted. "I have a question for you. I assume the dentist's office is closed right now, but that filling I got needs work." It was still bothering me, wrongly shaped enough that sometimes biting down hurt. I was hoping she would have suggestions for another dentist.

"I'm not working there anymore." She gave me a bright, fake smile and started to push past. "Sorry. Good luck with your filling."

That was odd. Had Gretchen quit—or been fired? Dental hygienist positions paid well, and Gretchen had a son, so I somehow doubted she would up and quit. But conversely, qualified personnel didn't grow on trees, especially in rural Maine. However, deciding the situation was irrelevant to Lance's death, I put it aside for now.

Madison and Sophie had saved us seats in the front row upstairs, next to Ian and Jake, which gave us a bird's-eye view of the proceedings. As time ticked on toward the start of the hearing, bailiffs were urging people to sit. I spotted Gretchen's tawny mane in the crowd, and Kyle, sitting beside his cousin, Derek, the mechanic.

Derek must be horrified that his loaner vehicle had been involved in a hit-and-run. I wondered if the police were going to subpoena his records and see who else had borrowed the Beast, since it was simple and cheap to make duplicate keys for older cars. But that would mean premeditation, and I wasn't entirely convinced that Lance's death had been planned to that extent. No, it seemed impulsive, as if someone had known Bella borrowed the Beast—and also that Lance was out jogging. Did he go out every morning? I'd have to ask Bella.

Doors at the side opened, and Bella was led in by bailiffs. With a gasp, I grabbed Grammie's arm. My fashionista—and not to mention innocent—friend was wearing an orange jumpsuit. I wanted to curl up and die, I felt so awful about this very visible humiliation. "We *have* to get her off," I whispered to Grammie.

"We will, dear," she whispered back. "Hang in there."

As they settled Bella at the defendant's table, I noticed Alan sitting in the row right behind her. To me, Alan's presence meant he was supportive of his ex-wife, instead of distancing himself from her. *Point to Alan.* I wondered how Bella felt about his help, whether it was welcome or perceived as intrusive. He was also a key witness in the case, which would probably complicate things for the prosecution. It was doubtful he would willingly give testimony that incriminated Bella, even if he swore to tell the truth. Unfortunately, as an ex-husband, he no longer fell under spousal privilege.

"All rise," the head bailiff intoned. Feet shuffled as everyone in the courtroom stood up in deference to the judge.

"Oh, good, it's Judge Nguyen," Grammie commented behind her hand.

Judge Lien Nguyen had a reputation for being fair, smart, and no-nonsense. She also ran a tight courtroom, which explained the no-media order. She was trying to prevent the bail hearing from becoming a media circus, although Lars by himself could make it into a sideshow.

The judge sat and so did we. The prosecutor presented the charges that he would be explaining to the grand jury. Rather than vehicular homicide, standard for hit-and-runs resulting in death, he planned to charge Bella with homicide, claiming that hitting Lance was a deliberate act.

I found myself clutching Madison's and Grammie's hands as we listened to this horrible litany of Bella's supposed crimes. Would the judge even grant her bail? I was worried she wouldn't.

But then Cookie Abernathy gave a reasoned case why Bella should be granted bail. She cited her tight family and business ties to the community, a lack of any criminal record, even a speeding ticket, and the willing surrender of her passport.

We held our breath while the judge pondered. Finally, when I was about ready to scream, she tapped the gavel. "Bail is set at—"

I threw myself into Grammie's arms, tears of relief springing to my eyes. All around the courtroom, people reacted, loud chatter breaking out. From the general tone, I gathered that many were supportive of Bella, although a few shouted out condemnation for Lance's death. I tried to forgive them. After all, Lance was a local icon, Blueberry Cove's claim to fame.

Judge Nguyen gaveled furiously, trying to restore order to the court before adjourning it. At her signal, the onlookers jumped up and began milling about, pressing toward the exits. The bailiff led Bella out, followed by Alan. There would be paperwork before she was released. And she could take off that horrible jumpsuit, too. I couldn't wait to see her in normal clothes again.

"Do you mind if I wait for Bella?" I asked Grammie. "I really want to talk to her."

"Go ahead, dear," she said. "Take your time. I'll open the shop this morning."

Ian caught up with me on the stairs. "What a relief," he said as we made our way toward the closest door. "I was really worried at first."

"Me too," I said. "The prosecutor really painted a dark picture." He'd made her sound like a murderous fiend, hell-bent on racing up the road to flatten Lance. A witness, Anton had said. If that witness was wrong, then the case would fall apart.

We emerged into the summer morning, watching as the crowd began to disperse. The press, however, did not. They waited like a pack of vultures to swoop down on Bella when she left the building.

And speaking of the media, Lars came bouncing down the courtroom steps, his fingers busy on his phone. His steps slowed when he saw me. "Already filed a story," he gloated. "This is huge, really gonna make my career." He paused, then said, "Bella Bags Bail. Has a real ring to it, doesn't it?" Lars got a real thrill out of creating tabloid headlines for our tiny paper. As I knew all too well.

"Lars," Ian said, his voice deliberately slow and calm. "You do realize this is our friend you're talking about?"

Lars thumbed his glasses back into place. "Oh yeah, man, sure. I like Bella, too."

"And hopefully your next headline will be All Charges Dropped." I said, my hands curling into fists.

The reporter stared at me, eyes big behind his

lenses, opened his mouth as if to say something, then clamped it shut. With a headshake, he pushed past and sauntered toward the gathered press, preening as they called out his name.

"I'm not going to cooperate with that weasel any more," I said. "With any luck, he'll get a new job and leave town."

"We can only hope," Madison said. "This is a new low, even for him."

As we moved to the side of the courtyard, Ian said, "Captain Greg and I are going to go see his friend Stan Perkins this afternoon about the foghorn. Can you go with us?"

"I'd love to." Stan Perkins was the friend Captain Greg had said kept in touch with other Korean veterans. "It would be great to take my mind off things for a bit. Let me know when."

"Mid-afternoon, I think," Ian said. "He doesn't live far out of town, so we won't be gone long."

"That should work," I said. "I'm sure Grammie won't mind."

With the instinct of herd animals, the press corps turned as one and surged forward, signaling that something was happening. A second later I spotted Bella, Alan, Cookie Abernathy, and two police officers emerge from a side door.

"Bella, Bella," the reporters cried. "Did you do it?" "Why did you do it?" "Was it a lover's quarrel?" Alan and Anton shielded a cowering Bella while Cookie strode forward, barking at the press to stand back. Rhonda Davis went to stand beside the attorney as backup, glowering threateningly at the media. Bella was escorted to Alan's black BMW, which was parked at the curb, and helped inside. Then Alan ran around and jumped into the driver's seat. He started the car, pulled onto the road, and drove away.

"I guess we're not going to get a chance to talk to her," Sophie said as we watched the car recede into the distance.

Then my phone bleeped, as did Madison's and Sophie's. "It's Bella," I said. She'd used Alan's phone. *I'm going to the resort to chill. Or have a nervous breakdown. Girls' night, Alan's suite. Pool time 6, dinner at 7?*

Grammie and I will be there, I wrote back. *What should we bring?*

I took it as a very good sign that Bella wanted to convene one of our regular girls' nights. But I wasn't so sure about her staying at the resort. Was this crisis driving her back to Alan's arms? I prayed she wasn't making a hasty—and wrong—decision.

CHAPTER 11

The next potential Ruffles & Bows employee I interviewed was exactly opposite of the first. During our half hour together, I don't think she said a word that wasn't pried, coaxed, or urged out of her. Young, casually but neatly dressed, she sat slumped in a seat, her eyes darting to her phone every few seconds. She seemed nice enough but incredibly introverted.

"I'm sorry," I finally said, deciding to rip off the bandage. "I don't think this will be a good fit. We spend a lot of time talking to our customers."

Her eyes widened in alarm. "Like actual interaction? I thought I just had to ring up purchases, like at the grocery store." She presently worked as a cashier at a supermarket.

"Yes, there's a lot of interaction here," I said, doubling down. "They often want our advice about their purchases. Plus they like to learn the background behind certain pieces. When they were made, the fabric used, the history of the item."

She jumped to her feet, the most energy I'd seen her display yet. "You're right, Ms. Buckley. This won't work for me. I don't *like* people that much."

"Honesty is a good start," I called after her. "Maybe you should find a profession where you can work alone."

The shop door slammed behind my once-future employee and she practically ran away down the sidewalk. "That went well," Grammie said wryly as I walked into the main room.

I went around the counter and perched on a stool, bracing myself for Quincy's jump onto my lap. "Better to find out now than later. But gosh, I sure hope we find someone soon." I glanced around at the empty shop. "Slow today, huh?"

"Sure has been, after that flurry this morning." Grammie continued to tie tags on aprons with apple, autumn-leaf, and school motifs for our fall display. "Everyone is outside enjoying the last days of summer, I guess."

I opened a browser, my other hand steadying the purring cat. "Unless you need my help, I'm going to do some research." Now that charges against Bella were moving forward, we really needed to dig into the other suspects.

"I'm all set, so go ahead," Grammie said.

Lance's death was big news, flooding the search results. But I needed to go back further, to when Kyle still sailed with him. And when Lance was dating Donna.

The split with Kyle came right before the 2016 Olympics. I found an article saying "Pedersen picks new crewmate," and worked backward. As a good-looking and talented athlete, Kyle had gotten his share of attention. But after the 2012 Olympics, stories began to feature his party-hearty ways. Drunk outside London nightclubs. Wild parties at Caribbean resorts. Skiing under the influence in Switzerland. Some articles mentioned that Lance was also present, but somehow he escaped the negative attention. Quite the opposite in fact, as Lance was featured in advertisements for watches, clothing, and, ironically enough, expensive liquor. Endorsement deals brought in more money than winning races, so Lance had probably been set for life.

Who was going to inherit his money? Peter—or his parents?

The last article featuring Kyle was about a drunk and disorderly charge at the Captain's Pub here in Blueberry Cove. He'd been fighting with some well-known local troublemakers. What a contrast to his binges with the moneyed elite. Naturally Lars raked up Kyle's salacious history to pad the account. Sailor Sinks in Rough Waters read the headline. Hats off, Lars.

While it was obviously Kyle's own actions that had tanked his sailing career, I had to wonder how much he'd resented no-stick Lance. Life was like that. Some people got away with everything while others were lightning rods for trouble. The contrast between this pair seemed especially brutal. One man was worshiped and set for life while the other tended bar at a tiny yacht club and no doubt struggled to make ends meet.

Donna had also been part of the pro sailing circuit for a while, but she'd dropped out long before Kyle. Her decision apparently warranted barely a paragraph, even in the *Herald*. Going further back, I found an article or two about the sailing program at the club, with mention of Donna and Lance as instructors. That must have been when they dated.

"Want a sandwich?" Grammie asked. Quincy, still curled up on my lap, mewed. "Not you, young man." Then she relented. "It's tuna, so maybe a taste."

His heavy body thudded to the floor like a ton of bricks. "You're spoiling him," I said, accepting a plate. "And me." The tuna was studded with celery and onion and thickly spread between slices of homemade bread. Perfection.

* * *

Around three in the afternoon, Ian swung by the store in his truck. As planned earlier at the courthouse, we were going out to pick up the foghorn equipment promised by Captain Greg's friend.

"I'll be back before we close," I told Grammie. The afternoon had continued to be slow or else I wouldn't have left her alone. We really needed that part-time employee.

Grammie waved a hand in dismissal. "I'll be fine. Have fun."

As I crossed the sidewalk toward the truck, Captain Greg slid out of the passenger seat. "You stay there," I told him. "I'll sit in back." I climbed into a rear seat, and after I was safely belted in, Ian set off down the street.

"Where are we going?" I asked, leaning forward.

Captain Greg glanced over his shoulder. "Stan lives out toward Appleton." Appleton, a tiny, quaint farming town, was inland and off the beaten path.

With the truck windows open, I couldn't hear much as the men chatted about this and that, so I sat back and tried to relax. But as I watched the lush summer countryside spool past, my mind kept turning over Lance's death, a process like searching an egg for cracks. We didn't have any clues pointing to one person or another—yet. We had proximity to the vehicle and motives aplenty.

"Here we are," Captain Greg said as Ian slowed the truck. Stan's house was a small white farmhouse with a side porch and dormers. A barn converted to a two-car garage sat at the end of the drive. As we pulled into the dooryard, a Border collie came running to greet us with barking and tail-wagging.

An older man eased himself out of a chair on the

porch with a wave. He slowly made his way down the steps while we parked and climbed out of the truck. "Hush, Mollie," he said to the dog, who subsided, tail still beating like a metronome.

The two veterans greeted each other with handshakes and backslapping, then Stan turned bright, inquisitive eyes on us. "Who do we have here?" he asked Captain Greg.

Captain Greg introduced us before saying, "Iris is on the committee putting together the museum displays, and Ian is fixing the old foghorn."

Stan nodded in approval. "Good for you. I can't wait to hear it blasting away again. Can't tell you how many times that horn saved my skin when we were out fishing and got caught in the fog."

"I'm looking forward to hearing it, too," Ian said. "And I was really excited to hear that you have some of the equipment we need."

"It's in the barn," Stan said, waving for us to follow. He shuffled across the dirt drive, Mollie on his heels. "After the keepers left and they put in automated equipment, the Coast Guard disposed of a lot of stuff. Many of us around here took it into safekeeping." He pulled on the sliding door, which moved with a squeal of wheels.

"I'm glad you did," I said, thinking this was the perfect opening to talk about the Bailey family—and when the time was right, Chester Chapman. "Florence Ricci, one of the Bailey daughters, is in town right now. Do you know her?"

Stan's head jerked up. "Know her? Of course I do. Florence and her sisters were the belles of Blueberry Cove. Everyone wanted to date 'em." He chuckled. "Except me. Sally tied my heartstrings good and tight from the moment I met her."

"Sally was a great gal," Captain Greg said. "I was real sorry to hear about her passing."

Stan's face grew sad. "Yeah. Hard to believe it's been two years already. But I have the children and grandchildren to keep me company."

I was glad to hear that. Grammie had lost her husband, my grandfather, last year, and I was thankful that I could be here to support her.

Stan led the way into the barn, pulling on a long string to turn on an overhead bulb. "It's back here," he said, crossing wide, soft boards toward a row of empty stalls. In the light streaming through high windows, dust motes swirled and danced. At one time this barn had housed animals, and their distinctive, sweet aroma still lingered, mingled with that of hay and old wood.

He threw the tarp off a bulky shape resting on sawhorses, and Ian and Captain Greg gathered around to admire the array of wheels, gears, and metal. Not being conversant in engine-talk, Mollie and I stood aside, watching a pair of swallows fly in and out of an open window in the loft.

Between the three of them, the men got the equipment loaded into a cart and then onto the truck bed, using a ramp. Ian secured it with ropes and cords, making sure it wouldn't slide around. While they did this, I made a circuit of the yard with the dog, admiring the neatly kept flower and vegetable beds.

"Want a glass of iced tea 'fore you head out?" Stan asked.

"I'd love one," I said, planning to ask him about Chester.

The four of us settled on the porch, tall frosty glasses in hand, me in a rocking chair that creaked pleasantly with every movement. "We're having a grand opening

at the lighthouse on Labor Day weekend, Stan," I said.
"You'll have to come."

"That's right," Captain Greg said. "Plan on it. It's
going to be terrific to see the place all fixed up." He
tipped his chin toward Ian. "This young man and his
friend are painting the place. Hasn't looked that good
in decades."

"I'll mark my calendar," Stan said. He laughed. "Not
that it's terribly full these days."

"Stan," I said. "Captain Greg told me that you're in
touch with a lot of Korean War vets."

Our host nodded. "I'm involved with a group that
plans reunions. Part of our work has been tracking
people down, creating a directory of sorts."

My pulse leaped. "We're looking for a man from
Blueberry Cove named Chester Chapman."

"All I know is that Chet was taken captive," Captain
Greg put in. "Do you know if he returned home?"

Stan leaned back in his chair, gazing up as if con-
sulting his memory banks. Then he pulled out a phone
and swiped the screen. "Yep, I was right. Chet was released in fifty-five. One of that last group in Mukden.
What a scandal, keeping them imprisoned so long."

"That's great news," I blurted. "So he did return
from the war. He lived." Tears sprang to my eyes as if
hearing about a close relative. Somewhere along the way
I'd really gotten invested in a happy outcome for Chet
and Florence, if it had been her letter in the apron. We
needed to find out for sure.

Stan put up a cautionary hand. "But I'm afraid we
don't know if he's still alive or not. He hasn't joined our
website or been listed in the directory."

My excitement and joy drained away. What were the
chances that he was still among the living? Over sixty
years had passed.

"Tell you what, Iris," Stan said. "I'll tap my network, see if anyone knows anything. If he's alive, we'll find him."

At six o'clock that evening, Grammie and I arrived at the Sunrise Resort for girl's night with the finally free Bella. I was driving, and Grammie held a large container of homemade Caprese salad, made with garden tomatoes, basil, and local fresh mozzarella. My mouth was watering already.

As we climbed out of Beverly, Sophie pulled into the adjacent parking space. "Hi, guys," she called as she slid out, a bakery bag in her hand and a gym bag over her shoulder. "I made cream-cheese turtle brownies for dessert."

"Oh my," Grammie said. "They sound sinfully delicious."

"That was my goal." Sophie laughed as she swung into step beside us. "Iris, do you want to take a quick tour of the resort before we swim? Mom's been on me to check this place out."

"I'd be happy to," I said. Sophie's reception gave us a good excuse to poke around the resort.

"I remember when this place was a lot smaller," Grammie said, gazing up at the sprawling façade. "They've really expanded over the years. But it was always exclusive. Snooty, even."

A crease appeared between Sophie's brows. "Snooty is definitely not my style. I want people to feel comfortable."

"One strike against the Sunrise, then," I said lightly.

Inside, we took the elevator to the third floor. Bella and her children were in the suite, getting ready to go down to the pool. After greeting us with hugs, Bella pointed to the refrigerator. "Go ahead and put the salad in there, Anne. Thanks for bringing it. And these, Sophie." She set the bakery bag on top of a platter, to be used later.

As Grammie opened the fridge door, she nodded toward a slow cooker on the counter. "What smells so good?"

"Something heavenly." I picked up the lid and peeked at a mélange of chicken pieces, mushroom caps, and peppers in a thick tomato and red-wine sauce. Pello, who stood beside me licking his lips, seemed to agree.

"Chicken cacciatore," Bella said. "From a family recipe. Right, Florence?"

"My mother-in-law's," Florence said. She picked up a big bottle of tequila and poured a healthy slug into a blender. "And this margarita recipe is mine."

Madison, who had just arrived, hooted. "Now there's a family recipe I can get behind." She placed a sleeve holding fresh-baked Italian bread on the counter and gathered Bella into a big hug.

"Me too." Grammie sighed. "I think we all need a drink right now."

"I sure do," Bella said, returning Madison's squeeze. Alice and Connor came bombing out of their bedrooms, dressed in swimsuits and sword fighting with pool noodles. "Go ahead and get changed, everyone. I'm heading down with the kids before they destroy this place."

"Want to play Marco Polo?" Madison asked the children. They cheered in response and raced to the door, ready to go.

"See you soon," Florence said. "I'll bring down a pitcher of drinks and plastic cups. And nibbles."

"I can help you," Grammie offered. "I'm not going to swim tonight."

"Great." Florence elbowed her. "We'll sip cocktails and gossip instead."

After donning suits and dressing again, Sophie and I went down to the lobby, accompanied by Pello on a leash. We were going to take him for a walk while checking out the grounds.

Sophie approached the front desk. "I'm getting married next summer," she said to the clerk. "Is it okay if my friend and I look around?"

"Of course," the gracious clerk said. "We don't have a function going on tonight so feel free to check out the space." She put a map of the building onto the counter top and circled rooms with a pen. "The ballrooms are here and here. And you can also have the ceremony outside in the pavilion, if you wish." She showed us the spot on the grounds.

Using the map, we found our way to the Sunrise Ballroom and, on the other end of the building, the Moonrise Ballroom. Both were empty, cavernous spaces, with stacks of gold princess chairs along the walls and sky murals on the ceilings. Velvet drapes lined tall windows overlooking the water.

"I like the veranda," I said, opening a French door to step outside the Moonrise. A tiled floor and stone pillars gave the roofed porch a Gilded-Age ambiance.

"Me too," Sophie said. She led Pello toward granite steps leading to the lawn. "Want to check out the Pavilion?"

The Pavilion was a large white tent set up next to a rolling lawn featuring a pergola. "You could do your vows here," I suggested, taking the dog so she could walk around. The spot was right on the water, with the sound of the surf clearly audible. Pello liked it too, especially when I extended his leash so he could sniff around.

Sophie turned in a circle, snapping photos for later reference. "It would be great unless it rains." She glanced up at me, gnawing at her bottom lip. "I'm not sure about this, Iris. It doesn't *feel* right to me." She waved a hand. "I can't imagine me and Jake getting married here."

"Not the reaction they want you to have, I'm sure," I said. "So tell your mother that."

Her eyes were troubled. "What do you think? I'm so confused I don't even trust my own judgment."

I took a moment to formulate an opinion. "It's beautiful but kind of impersonal," I finally said. "I see you somewhere smaller and more intimate."

Sophie pointed a finger at me. "Exactly. Thanks, Iris. I'm going to tell Mom that." Her fingers worked busily at her phone. Her lips curved in a sly smile. "And I'm also going to say that eloping is starting to look pretty good."

After she finished sending her text, we strolled back to the main building, taking Pello on a detour through the flower gardens so he could stretch his legs. The evening sun slanted low, touching the trees and buildings with gold while casting long dark shadows. The air was soft and warm, the tiniest of breezes ruffling our hair.

"Oh, I love this time of year," Sophie said. "I am so not looking forward to winter."

I shuddered. "Don't remind me." I paused to look at the bay, where the *Lucy Ann* was clipping along. "One thing I am looking forward to is our sunset sail." Jake and Sophie were going as well.

"Me too," Sophie said. "It's going to be so romantic."

For her and Jake, maybe. But I didn't mind taking Grammie along. Ian and I could get romantic anytime.

From this side, screened lattice and hedges blocked

the pool area from casual view, but I could hear splashing and shouts of "Marco" and "Polo." Madison and the kids were still playing the pool game.

The murmur of voices drifted from behind the hedge, one male, one female.

"How are you holding up?" the woman asked.

Who was that? She sounded familiar. After thinking for a few seconds I realized it was Donna.

"It's been a rough couple of days," the male voice answered. His voice lowered, deep and laden with concern. "And what about you? I've been planning to call, see how you're doing."

I reached out and gripped Sophie's forearm. *Alan.* Was he up to his old tricks again?

CHAPTER 12

Sick anger churned in my chest. Why had he been planning to call Donna? Was she another of his women? We had to find out. Without the slightest twinge of guilt about eavesdropping, I put a finger to my lips and tiptoed a little closer. Sophie crowded right behind me.

"I'm just *devastated* about Lance's death." It had to be Donna he was talking to. "But you actually . . ." Her voice trailed off.

"I couldn't believe it," he said. "I'm just glad I spotted him before . . ."

The couple fell silent. My mind easily filled in the blanks. Alan had come across Lance after the accident.

"It's too bad you didn't see the driver," Donna said. "Or anyone else up there." Her voice rose into a question.

"I sure wish I had. This case would be going in a totally different direction."

Donna didn't say anything for a moment. "Well, if you think of anything," she finally said, "let me know, okay? We can work together to put a cowardly killer behind bars."

I had to suppress a yelp. Last time I'd talked to Donna, she'd been certain that Bella had killed Lance.

Now she was pretending to *Bella's ex* that she was on *his* side.

"I'm glad to have your support, Donna," Alan said. "The rest of your colleagues don't believe Bella." And neither did Donna, I wanted to shout.

After thirty seconds of silence, I poked my head around the hedge. They were both gone, and although Alan was standing by the pool watching his children play, I didn't see Donna anywhere.

Donna puzzled me. Did she still believe that Bella was guilty? That would mean she had been playing Alan, which wasn't nice at all. Or maybe she had started to suspect someone else. I hoped so. Anyone but Bella. And then there was a third possibility: she was guilty and was trying to find out what Alan knew or suspected that might point to her.

Putting aside my speculations for now, Sophie and I took a refreshing swim in the pool, dodging the Marco Polo players. Then we all went upstairs for dinner. Alan didn't join us, and I gathered he'd gotten another room at the resort, which was very tactful of him, to give Bella space. The kids ate first, before disappearing into one of the bedrooms to play a video game.

We served ourselves from the slow cooker, grabbed chunks of bread and plates of salad, and then sat around the balcony table. Florence filled glasses with white or red wine, as we directed.

"This is wonderful," Grammie said, taking in the spectacular view of the bay and islands from this height. "Look, you can see the lighthouse from here."

Five miles to the south, the white tower glowed even whiter against the deepening twilight. The beam flashed, paused, and flashed again. Ever vigilant in keeping sailors safe.

"I love our lighthouse," Madison said with a sigh.

"Wait until you see the marketing materials I drafted for the museum website and brochures. They practically wrote themselves."

Florence cleared her throat, drawing our attention. "After dinner, do you want to look at my old photo albums? You might find some pictures you want to use."

Madison nodded with enthusiasm. "Absolutely. Iris and Anne are going to get some enlargements made as well. Isn't that right?"

"Our idea is to display photos of how the cottage used to look in each room," I said. "Plus they'll guide us in looking for furniture and other items so we can set up period-correct exhibits."

Florence clasped her hands. "Oh, how wonderful. The day we left the lighthouse was one of the saddest days of my life. I was born there, you know. My mother didn't make it to the hospital."

"Really?" Bella shuddered slightly. "I can't imagine having a home birth. *Mamma mia!*" Since she was the only one of the gang who'd given birth so far—besides Grammie, obviously—I took her word for it.

Florence told us about the stormy winter day she was born and then shared a few more memories from what was obviously a rich trove.

I glanced at Grammie, who nodded. The time was right. "Florence," I said tentatively, "we are just loving your stories. Would you be open to doing a filmed interview at the lighthouse? I know our visitors will enjoy seeing it."

Florence spun her wineglass by the stem as she considered our request. Finally she dipped her head in assent. "All right. I'll do it." We burst into cheers, which made color flame in Florence's pale skin. Guests strolling on the paths below even glanced up to see what all the commotion was about. Madison lifted a glass in a toast toward them.

Bella slung an arm around her grandmother-in-law's neck and kissed her cheek. "Love you, Nonna. Thank you for letting us record your stories for posterity."

"How can I refuse?" Florence fluttered, waving her hands. "If you really think people will be interested . . ."

"We do," we all said in unison.

I glanced around the table at the smiling faces, flick-ering candlelight highlighting their beauty. Yes, we still had a serious situation to deal with, namely, solv-ing the mystery of Lance's death, but at the moment, Florence, the museum, and a fine meal were proving a much-needed distraction.

After we finished dinner, Bella sent Alice and Con-nor to bed and we settled in the living room to look at the albums with the platter of brownies and glasses of iced tea close at hand.

Florence carted a huge bag out from her bedroom and set it by her feet. "After my mother died, I took all the family photographs. After sorting through every-thing, I made duplicates of the best pictures for my sib-lings and their families."

I had to ask. "Did your brother make it back from the war?" I remembered Florence saying that he'd been wounded in action.

Her soft features creased in a smile. "Yes, thank God. Roger was in the hospital for a while and then dis-charged. He ended up marrying his high school sweet-heart and going to college on the GI Bill. He ended up teaching at Orono." Located near Bangor, Orono was home to a branch of the University of Maine.

Talking about Roger made me think of Chet. Did Florence know he'd finally been released? Had she been the one he proposed to? But instead of asking, I sat closer to Grammie and watched as she flipped through an album with black pages, the photos held in place by tiny clear triangles.

The black-and-white pictures had great clarity and resolution. "We need this one," I said. The shot showed Florence's beautiful mother in the kitchen, smiling as she stood at the stove flipping pancakes. I eagerly took in every detail—the wallpaper, which was still the same, the stovetop percolator, the full floral apron Mrs. Bailey wore over her dress. Even the same clock was on the wall.

"I agree," Grammie said. "What shall we do with the pictures we want to copy?" she called to Florence. "We can get duplicates made right here in town." The drugstore had a machine that made reprints.

"Go ahead and take them out of the album," Florence said. "I trust you to bring them back."

Grammie teased the photograph out from the triangles and set it on the coffee table. We continued to turn pages, finding a number of pictures that were truly delightful. One showed the whole family on the bluff below the lighthouse. The children looked to be pre-teens. I loved the thick wool sweaters they each wore, which had to be handmade. Everyone in the family was wearing denim jeans and work boots. That was a keeper.

And so was the picture of three lovely young women and their handsome dates standing in front of the fireplace in the main room. The women wore long formal dresses and corsages, while the men wore black suits and bow ties.

Florence had been making the rounds to answer questions, and she happened to be standing near us.

"Which one are you?" Grammie asked. "You're all so pretty."

Florence perched on the sofa next to Grammie. She pointed to the girl in the middle, who had blonde waves. "That's me." She pointed to one with a dark pageboy haircut. "Gloria." The third girl had bangs, short hair, and glasses. "And Doris."

"Who are your dates?" I asked, my heart beating a little faster. Her date had a long face with features that resembled a young Jimmy Stewart. Oh my.

Florence's arthritic fingers clenched then straightened slowly. Her gaze didn't leave the young man's face.

She was obviously distressed, and I felt like a complete and utter jerk. "I'm sorry," I said. "I didn't mean to be intrusive."

"It's okay," Florence said through stiff lips. "You didn't know. And it was a long time ago." She pushed herself to her feet. "My date was named Chester Chapman. And he was a real dreamboat. If only . . ." Her voice trailed off. If only what? If only he had returned before she married Alan's grandfather? Or if only he had never been taken captive at all? History would be different, that was for sure. Alan probably wouldn't exist, which meant he wouldn't have married Bella and brought her to the United States.

Madison waved from across the room. "Florence. We have a bet going over here. Is this the old drive-in?" Florence hurried to answer, and as I watched her carefully, to my relief, she seemed all right again.

I'd gotten my answer about the letter—and at what a cost. Florence remembered Chet all right, and those memories still hurt. Maybe my romantic notion of a reunion wasn't a good idea.

A while later, Florence went to bed, and we held a

council of war around the kitchen island, fresh glasses of iced tea and the decimated platter of brownies close at hand.

"So," Bella said, the bright mask she'd worn for Florence slipping away. "Where do we go from here?"

"First of all," Grammie said, "how are you holding up?"

Bella shrugged. "I'm okay. Taking it moment by moment. Cookie Abernathy is pretty confident that the case is weak and I'll get off. There isn't much beyond the witness and my possession of the vehicle." Her lips trembled. "But what if she's wrong?"

I pulled a notebook and pen out of my bag. I always felt better when I could make a to-do list. "We're going to launch our own investigation and get you off."

Bella threw back her head and laughed, the brilliance returning to her dark eyes. "I love your confidence, Iris."

"It's not as if it's our first rodeo," Madison said. "With all due respect to Anton"—here we cheered and whistled—"he's not in charge of the case. Unfortunately. So it's up to us to do what we can. To help Cookie."

"We have other suspects already," I told Bella. For the next few minutes, we showed her the town map Madison had marked up and discussed the logistics of the case.

I talked about my encounters with Donna and Kyle, detailing their possible motives. I also mentioned Peter. He lived up the street from Bella, had access to the Beast, and would certainly know when his brother went running. I wasn't certain of a motive for him yet, but one thing was clear—Lance completely overshadowed Peter in the family. Everyone agreed with that assessment.

Bella studied the map, teeth gnawing at her bottom lip. "Laying it out like this really helps." She put a finger on the approximate location of the Pederson home. "So Lance leaves the house and runs up the hill." She traced an alternative route. "Or goes along this street and then up." She traced a wider circle.

I thought of an earlier question I'd had. "Did Lance go running every morning?" I was wondering how someone outside the family might know he'd gone out, whether it was a predictable ritual or if the person had been watching for an opportunity. Or had grabbed one presented to them.

"No, he didn't," Bella said. "He is—I mean, wasn't a morning person. He told me he'd seen enough sunrises while on the sailing team."

"Someone must have known he was taking up the habit, then," I said. The more I thought about it, the less impulsive the act seemed. The time of day was perfect, with very few people on the roads or even awake, which meant few witnesses. *The witness.* Grammie must have read my mind, because she asked, "Was Cookie able to get any information about the witness who said she saw you driving, Bella?"

"Yeah," Madison said. "We want name, address. Serial number." The latter was a joke. "Not that we'd interfere, but it'd be good to know where they live, at least."

Bella shook her head. "No details yet. But we do know that it was an elderly woman. And she saw the driver wearing a white hat and something that looked like my white robe." She grimaced. "Which they took into evidence, believe it or not."

"Ugh." Sophie wrinkled her nose. "That's awful. We'll have to burn it when you get it back." She pointed at me. "The killer wore white. Write that down."

"Sounds like a book title," I said, complying. But this was another clue. Why white? An idea nudged at the back of my mind, but a text bleeping on my phone distracted me.

Your appointment is confirmed for eight a.m. Please text yes to confirm.

My filling was finally going to be fixed. "Guess what?" I said as I confirmed the appointment. "I'm going to Dr. Pederson's tomorrow morning. They're actually taking appointments right now. Maybe I'll find out something about the case."

"Iris Buckley investigates," Madison said. "I like it."

CHAPTER 13

The next morning, Grammie and I drank our coffee in the garden so we could admire the tomato crop. Happy to have us outside, Quincy darted about, chasing a white moth and playing hide-and-seek under huge squash leaves.

"Look at the size of this beauty," Grammie said, holding a beefsteak tomato that filled her palm. "This is shaping up to be a banner year."

"It sure is," I said, picking a cluster of Roma tomatoes. We used those to make sauce, since they thickened up beautifully when simmered with red wine and herbs. "Everything is peaking right now," I added, moving on to some heirloom plants. We grew about a dozen different types. Purple, yellow, and so-called chocolate varieties were new this year.

"I'm having this for lunch." Grammie was still admiring the gorgeous beefsteak, which sliced and salted would fit perfectly on fresh white sandwich bread slathered with mayonnaise. One of our summer rituals.

I studied my grandmother, so content and at peace here in her garden. She needed a serious break. "Why don't you stay home today?" I suggested. "I can handle the store. It hasn't been that busy this week." My dentist appointment was at eight, so I had plenty of time to get to the store in time to open.

Her eyes lit up. "I could get a good start on the canning."

"Or sit on the back-porch swing and read a book," I said. "I can help with the canning after work." Then I remembered. "Not tonight, though. We're going on the sunset cruise."

"I'm really looking forward to that," Grammie said. "So I'll do what I can today." She put the large tomato on the porch table. "Help me fill some buckets. If these sit on the vine another day, they'll overripen."

After we picked tomatoes and set the containers on the back porch in the shade, I got ready for work. Today I felt girly, so I chose a full-skirted dress printed with pink roses and a pair of pink flats. I'd slip on a Ruffles & Bows pinafore apron once I got to the shop.

Drive time was often when I thought about the business. People were continuing to order pinafores almost every day, so we really needed to find someone to help sew. I could see us adding other custom garments later on too, and ideas floated into my mind. Some of the vintage aprons were so adorable, but they were often one of a kind. If we reproduced them, then everyone could have one.

This train of thought took me all the way into town, where I cut up the hill toward the dentist's office. It was really good of them to take me in right now, when they were grieving the loss of Lance.

The parking lot was empty when I pulled in, and the whole place had a deserted feel. When I shut my car door, the sound echoed, and my footsteps seemed really loud on the asphalt drive. I felt as if I should tiptoe.

But the office door was open so I walked right in, setting off a buzzer in the mat. The fish tank burbled away, but otherwise the place was deserted. "Hello?" I called. "Anyone here?"

"I'll be right out," came Peter's shout from the back. Instead of sitting down, I hovered near the reception desk, noticing that one computer was on, but otherwise there was no sign of life. A red light flashed on the desk phone. Other emergency patients?

Footsteps thudded in the corridor and Peter emerged. "Good morning," he said, picking up a file and flipping through. "Here about that filling? Come on back." He turned and began walking down the hall, so I hurried to follow.

"Yes, it's the filling," I said. "My bite isn't quite right."

We reached an examination room, and Peter gestured to the chair. "That can be quite annoying. Go ahead and take a seat, and we'll get started."

I set my handbag down on the floor and slid into the reclining chair. He gave me a pair of plastic protective glasses that matched his own and clipped a napkin around my neck, then began to fiddle with a tray of utensils.

Once I was lowered and the lamp shining in my face, he began to probe around, making little sounds. "It looks okay," he finally said. "Firmly in place. I'll file off a couple of edges."

Free from his scrutiny as he prepared, I said, "I was so sorry to hear about your brother."

At first he didn't look up, and I thought maybe he hadn't heard me. Then he nodded, still not making eye contact. "Thank you. My parents took it really hard, as you might expect. They're out of town for a few days, at their camp up north."

That explained the deserted feel of the property. "But you're holding down the fort," I said. "Gretchen's not here to help?" I was curious to hear what he had to say about her position here.

"No, she's not with us any longer." A brief smile flashed. "Sometimes it just isn't a good fit, you know."

Moving closer, he peered down at me. "Open wide; let me take a look."

I closed my eyes and lay back, hoping that it wouldn't take long. At least he wasn't injecting me with Novocain this time.

As he did mysterious things to my tooth, he started muttering. "Big loss to our family. Lance was always the favorite, you know. My parents thought the sun shone out of his—" Metal clanked on the tray as he sought a new tool. "Not easy being the younger brother in a situation like that, don't you agree?" The volume of his voice rose a notch. "No matter how hard I tried, Lance always got there first. At school, at sports, with girls . . ."

"He was popular with the ladies, all right," I said. "Dating Bella . . . and maybe Donna too, it looks like." A shameless probe for more information.

Peter made a scoffing sound as he loomed over me with a scary metal implement. I hastily closed my eyes. "He was *such* a player. But every woman thought she could change him." My heart was crushed just a little for Bella. With a huge sigh, Peter returned to the topic of his parents. "I even asked my mother once why they bothered to have me. Why they didn't just stop after the *perfect* one was born."

My hands clutched the armrests. This was getting into TMI territory, for sure. Feeling that a response was needed, I grunted.

"Mom didn't get it, of course. Didn't see it." His

laugh was bitter. "She told me to stop being jealous, that it wasn't becoming." He put a piece of paper in my mouth. "Bite down. . . . Good." A pause as he examined the bite marks. Then he continued his work. "I used to wish Lance would disappear. That maybe he wouldn't come back from one of his races. Then maybe my parents could see how much I do for them, how much I sacrificed."

The mat buzzer in the front office sounded, and Peter's fingers left my mouth. "Excuse me. I'd better go see who that is."

Saved by the buzzer. I lay back in the chair, limp. When he returned, I'd let him finish and then get out of here fast as I could. I needed to find a new dentist ASAP.

And Peter was definitely a suspect in Lance's death. He knew his brother's schedule, of course, and he lived right up the street from Bella. The loaner vehicle was less than a block away, and better yet, it couldn't be traced back to him.

Had Peter's anger and resentment toward his favored brother finally boiled over? This theory seemed plausible to me.

"What a perfect night for a sail," Grammie said. We were in line to board the *Lucy Ann*, along with Sophie, Jake, and Ian. Grammie and I were carrying picnic baskets for an onboard snack, since we'd still be out at dinnertime.

As we drew closer to the kiosk, I recognized the woman collecting tickets. "So we meet again, Gretchen," I said with a laugh.

She didn't respond in kind, merely grunted as Ian handed over the tickets. She punched them and handed them back. "Have a nice cruise. Next?"

As we strolled up the gangway, Grammie turned to study Gretchen. "Doesn't she work for the dentist?"

"She did," I said, taking Grammie's arm to help her over the lip and onto the deck. The *Lucy Ann* was spacious, about sixty feet long, so it had plenty of room for the dozen or so passengers to spread out.

Our little group found a spot in the stern near the wheel and settled in. The evening air was warm, the sun still hot, but we'd brought windbreakers and jackets against the inevitable cooler temperatures out on the water. To my surprise, I saw that our captain was Kyle Quimby, who also tended bar and gave lessons at the yacht club. He really was a versatile guy, like so many of us in Blueberry Cove.

Before casting off, Captain Kyle introduced the crew—Gretchen and two lanky teenage boys—and gave us safety instructions. Then he told us about the boat, its history, and the planned itinerary tonight. Our voyage would take us out around several islands and then back into harbor, with a total time of about two hours. Next he drafted a few volunteers to help raise the sails and run the lines, including Ian and Jake, and soon we were underway, the large craft cutting cleanly through the sparkling bay, all three sails billowing. It was as if we had stepped back in time two hundred years.

Grammie flipped open a basket lid and began to lay out cheese, fruit, a log of smoked meat, and crackers on a cloth. Sophie uncorked a bottle of wine and handed around plastic cups. We toasted one another and drank.

"By the way, Mom finally responded to my text saying I didn't like the Sunrise Resort," Sophie said, making a face. "She was not happy."

"You'll find the right place," Grammie said. "Just like when you met Jake, you'll know."

"I hope it goes a little smoother than that," Sophie said. She and Jake had faced some bumps but had come out of those setbacks stronger and more in love than ever.

We talked about the wedding a little, with Sophie showing Grammie the dress and flower arrangements she wanted on her phone. In between, we gazed out at the rippling water where dolphins, seals, and even a whale cavorted.

The sight of that big tail rising up against the sky then slipping under gave me goose bumps. It was probably a humpback, I guessed, which was confirmed by Captain Kyle a moment later.

"Oh, I love whales," I said. "I need to come out here more often. Too bad we don't have our own sailboat."

"Like that one?" Sophie asked. A smaller sailboat was approaching at speed, heeling over against the steady breeze.

"Exactly." I watched the boat zipping along, admiring how it appeared to glide across the water. Two people were crewing the boat, which looked to be about twenty-five feet long. Painted on the hull were the boat's name, *Nixie*, and the Maine registration number.

Sophie rested a hand on my forearm. "Isn't that Donna Dube? And Peter Pedersen?"

It took a moment to confirm that, since both wore billed caps pulled low. "It is. I didn't know they were such good friends." Of course they knew each other, since Peter kept his boat at the club and Donna worked there part-time. But suspicious me couldn't help wonder why they were together right now. Although they could be comforting each other over Lance, despite Peter seeming more angry than sorrowful, at least in my eyes.

I couldn't help but remember Donna talking to Alan

about identifying the killer. Did she suspect *Peter*? I hoped so, if it took her focus off Bella.

The sailboat skimmed off, leaving a creamy wake, and I tried to let my speculations go with it. This was the worst thing about a murder investigation. Analyzing everything people said and did could create a big a tangle as Quincy with a stray spool of thread.

Ian and Jake returned from their sailor duties, chatting and laughing. Ian sat cross-legged beside me, warm and tanned and smelling of sunscreen and clean male. "That was fun," he said. "Kyle said we could help put the boat away when we get back in."

"Only *you* would think that was fun," I said, handing him a cold beer. I passed one to Jake, too.

They clinked bottles and drank. "We were just saying we should do this more often," Ian said. "What a perfect way to relax."

I slipped my hand into his, warm and callused. "I just said that exact same thing to Grammie and Sophie. Did you see the whale?"

"Sure did." He pointed out into the water. "And there it is again."

"He or she has a friend along this time," Grammie said.

"There's another," someone else shouted.

Another whale joined the three, and we watched in awe as the pod showed off for us. They breached, blew air, flipped their tails, and came crazy close to the ship, making us scream in delight. Finally they disappeared into the depths, leaving us bereft.

"I'm going to the restroom," I told Ian, taking advantage of a lull in the excitement. The compact space was down below, and occupied. So I took a moment to give myself a tour of the lower deck, checking out the efficient galley, the bench seats around the wall in the main room, and the small crew quarters with their berths. Some schooners allowed guests to stay overnight, which would be a blast.

The lock clicked open on the restroom at last, and the door opened, revealing Gretchen. "Hi there," I said. "We're having such a great time tonight."

"That's good," she said, pushing past me.

"Do you like working on the *Lucy Ann*?" I asked, reluctant to let her go. Gretchen always seemed so unhappy, whether at the dentist's office or here, at a new job. What was the matter? Then a possibility hit me. "I'm sorry for your loss."

She reared back, her eyes wide with confusion. "What do you mean?"

"Lance," I said. "Did you get close while working at the dentist practice?"

Gretchen backed away, shaking her head. "I have no idea what you're talking about." She turned and rushed off, and a moment later I heard her footsteps on the ladder to the deck.

Strange behavior, but I was starting to realize that such was par for the course with Gretchen. As Madison might say, she had issues.

All too soon, we skirted the islands and were headed toward home. I tried to imprint every precious sensation into my memory: the gurgle of water sliding past the hull, the snap of a sail as the wind began to soften, the lighthouse beam welcoming us home. From out here, Blueberry Cove was indistinct, but as we swooped toward shore, details emerged, as if a lens were coming into focus.

Ian leaned close, his shoulder bumping mine. "Did you enjoy it, babe?"

I nestled into his bulk. "I loved it. What a treat." I glanced at Grammie, who was watching Kyle expertly maneuver the boat toward its waiting berth. "And thanks again for inviting Grammie."

He kissed my hair. "My two favorite girls." When I pulled back in mock surprise, he laughed and said, "I should include my own mom, right?"

"Yeah, you should," I agreed, resting against his chest again. I liked his intelligent, incisive mother, Fiona, who worked at the library as well as helped run the family bed and breakfast. But she'd intimidated me at first and I was very glad we were past the awkward stage.

Once we docked, the rest of the passengers filed off, but our group stayed behind with Kyle and the crew to put the boat away. Grammie and I ended up swabbing the deck and picking up stray trash before it blew into the harbor.

"I should give you ladies a discount," Kyle said. "Really above and beyond."

"I don't mind," Grammie said, pushing the mop with gusto. "Yo-ho-ho, and a bottle of rum."

Kyle laughed. "Speaking of which, I've got something really special for a nightcap." He wiggled his eyebrows. "Artisan rum from Barbados."

"Lovely," Grammie said, giving the mop an extra swirl. She was such a good sport. I loved that about her.

Once we finished cleaning up, the crew left, including Gretchen. Kyle called after her. "Hey, Gretch, you aren't going to stay?"

"Got stuff to do," was her brief answer, and with a hunch of her thin shoulders, she headed down the gangplank.

Kyle watched for a moment, then said to us, "Go ahead and get comfortable up by the wheel. I'll bring out the goodies." He descended into the hold.

After twilight, the crew had switched on battery lan-

terns to light the deck, so we gathered a few to illumi-
nate our seating area. A couple of minutes later, Kyle
climbed the ladder, whistling, and emerged carrying a
tray. It contained the promised rum, shot glasses, and
bowls of nibbles. "We keep some food on hand," he explained. "For group functions." He dispensed servings
of rum and then our shaggy-haired captain sat cross-
legged at the head of our circle.

I touched my tongue to the rum for a taste. It was
rich and spicy with a deep banana flavor. "What do you
think, Grammie?"

"I'm thinking it might be a nice addition to my banana bread." She lifted her empty shot glass with a
wink. Everyone laughed.

"We've got extra beers for a chaser," Ian told Kyle,
flipping open his cooler.

Kyle took one and popped the can open. "This is so
nice," he said with a sigh. "I'm savoring every single
day of summer we have coming to us."

Full night had fallen now and lights from shore
and rigging on other boats were reflected in the water.
Voices drifted from the yacht club where the guitarist
from the other night wailed and strummed.

"I was surprised to see you tonight," I said. "How
many jobs do you have, anyway?"

Kyle laughed. "Well, as any Mainer knows, you have
to make money while the sun shines. The club shuts
down right after Labor Day." He shrugged. "Then it's
either go south or find something to do all winter."

"I might need a guy," Jake said, tossing mixed
nuts into his mouth. "But we go out all winter. While I
love my job, it can be brutal out there."

"You're a lobsterman, right?" Kyle said. "It's the
same in competitive sailing. It sure wasn't all turquoise
waters and rum drinks. No sir." After offering us the

rum, he filled his own glass. "We sailed in some really nasty stuff. Cape Horn, the Tasman Sea, the North Sea. All over the world."

"Sounds amazing," Jake said. "The all-over-the-world part, that is."

Kyle threw back the shot. "Yeah. It was." His brows drew together in an expression of regret. "You know what? At first I thought it might be fun to have Lance back. But it only took a week or two to realize that things hadn't changed. That *he* hadn't changed." Staring into space, he fell silent for a beat. "He even had to mess with my cousin Derek. Lance was going to give him a loan so he could take over the garage and Roy can retire. Easier than going through the bank, and better terms, too. But no, he kept jerking Derek around for weeks waiting for a final answer. Poor guy almost went nuts." Another pause. "And now he's back to square one."

It took me a moment to wrap my head around this revelation. Derek's garage owned the Beast, so he probably had a key. Had he known that Lance was going to be jogging that morning? If so, then we had another suspect.

CHAPTER 14

"ood morning, you two," Sophie called from behind
the counter at the Belgian Bean, where Madison
and I were meeting for breakfast. "There's a table open
in the back." The cheerful café was a hive of activity
this morning, with all seats in the front room full and
a line waiting at the counter. The Bean was now one
of Blueberry Cove's favorite eateries, and I was glad to
see Sophie's hard work paying off.

"Perfect," Madison said, giving her two thumbs-
up. "We'll have our usual coffee orders and two Bene-
dicts."

Sophie's brows rose. "Oh, splurging today, I see." She
grinned.

"You bet," I said, my belly already rumbling. Her
concoction of poached eggs resting on ham and a Belgian waffle with hollandaise sauce was absolutely to die
for.

We made our way to the back room, which was
slightly quieter and overlooked the harbor—a major
point in its favor. As Sophie had promised, a two-top
next to the windows was free, so we grabbed it.

"Breakfast at the Bean," Madison said with a sigh
as she slipped into a seat. "My favorite." She gazed out
at a lobster boat chugging across the harbor.

"Mine too." I set my tote bag on the floor, then sat, smoothing my full skirt under my bum. Today I wore a cute new dress with a bluebird print, trimmed with matching blue piping.

"Love that dress," Madison said. "Did you make it?"

"Thanks. I did. It's from a great nineteen-fifties pattern I found." I fiddled with the packs of sugar, hoping that we wouldn't have to wait too long to eat.

Madison was still eyeing my dress. "That style really suits you. I'd like some retro outfits, but with my bony bod . . ." She scrunched up her nose.

"Cut it out. You're gorgeous." I thought for a moment. "If you're serious, I'll gather some ideas."

She shifted in her seat. "Would you? I would love that."

Sophie hurried into the room, carrying a tray. She set our plates on the table, followed by huge mugs, condiments, and wrapped utensils, then pulled over an empty chair. "I can sit for a few. The team up front has it under control."

"Awesome," I said. "That gives us a chance to visit." I stared down at my plate, admiring the presentation before grabbing my fork and knife and attacking.

Between bites, we talked about the menu for the museum open house. Sophie offered to make some of the appetizers for us. "I have a great old cookbook with really cool canapé recipes. I've been wanting to make them for ages."

"Oh, I adore trying vintage recipes." My phone rang. Bella. Then I had an idea. "Hey," I said when I answered, "want to do a video call? I'm with Sophie and Madison." I set up my phone up against the napkin dispenser so we could all see.

After a round of greetings, Madison asked, "How are you doing, Bella?"

Bella sighed, pushing hair off her forehead. "Not too bad, considering. Trying not to think about anything, or worry. I'm just focusing on the kids and taking care of myself." A wicked grin flashed. "I'm having the full spa package later."

Her comments made me decide not to mention the investigation or Lance. But then I found myself blurting, "How's it going with Alan?" *Smooth move, Iris.*

But she didn't seem upset, just tipped her head back and forth, thinking. "It's okay. He stays out of my face, which is a good thing. And he's been doing a lot with the kids. Today he rented a boat and took them and Florence out to one of the islands. Hence the spa day."

"Good for you," Madison said. "I want a spa day."

Sophie and I echoed her.

"But that brings me to why I called," Bella said. "My car is ready but I really, really don't feel like going to pick it up." She winced. "I don't want to see people in town yet. I'm so thankful my assistant is running the store. She said sales are up because everyone is coming in out of curiosity to see me. Then she guilts them into buying stuff."

"That's great, Bella." I needed an employee like that. "I can go get your car later. Do you want me to leave it at the resort or at your house?" Not only was I doing a friend a favor, I could talk to Derek about his relationship with Lance.

"Thanks a bunch, Iris." Her features relaxed. "Leaving it at the house is fine. I don't need a car right now."

Madison consulted her phone. "I have time this afternoon between appointments to run you to the garage," she said. We set a time to meet at the store.

"Thanks so much, guys," Bella said again. "Oh, one more thing. Sophie, I might have a lead on a fantastic place for your reception. The ceremony too, if you want to have it there."

Sophie leaned forward. "Really? Tell me more. My mother wasn't too happy when I said no to the resort. She's threatening to come up here and look around herself." She rolled her eyes with a groan.

"We can't have that," Bella said. "I'd tell you more right now but the information was from someone I bumped into here. The place doesn't have an online presence yet so I need to get more info first."

"That's fair," Sophie said. "But I'm dying to find out about it."

"Soon as I know, you'll know, *amica*," Bella assured her.

Out of the corner of my eye, I spotted a young man sauntering into the back room, coffee in hand, laptop bag strap over shoulder. Oh no. Lars Lavely, cub reporter. He gazed around, looking for a free spot, of which there were none, then saw us.

"Reporter, incoming." I lay my phone flat and placed a napkin over it. Bella squawked something but it was too late to say more. "Hey, Lars," I said, giving him a big, fake smile. "How are you this morning?"

Using his free hand, he thumbed up his glasses, his gaze studying each of us. "Hey, ladies. I was wondering, have you seen Bella around? She seems to have disappeared. Heh-heh." He shifted his stance. "Not that I'm going to try to talk to her. Cookie Abernathy won't let me interview her. I just need an update for my story." So he was being nosy, maybe hoping to snag a photo or two of Bella. And that was a hard no.

Leaning on the table to bring my mouth closer to the phone, I said loudly, "Bella? No, *Lars*, we haven't seen her. Did you try her house? Or the store?" Although I couldn't see if Bella was still on the line, I sensed she was.

"Went to both. The woman at her store blew me off." His lips twitched. "Tried to make me buy a present for my girlfriend."

Lars had a girlfriend? I tried to imagine the woman and failed. I shrugged it off as a topic of investigation for another day.

"Sorry we can't help you, Lars," Madison said in her creamiest voice. "But I'm so glad to catch up with you. I'm hoping we get a lot of free promo when the museum opens. Maybe we can talk about that?"

The reporter began to swivel his head as though seeking escape. "Um, sure, but not right now. Call me." With that, he pivoted and strode for the doorway, no doubt deciding to make his changes in the other room.

I lifted the napkin from the phone and set it upright again. "Sorry, Bella. I didn't want him to see us talking to you."

"That's okay," she said. "At first I thought your video went off." She blew air through her lips. "Thanks for running interference." She glanced down, then said, "And I'd better scoot. Talk later?"

After we hung up, I said, "Mads, we have another suspect to add to the list." I paused dramatically before whispering, "Derek Q."

"Really?" Madison's eyes widened then narrowed. "I can see he'd have means, but what's the motive?" She popped a last piece of Benedict into her mouth and chewed.

Between us, Sophie and I filled her in about the conversation we'd had with Kyle on the schooner.

"When we go pick up Bella's car," I said, "I'm planning to ask Derek about the loan." I laughed. "Well, not that bluntly."

"My dad invests in local businesses," Madison said. "If the garage numbers look good, he might help him." She shrugged. "Unless he's guilty of murder. That would kill the deal."

"One more thing." I touched my cheek. "I went to the dentist yesterday to get my filling fixed. Again." I gave them a rundown of what Peter had said. "So I think he's worth keeping on the list."

"And it's time to find a new dentist, regardless," Madison said, wrinkling her nose. "Wow. He's a freaky one." She leaned close and whispered. "Did I tell you he asked me out?"

"No," Sophie and I chorused. Before she started seeing Anton, Madison had dated a string of odd ducks, guys who looked good on paper but definitely were quirky. Or just plain wrong for her.

"I was so thankful I could tell him I already had a boyfriend." Madison's expression was starry-eyed.

"And a real keeper at that." Sophie glanced over her shoulder then pushed back in her chair. "I'd better get back to work." She peered at our mugs. "Want refills?"

"Maybe a splash," I said. "If you have time, Madison." I still had half an hour before the store opened.

"I do. And I'd love a refill."

Sophie cleared our empty—practically licked-clean—plates and a moment later, a server popped out and filled our mugs.

"How was the schooner cruise?" Madison asked as she splashed cream into her cup. "Was it romantic?"

"Very. We all loved it. You and Anton—" I broke off when she touched my arm.

"Hold on," she said, her eyes on the doorway. She got up and hurried into the next room. A moment later she returned, with the man in question in tow, in uniform and carrying a to-go cup. A citrus aftershave wafted from his fresh-shaved cheeks. "Look who I found."

I pushed out the chair Sophie had used. "Have a seat, Chief."

"I guess I can sit for a few minutes," he said, settling his bulk onto the seat. "Long as you two don't grill me." His crooked smile let me know he was joking. Sort of.

"We won't do that," I promised. "I was just telling Madison about our sunset cruise on the *Lucy Ann*. It was fabulous."

His shoulders came down a notch at my reassurance but then an odd expression flashed through his eyes.

"Wouldn't it be fun, babe?" Madison said. "I'm dying to go. We can bring a picnic and wine." With every word, Anton shifted lower in his chair, turning his cup in a circle on the tabletop. "What? You don't want to go?" She thrust out her bottom lip in disappointment, looking confused.

Anton continued to fiddle with his cup. "It's not that. I'd go anywhere with you, Mads. But I . . . I don't like boats." He exhaled a rush of air at this confession.

Madison rocked back. "What? You grew up in Maine, on the coast, and you don't like boats? How did that happen?"

Anton shrugged his massive shoulders. "When I was a kid, I used to get awful seasick every single time I went out. Made field trips a whole lot of fun." He shuddered. "Thankfully it doesn't happen when I have to go out with the marine patrol now and then, but it's always a concern."

Madison's gaze grew distant and I recognized the signs. She was thinking about how to fix this. "Okay, we won't go on a cruise. Right now. We'll find something else fun to do."

Relieved, he turned to me. "Madison told me you're

looking for an employee. I might have someone for you."

"Who is she?" I asked, cautiously hopeful. If the person wasn't a good fit, I'd have to handle the situation extra carefully. That was the downside of a recommendation from a friend.

Anton leaned back in his chair, holding his cup. "Faith O'Brien, Tade's wife." Tade O'Brien was one of the local officers. "She's looking for part-time work after the kids go back to school. Youngest is going to kindergarten this year."

"Does she have any experience?" I asked.

"She's worked a lot of retail, Tade said," Anton told me. "And she sews like crazy. Makes a lot of the kids' clothes."

Now that sounded promising. "Have her give me a call," I said. "I'd love to talk to her."

"Will do." Anton glanced at his military-style watch. "I'd better get back to work."

"Too bad," Madison said, batting her lashes. "But I know you need to go keep us safe." With a giggle, she glanced around then planted a quick kiss on his lips. He was on duty, after all.

Taking the opportunity, I made a list on a scrap of paper. As Anton stood, duty belt clanking, I handed it to him.

"What's this?" he asked, his brow furrowed.

Smiling up at him, I laced my fingers together and stretched. "Oh, just a few other people to consider. You know, suspects." I'd promised not to question him but I hadn't said anything about passing along my thoughts. Valid loophole, right?

CHAPTER 15

Maybe it was the Belgian Benedict, but I had a really productive morning. In between customers—and Quincy pats—I located second-hand mannequins for our museum, ordered a line of children's art aprons, and set up a meeting with Faith O'Brien, Anton's recommendation for us.

"She sounds great on the phone," I said after hanging up. "Fingers crossed we have a good interview."

"When is she coming in?" Grammie asked. She was ironing a stack of aprons we planned to put out. We'd come across a stash of Depression-era flour sack aprons in the prettiest floral fabric. I loved how the companies had changed flour-sack fabric after finding out women were using empty sacks for aprons and other clothing. Now they were collectors' items.

"Tomorrow morning," I said, making a note on the desk calendar. Despite using our phones and store computer to keep track of things, I liked to write things down. Frankly, I tended to ignore digital beeps and flashes. Pen on paper worked for me.

Then a notation made by Grammie jumped out at me and panic lanced through my veins. "We're filming Florence tonight at the lighthouse. Are we ready?" I hadn't even given the project a thought since she had agreed to do it.

"We're all set," Grammie said, calmly standing the iron and shifting the apron on the ironing board. "Madison and I arranged it all yesterday. Florence will meet us there at six. We'll do the interview and then have supper."

I slumped back against a stool. "Thank you. For a minute, I thought there was something I'd forgotten to do."

"Nope." Grammie glanced at the wall clock. "When is Madison coming to pick you up? I thought we could have lunch once you get back."

"Around noon." I patted my midriff. "And good idea, because I'm still full from breakfast."

"I made us a big salad," Grammie said with a wink. "Nice and light."

"My waistline thanks you." I bent to pick up Quincy, who was curling around my ankles. Carrying him in my arms, I went to the front of the store to look out the big picture window. Traffic was fairly light today, with clusters of people strolling down the sidewalks window-shopping. We had a view of the harbor from here too, due to a fire decades ago that demolished the building right across the street.

Sailboats were out in force, reminding me of last night's wonderful experience—and Lance's death. All we had right now were suspicions—and an eyewitness who thought she saw Bella. Well, someone wearing white. Was she certain it was a woman? Or were the police assuming that based on Bella's robe?

All our suspects—Peter, Kyle, Donna, and Derek— seemed to have means, motive, and opportunity. Any of them could have slipped over to Bella's house early in the morning and stolen the Beast right out from under her nose.

Quincy made the cute little snort purr that let me know he was falling asleep. That plus the fact he suddenly weighed double in my arms. How did cats do that?

I gently placed him in an armchair, one of his favorite napping places, especially when we accidentally left merchandise on the seat. We'd taken things home to be washed more than once due to this little habit.

My cell phone rang over on the counter and I hurried to see who was calling. It was an unfamiliar number but I answered anyway, in case it was a customer or someone with aprons to sell.

"Good morning," an elderly male voice said. "I'm looking for Iris Buckley."

I reached for a pen and paper, just in case. "This is Iris. How can I help you?"

"This is Stan Perkins." Captain Greg's friend. He cleared his throat. "I have some news for you."

Spit it out, man. "Good news, I hope." My laugh was nervous, and Grammie glanced over, frowning. I shook my head to let her know it wasn't anything serious.

"Very good news, Iris. Good news indeed." Stan paused again. "Chet is alive and well. He's living in Massachusetts with his daughter."

Whew. I leaned back against the counter in relief. "That's wonderful, Stan. Um, another question. Is he married?" That sounded strange even to me so I hastily added, "Asking for a friend."

Stan chuckled. "And I can guess which *friend* you're talking about, young lady. I heard Florence Bailey is in town."

"I can't keep any secrets from you," I said, charmed at the idea that this older generation still had a lively social network. "So is he?"

"Chet's a widower," Stan said. "Wife died quite a few years ago, I gather. I've got his phone number if you want it."

I picked up that pen. "I sure do. Fire away." After I thanked Stan and hung up, I told Grammie the news.

"That's wonderful, Iris," she said. "We can share the news with Florence tonight."

I felt a pang of trepidation. "If we can do it without upsetting her. I could tell when she saw his picture that it still hurt."

"We'll take our cues from her," Grammie said. "How's that sound?"

"Brilliant as usual, Gram," I said. I spotted Madison coming along the sidewalk. "And there's my ride now. We'll be back well within half an hour."

Madison had snagged a street parking spot, so we were soon on our way to Quimby's Garage. On the way, I told her about my call from Stan.

She bounced a little in her seat. "Oh, I'm so glad to hear that. Reuniting sweethearts after more than sixty years. Wow."

"Maybe," I cautioned her. "If Florence wants the reunion."

"She will," Madison said blithely. "Sure, it's bittersweet, but they're getting a second chance. How many people get that, especially after a lifetime?"

I hoped she was right. "I'm going to let Grammie take the lead on this one, okay? If it's too upsetting for Florence to talk about, we're just going to let it go."

Madison waved a hand. "Of course. The last thing I want to do is upset Florence. I love her."

"I do, too. And thanks for planning the interview. It's going to be fantastic."

She gave me her thoughts about the interview's format the rest of the way to the garage. Madison was going to record it on video, and she had lists of questions to cue Florence in each room of the cottage and the lighthouse. "We can go off script, of course," she said. "But the questions will prime the pump, so to speak."

"It's brilliant," I said. Her plan was thorough but short enough that Florence wouldn't get overwhelmed or fatigued.

Business was brisk at Quimby's, with all three bays full. Bella's Volvo was parked on one side, ready to go. Madison rolled to a stop near the office and we both got out.

A plump older woman smiled at us from behind the desk. "Help you?" she asked.

I recognized Gladys Quimby, the owner's wife. "Morning," I said. "We're here to pick up Bella Ricci's car."

The smile dropped. "Oh, yeah, I have the slip for you." Her expression was grim as she began to sort through a stack of invoices in a tray. I was sure she didn't appreciate the reminder of the hit-and-run, since the garage owned the vehicle used. Was there insurance for such a thing? Would the Pedersens blame the garage? I really hadn't given those angles much thought.

We stood in uneasy silence as she sorted, losing her place and starting over again. Definitely flustered. "Is Derek here?" I asked. "I want to talk to him."

She turned hot eyes on me. "What about?" She'd finally found Bella's bill and she slapped it down on the counter, followed by a set of keys.

"Uh, not much," I said, now flustered myself. "Isn't

it typical to talk to the mechanic when you pick up a car?"

"He's not here," she said shortly. Then she sighed and pushed back from the desk. "But I suppose Roy can talk to you."

"Whoa," Madison said after Gladys went into the shop. "A wee bit hostile, don't you think?"

"I'll say." That annoying Pirro Auto jingle came on the radio again, assaulting our ears. It was going to haunt me for sure.

Roy Quimby, a short, heavyset man with cropped gray hair, followed his wife back into the shop. "Good morning, ladies," he said, wiping his fingers on a rag. "You picking up Miss Bella's car?" He at least was friendly. He ushered us toward the door. "The car's out this way."

Standing next to the Volvo, Roy went over the bill, even showing us the used parts while explaining what the mechanic had done. "She should be all set now. But holler if you have any questions." As he handed me the bill back, he said, "How's the Falcon running?"

They'd done some work for me recently. "Humming like a top," I said. Spotting an opportunity, I said, "I understand Derek is planning to take over the garage. He's a great mechanic, a perfect choice to continue the Quimby legacy."

Roy smiled at this compliment. "We've been talking about it," he said. Then his face fell. "Toughest part has been getting a loan. I was hoping he could buy the place outright but I might have to give him terms myself. Have him pay me monthly."

"Lance Pedersen was going to lend him money, right?" I asked. "Too bad that fell through."

Roy barked a dry laugh. "Not to speak ill of the dead, but that guy was a flake. He dangled Derek for months with his promises." He grimaced. "Then pulled the plug without warning. Derek was pretty upset. Never seen him like that."

"I'll bet," I said lightly, hoping my glee didn't show on my face. Roy had just confirmed what Kyle told us about Derek's anger toward Lance. "I'm sure something will work out." I turned to my friend. "Ready, Mads?"

Madison followed me back to Bella's house so she could run me back to the shop. A few minutes later, I was pulling the Volvo into Bella's drive. All was quiet in the neighborhood except for cheerful music drifting from Kyle's house next door. His Triumph was in the yard, which meant he was home.

Madison pulled in behind me, waiting in the Mini for me to get in. I pointed to Kyle's house. "I'm going over to talk to him a minute."

She shut off her engine and joined me as we skirted the hedge onto the other property. The music had stopped and an announcer was giving the weather report. . . . Then, before I even had a chance to call his name, the sight hit me like a blow.

The Triumph was sagging down on one side, and the pair of legs underneath revealed the shocking truth. Kyle was pinned under the car.

A scream ripped out of my chest as I ran to the bumper of the car. Instinct had taken over and I needed to do something, anything to help. I saw one of the jacks had fallen over, so I slid it back under the frame and began to pump. My late grandfather had restored vehicles, including Beverly, and from helping him, I knew my way around an automobile.

Madison had her phone out and was already dialing 911. While holding the phone, she crouched and put two fingers on his ankle to check for a pulse. "He's still alive."

Good news. I continued to work the jack handle, praying help would get here soon. What if we hadn't dropped Bella's car off when we did? How long would Kyle have lain there undiscovered?

Madison kneeled on the driveway. "Kyle? Kyle. Can you hear me?" No answer. He must be unconscious.

A woman came jogging up the sidewalk, pausing to drink water and wipe sweat off her brow. Donna Dube, dressed in shorts, V-back top, and sneakers. Her eyes flared then narrowed when she saw us. "What are you doing here?"

"I could ask you the same." I ran a shaking hand through my hair. "Kyle is hurt. His car fell on him."

Her body tensed as if a shock had gone through her. "What? Where?" She charged forward. When she saw Kyle's legs under the car, she shrieked. "Oh no. This is awful. Is he dead?"

Madison shook her head. "No, thank God. An ambulance is on the way."

Donna bent over, resting her hands on her knees. Her complexion was dead white, freckles standing out on her fair skin. "Oh, I can't believe this. He had something to tell me about Lance."

My head whipped around, my gaze meeting Madison's. "About Lance?" I asked. "You mean concerning his death?"

Donna nodded, her head still bent. She inhaled and exhaled audibly.

"You'd better sit," Madison said, coming to take Donna by the arm. "I don't want you going into shock." She sent me a sharp glance when my teeth began to chatter, one of my responses to severe stress. "And you neither."

Donna and I ended up sitting on Kyle's steps. Madison fetched a water bottle from her car and handed it to me while Donna sipped on her own. Then Madison paced about, back and forth, watching for the ambulance.

Sirens echoed down the hill. Help was on its way. I pictured the emergency vehicles tearing out of the station, racing along Main Street, and then zooming up the hill.

After a few sips of water and some deep breathing, I'd gathered myself enough to ask Donna a question. "What were you and Kyle going to talk about?"

At first I thought she wasn't going to answer me. Finally she said, "Last night at the club, he said something didn't add up about Lance's death. But when I pressed him, he clammed right up. I was hoping he might tell me more today."

Did Kyle know who the killer was? Had he seen or heard something that gave rise to suspicions? He lived right next door to Bella and down the street from the Pedersens. It was entirely credible that he had witnessed something important and maybe not realized it at the time.

Another question nudged at my mind. Why was Donna talking to Kyle about Lance's death? Protocol would dictate that she would pass along the tip to Anton or the State Police. I remembered her cryptic conversation with Alan. She'd been prying and probing then. Did she fancy herself a detective or was her motivation more nefarious? Maybe she was trying to cover her tracks or build a case against someone. Like Bella? I couldn't help remember our conversation in the bathroom before the sailing lesson—she'd seemed so sure, then, that Bella was guilty.

I found myself unconsciously edging away along the stair tread. Then I spread my arms and legs wide to cover the movement. Since Donna might know something, I had to be careful not to alienate her.

The sirens grew louder, almost deafening, and an ambulance arrived. Madison went out to the street to direct the EMTs. Anton, at the wheel of the police SUV, was right behind them. He opened the door and leaped out. After conferring with Madison, he came trotting over to us.

"I'm going to need you two to wait next door at Bella's," he said. "But stay put." He rested hands on his hips. "What are you doing here, Donna?"

She fidgeted on the step, extending her long legs, one, then the other. "I was taking a run." I could feel her mind tumbling over as she tried to decide what to tell her boss.

"We think Kyle knew something about Lance's death," I said. At a later time I would fill Anton in about Donna's seemingly underhanded movements.

Donna threw me a look I couldn't quite read. "Yeah, I was going to tell you, Chief, honest. He said things didn't add up, but he wouldn't say what exactly."

And now Kyle was lying underneath his car, injured and perhaps dying. More vehicles arrived, officials pouring out to help the stricken man.

As Anton suggested, Donna, Madison, and I made our way back to Bella's house. She had a comfortable front porch furnished with wicker chairs, so we sat there to wait. After a few minutes, once my wobbly knees regained their strength, I stepped into the side yard to call Grammie. She must be wondering where we were.

"Oh, that poor man," Grammie said after I filled her in. "I pray he'll be all right."

"Me too." I tried to swallow the lump in my throat.

"Anyway, I'm going to be here for a while. Until the police release us."

"Take your time, honey." Her tone was warm and reassuring. "Quincy and I are holding down the fort just fine."

The ambulance took off right then, siren wailing. Once it died down a little, I said, "I'd better go, Grammie. See you soon." The other police cars also left, one by one.

Anton made his way around the hedge, and Donna got up and went to meet him. Although they spoke in low tones, I could tell by their body language that the conversation was tense. Finally she ran off down the sidewalk and he continued on to talk to us. I returned to my chair.

Part of me wanted to tell Anton my theory about Donna. After overhearing her talking to Alan and what she said today, I was almost sure she was unofficially investigating. But why? For her career? To avenge Lance's death—or another reason?

In the end, I decided to leave it alone. Maybe with enough rope she would hang herself. It wasn't up to me to rat her out, and after all, the only reason we really considered Donna a suspect was because of Kyle's assumption that Lance wasn't interested in a long-term relationship with her. Thinking of Kyle brought me back down to reality with a thump.

Anton regarded us both with sympathetic eyes. "Hey, you two. I need you to tell me exactly what happened. I'm assuming one of you jacked up the car again?"

I waved my hand. "That was me. I probably ruined any fingerprints but it was instinctive, you know?"

He tilted his head, continuing to study my face. "You

probably saved his life, Iris." After letting that sink in, he said, "Why do you think we need fingerprints?"

Uh, I probably shouldn't have said that. I shifted in the wicker, making it creak in protest. "Well, in case it wasn't an accident. Kyle worked on that car all the time. Why did the jack fail? It wasn't broken, just lying on the ground."

"As if he hadn't made sure it was level," Madison said. "But I personally don't believe he would make that mistake. Like Iris said, he was out there all the time. We've seen him."

Anton took this all in. "What would you think if Donna hadn't said he knew something about Lance's death?"

I shifted again, seeing how her insinuation had affected my thought process. "That it was an accident?"

He nodded. "Exactly. We have to work with the evidence, not theories. And he's in bad enough shape that we can't confirm what Donna said. It will be a day or two before we can question him." On that note, he went on to take our statements.

But my thoughts kept returning to Kyle. What did he know about Lance's death? Was it enough to get the charges against Bella dropped? And identify the real killer?

And most disturbing of all, was Anton wrong? Was today's "accident" an attempt to silence Kyle for good?

CHAPTER 16

Distracted and perturbed, I somehow muddled through the rest of the day. After we closed the shop, I was more than tempted to beg off Florence's interview and go home. But not wanting to let the others down, I forced myself to go.

The first thing I saw when we pulled up to the lighthouse was Ian, setting up a barbecue grill near the picnic table. "Ian is grilling steaks for us tonight," Grammie said. "Didn't I tell you?"

"No," I said, climbing out of the Jeep. "Well, maybe. I've been kind of preoccupied today."

Grammie lifted the back gate. "Help with this, will you, dear?" She'd packed salad fixings, pasta salad, and dressings in a large cooler. We each took a handle and lugged it over to the picnic table. Then I grabbed a tote containing dishes and utensils, plus napkins and condiments.

"Hey, babe," Ian said, pecking me on the lips. "How was your day?"

I froze, realizing I hadn't told him the news. He'd been working on one of the islands today, out of cell phone range. And then I'd totally forgotten. Seeing my expression, Grammie patted me on the shoulder.

"Why don't you go say hi to Florence and Bella?" she suggested. "I'll give Ian the update."

Bella was helping Florence get out of Alan's BMW. Florence looked lovely tonight, her silver hair freshly done and light makeup enhancing her soft features. She was dressed in a flattering lilac pantsuit.

Time to tuck everything away and focus on Florence. I thought again of the letter we'd found and the bombshell news that Chet was alive. My belly clenched in anticipation. Would tonight provide an opportunity to share both?

"Hey, ladies," I said, giving each a hug. "I'm really looking forward to tonight."

"Me too," Florence said with a little laugh. "This place was a huge part of my life. It was all so long ago, but it feels like yesterday."

The three of us looked at the lighthouse, standing proud against a misty sky. Clouds were coming in and the setting sun was a band of orange in the west. Pink and lavender and gold wisps of cloud drifted above the milky bay, and seagulls squawked and soared. What a special landmark it was, and I felt proud to be part of the team preserving it for future generations.

Madison buzzed up the road in her Mini and hurried to join us. Tonight Sophie and Jake were busy with his family, so we were it.

After several shots showing Florence on the bluffs below the lighthouse beam, we went into the keeper's cottage. We went through the place room by room, with Florence sharing stories of her childhood there. She spoke about the flock of chickens they'd kept, sweet Christmas traditions, and the horror and thrill of a shipwreck offshore.

In the kitchen, she told us about family meals and memories, Saturday night baked beans, and eating all the lobsters she wanted. The final shoot tonight was of Florence and Grammie seated at the kitchen table drinking tea. Florence told us about the last days here, when the order had come from the U.S. Coast Guard.

"My daddy knew it was coming," she said, blinking back tears. "All up and down the coast they'd decided to automate the lights. It would save a lot of money, you see." She tried to smile. "It was truly the end of an era. Two hundred years of lighthouse keepers all up and down the Maine coast."

Grammie sighed. "And the idea of living in a lighthouse still fascinates people today. It seems so romantic."

Florence laughed. "It was, I suppose. Hard work, yes. And often lonely. But we lived connected to the sea, and to those who depended upon our light for safety." Her words evoked the endless beat of the waves and the bobbing lights of boats passing by.

Madison switched off her camera. "Perfect. Absolutely perfect."

Florence's shoulders sagged. "Whew. I'm tired now." She picked up her teacup and sipped. "Long trip down memory lane."

"And we loved it, Nonna," Bella said. "The early fifties were quite a period of transition, sounds like."

"They were," Florence said. "We had the war going on, too. If we weren't caught up in that, it might have been worse leaving. As it was, I kind of associated the two."

I glanced at Grammie, who nodded. "Um, Florence, when we were sorting through boxes at the lighthouse, we found something in one of the aprons. Your apron."

Florence's brows lifted in interest. "Really? What was it?"

In anticipation of this moment, I'd placed the letter

in a plastic sleeve and tucked it into my tote. "It was a letter." I slid it across the table, holding my breath while she picked it up and glanced at it, back and front.

Her gaze grew distant. "Chet. Dear Chet. I sometimes wonder—" Breaking off, she turned to Bella. "Oh, I loved Louis. But Chet was my first love."

"I understand, Nonna," Bella said. "We all have one of those."

"Sometimes I wish . . ." Florence chewed at her bottom lip. "I don't even know what became of him after the war. I heard that he was released, but I was married and pregnant by then. I wanted to reach out, to express my relief and joy, but I didn't think I should. It might have upset Louis. Better to let bygones be bygones."

I inhaled deeply. "What if Chet is still alive? Would you want to see him?"

"We found him, Nonna," Bella jumped in. "He's living in Massachusetts. He's a widower."

A long silence fell. Then Florence said slowly, "You know what? I think I do want to see him. It's time."

"No, thank you," I said, refusing the pan of banana pudding making the rounds. "I can't eat another bite." Our little group was seated at the picnic table on the bluff, watching the hazy sunset while gorging ourselves.

Madison took a big spoonful of whipped cream and fruit. "Are you sure? It's totally delectable."

Where did she put it all? "Save me a little," I said. "I'll have it for breakfast." Since Grammie had made the dish, leftovers would be going home with us.

Ian, who was seated next to me, put a hand on my thigh. "How was your steak?" As chef today, he'd been sweetly concerned about cooking the meat the way each of us liked it.

"It was perfect," I said. "Medium rare." I didn't eat

tons of meat but my carnivore side adored the primitive pleasure of steak cooked over a fire. I looked at the lighthouse, the way the beam shone in the gathering dusk. "When are you going to start painting?"

"Tomorrow evening," Ian said. "Anton is going to help me and Jake so we can get 'er done."

Madison pointed her spoon at Ian. "You're planning on helping me tomorrow, right?" To the table at large, she said, "Ian and I are teaching the sailing class at the yacht club."

With a jolt, I remembered that Kyle was out of commission. But what about Donna? Maybe her hours at the police station had interfered with teaching.

"Alice and Connor are really loving their lessons," Bella said. "I'm so glad we signed them up."

"Well, we'll try not to wreck that for them, right, Madison?" Ian laughed. "Kyle and Lance left big shoes to fill," he added, quickly sobering at the thought of the two men.

"Any updates on Kyle?" I asked Madison, figuring that she had the best chance of learning anything.

She scraped the bottom of her bowl with the spoon. "Nope. Still stable, far as I know." Kyle had suffered a number of injuries when the car fell on him, and the word "miracle" was being bandied about.

"So glad to hear that," I said. "I hope he recovers quickly." My gaze was caught by a bicyclist slowly pumping the pedals as they climbed the sloping entrance road. "I wonder who that is." The lighthouse grounds were closed to visitors after six now, so we had time and space to rehabilitate it.

Everyone turned to watch as the cyclist continued to approach. He wore a bright orange helmet, shorts, and a tight sports top.

Then I recognized the beard and the dark-rimmed

glasses. "It's Lars Lavely. What the heck is he doing here?" Couldn't we shake him for one night?

Bella jumped up from the table, glancing around. "Quick. Hide me."

"Why do you need to hide, dear?" Florence asked.

"He's a reporter for the local rag," I said. "And he wants pictures of Bella."

Grammie groaned. "This is all on me. I invited Lars to come take some pictures for a newspaper article about the museum." She glanced at the darkening sky. "He's late. I thought he'd forgotten."

"It's not your fault, Grammie," I said. "He's a sly one." I was sure Lars was fully aware that Bella was on our committee. Sure, he was going to do an article about the museum, which we appreciated, but he was probably hoping for a twofer. Candid pictures of Bella were probably going for big bucks right now.

Ian patted his jeans pocket, then pulled out a key ring. "Here's the lighthouse key. Go hang out in there. We'll get rid of him quick as we can."

Bella took the key and sprinted across the grass, her sneakers flashing. Of course Lars noticed, and he halted on his bicycle to watch. But before he could get his camera out of his pack, she disappeared through the lighthouse door. It slammed shut.

Lars began moving forward again, his pace increasing as the road leveled out. Once he reached the grass, he hopped off his bike and wheeled it toward us. Then he engaged the stand and unclipped his helmet. "Whew. That was a bit of a puff." After hanging the helmet on his handlebar, he pulled a water bottle from the clip and drank deeply.

"Thanks for coming up," Grammie said. "We appreciate having you write a feature about the museum." She got up from the table. "Let me show you around."

"We'll clean up, Grammie," I said. If she could corral Lars for a while, we could sneak Bella out of here.

To my surprise, Florence also rose. "Hello, young man. So nice to meet you. I'm Florence Bailey. I grew up in this lighthouse, from birth to my early twenties."

"Whoa," Lars exclaimed. "Seriously? That's so cool."

"I'll tell you all about it, if you want," Florence said. "I've never spoken to the press before. Just to the lighthouse committee."

Perhaps the lighthouse story was small potatoes compared to a murder case, but Lars was taking the bait. His eyes now had a familiar wolfish gleam as he began to fumble with his pack. "Hold on, let me get my stuff."

"We just finished interviewing Florence on video for our exhibit and website," Madison put in. "I can give you a sneak peek after I edit."

Lars pursed his lips. "That'd be great. Appreciate it." He straightened his shoulders. "I bet a couple of the regional magazines will be interested." Although Lars worked for the *Herald*, he sometimes freelanced for other publications, like *Down East* and *Yankee*. Florence's story was perfect: a blend of human interest, history, and tourist attraction.

Madison, Grammie, and Florence escorted Lars to the keeper's cottage, leaving Ian and me at the table. We began to clean up, loading the cooler with containers of leftovers and dirty dishes to wash later. Scraps of food went into a trash bag to carry out. Ian had already loaded the grill and barbecue tools into the rear of his truck.

"How do we get her out of here?" he asked, staring over at the lighthouse tower. "She brought Florence, right?"

"She did." I studied the upper balcony, wondering if Bella would dare to venture outside. It must be awful to be the target of such relentless media scrutiny. "But I can drive Florence to the resort in the BMW, and Grammie or Madison can swing by and get me."

"Why don't I take Bella?" Ian suggested. "I'm not needed here." He pressed his lips together. "I was hoping for some you and me time later but . . ."

I swooped in for a hug. "Me too. You can go hang out at the house, if you want. We have beer in the fridge. And Quincy would love to see you."

He kissed me. "Okay. Sounds like a plan." After we loaded the rest of the stuff into Grammie's Jeep, he got into the truck and drove over to the lighthouse, where he pulled up close to the door. I sent Bella a text, and a moment later she was out the door and in his truck. They raced away.

I went into the cottage to see how things were going, discreetly giving my friends a thumbs-up to let them know the mission was accomplished.

Lars finished taking notes on his tablet. "I'd really love to go inside the lighthouse itself." Behind his glasses, his eyes gleamed as he waited for our response.

"We can do that," Madison said. "We'd better hurry though. It's getting dark."

When the reporter realized a few minutes later that his quarry had fled, his disappointment was palpable. In front of Florence and Grammie, he maintained a pleasant demeanor, but as we left the lighthouse, he hung back to walk beside me. "Good one, Iris," he said. "But she can't avoid the press forever."

"She will long as I have something to do with it," I said crisply.

A short distance away, Madison pulled her cell phone out and answered. By her greeting, I could tell it was Anton. My heart thudded into gear. Was there news?

"Ahh, don't be that way," Lars said, his tone whining. "I've done you a lot of favors, with your business and all. And now the museum."

What a weasel. "Lars, I like you, honest I do. But you're really getting on my nerves right now. Bella deserves privacy, like any of us."

Madison hung up, her eyes boring through the dusk to mine. The tilt of her head said plainly, *Get him out of here.*

His mouth opened, ready to frame a protest, but then he seemed to think better of it. With a grumble, he trotted across the lawn to his bicycle, detouring to say goodbye to Grammie and Florence. They fussed over him, which he ate right up of course, and then soon he was pedaling down the road, lights twinkling on his bicycle.

"What is it, Madison?" I asked, catching up to her as she reached Florence and Grammie.

"That was Anton," Madison said. She appeared to brace herself. "The police figured out that the car falling on Kyle wasn't an accident. Someone not only moved the jack, they kicked out some supporting blocks under the frame." Blocks were used as backup in case of jack failure.

It all came together in my mind. "Someone tried to kill him," I said, "because he knows something about Lance's death."

CHAPTER 17

Florence looked confused. "What's going on? Who is Kyle?"

We quickly filled her in. "I'm so sorry to hear about that young man getting hurt," she said. "But this time Bella has an alibi." She smiled. "She was with me all day."

"Call Anton back," I said to Madison. "Tell him that."

As Grammie locked up the cottage and lighthouse, Madison placed the call. While she was waiting to talk to Anton, I told Florence I would be driving her home. Bella had left her bag behind when she escaped to the lighthouse, so we had the keys.

"That's fine, dear," she said. "I still have my license but I prefer not to drive at night."

Madison spoke briefly into the phone, then hung up. "They're already sending officers to the resort to question Bella. We'd better get you back, Florence." She offered to follow us and pick me up, so Grammie went ahead home. I told her to reassure Ian that I'd be there as quickly as I could.

Alan's BMW was so new it still smelled like leather and money. The driver's seat cupped my body just so and the engine purred like a kitten. Although I was perfectly content with my vintage beauty, I could see the allure of the luxury automobile.

"All set?" I asked Florence, seated in the front passenger seat. After she assented, I put the car into drive and set off down the road. The BMW handled like a dream, hugging corners and responding to my every touch.

The route out to the resort was very familiar by now, and to save time, I went out to the main highway so as to avoid downtown, Madison's headlights shining cheerfully in my rearview mirror. This route led us past Quimby's, which was dark except for a light in the office. *Derek hadn't been at the garage this morning.* The thought swept over me like a splash of cold water.

Had he gone to pay his cousin a visit? And what of Donna? She came along at the most convenient time. Was she revisiting the scene of the crime to make sure Kyle was dead? And our third suspect, Peter, lived right up the street. He could have slipped down to Kyle's house, kicked the jack and blocks out and been back home within minutes.

Perhaps sensing my preoccupation, Florence remained silent, gazing out the window at the passing countryside. I was sure the revelation about Chet Chapman being alive had given her plenty to mull over.

At last we reached the resort entrance, the stone sign lit by spotlights. "This place is starting to feel like home," Florence said with a laugh. "I've been enjoying spending time with the children so much."

"I'll bet," I said. "They're great kids." I pulled up under the front canopy so Florence wouldn't have to walk far. "Tell Bella to keep us posted, okay?" I would love to go inside and witness the police interview but was sure they wouldn't appreciate it.

She opened the passenger door, holding Bella's

handbag. "I'll do that. Thanks for the ride, Iris." She hesitated. "And thank you for tracking Chet down. Until I found out there was a possibility of seeing him again, I didn't realize how much I wanted to."

"Ah, that's great, Florence," I said. "Maybe he can come to the museum opening. He can be one of our guests of honor." She was definitely the other.

She swung her legs around so she could get out. "I'll ask him. My plan is to e-mail him tomorrow." She smiled. "Hopefully he'll write back."

"I'm sure he will." I watched as she slid out of the car and stood, then shut the door. I waved and smiled goodbye.

Before I got out to give Alan's keys to the valet, I grabbed my phone to send Ian a quick text. But my fingers fumbled and the phone slid down between the seat and the console. Ugh. The space was narrow and I could barely get my fingers down there.

I fished around best I could, finally grabbing on to something. It wasn't my phone, though.

It was a dragonfly hair clip, quite pretty. Where had I seen one like this?

An image floated into my mind. Someone walking ahead of me . . . Gretchen Stolte, at the dentist's office. Gretchen, who had dated Alan, and judging by her attitude toward Bella, had hoped for more from him.

Was he up to his old tricks? First Donna and now Gretchen? What should I do with the clip? I didn't want to leave it for Bella to find and she well might, since she'd been driving this car.

The valet was coming toward me, probably puzzled about what I was doing, so I pushed the clip back between the seats. But it certainly wasn't forgotten. Soon as I could, I would read Alan the riot act. How dare he try to convince Bella to get back together while spending time with other women?

After finally locating my phone, I climbed out of the BMW, leaving the engine running. "It's all yours," I said to the young man. A tip. I should give him a tip. I opened my handbag and began to rummage for my wallet.

"No problem, miss," he said, sliding past me into the driver's seat. "Mr. Ricci is taking good care of me."

Madison had pulled up nearby to wait for me. "What's up?" she asked as I climbed into the passenger seat. "You look flustered."

"I am," I said with a laugh, fastening the seat belt. She knew me too well. "I found Gretchen's hair clip in Alan's car. Down beside the seat."

She put the car into gear and we set off. "Okay. Two things. How do you know it's hers? And if it is, maybe it's leftover from when they dated."

"Maybe, if she had more than one," I admitted. "Though it's a pretty expensive piece. Sterling silver. I saw her wearing it when I went to the dentist a few days ago. To me that says she's been in his car recently."

Madison halted at the resort entrance, flicking her left blinker on. "I sure hope not, for his sake. Bella will kill him."

For a second, this typical hyperbole silenced us. "I don't know what to do," I admitted. "I put it back where I found it, but I'm so tempted to tell her."

"It's a tough call," Madison said. "But if something like that ever happens to me, you tell me, okay? I promise I won't shoot the messenger."

"Same here." I leaned my elbow on the rest and watched the countryside whiz by. "I was thinking about talking to Alan, telling him to cut it out or I will tell Bella."

"That *might* work," Madison said. "But if he's still

hanging out with other women, then I really doubt his sincerity."

"Me too," I said. "What a jerk." Until now, I hadn't realized how much I was hoping to see a happy ending for Bella and Alan. We all love it when the bad guy reforms, right? And those poor kids . . .

A short while later, Madison slowed as she prepared to turn up my driveway. "Want to come in for a while?" I asked. Ian's truck was still parked near the barn, I was glad to see. I wouldn't have blamed him if he'd given up and gone home.

"Not tonight," Madison said, putting the car into park. "I'm due at the yacht club bright and early."

"That's right, you're subbing for Kyle," I said, opening the car door. "That should be fun."

"Come down for lunch," she called. "We're having sandwiches and pizza catered. There will be a ton, so come help us eat it."

"I'll try," I said. "I have that interview with Faith O'Brien tomorrow. Wish me luck—we really need to find someone for the store."

She did, then zoomed off for home. Instead of going in through the back door, I detoured through the flower gardens to the porch. As I hoped, Ian was seated on the hanging swing, Quincy in his lap.

"There you are," he said, straightening to a more upright position. "Me and Quince were falling asleep." At his movements, Quincy mewed and clung on to his jeans with his claws.

"He's not going to want you to leave," I said, sitting beside them. I reached out and touched Quincy's soft fur, trying to encourage him to settle again.

Ian laughed, looking down at the cat. "Trapped by a cat. Think my clients will accept that excuse?"

"I've thought about using it myself," I said. As we

gently rocked back and forth, I felt myself relax. Ian put an arm around me and pulled me close. Crickets chirped in the grass and the moon floated behind hazy clouds. My plans to discuss the case with Ian floated away. It could all wait until tomorrow.

Faith O'Brien was right on time for the interview the next morning—along with her three children. "I'm sorry," Faith said, her cheeks flushing. "But my babysitter cancelled at the last minute. If you want to reschedule, I understand." Faith was short and slight, with light brown hair, freckles, and elfin features. Her children were miniature versions of Faith—adorable, with good manners.

"It's not a problem," Grammie said. "I've got some coloring books and crayons if they would like to color." She smiled at the children. "What are your names?"

Thomas was ten, Madelyn was eight, and Grace was six. They wore beautifully stitched seersucker shorts, polo shirts, and matching sandals.

"Did you make their outfits?" I asked, smoothing Grace's collar.

"I did," Faith said, the blush deepening. "I just love to sew."

Grace looked up at me, her bobbed hair held back with barrettes. "Mommy makes lots of clothes for us."

I held out my apron skirt. "And we sew aprons here. We even make some that fit little girls."

Grace and Madelyn darted glances at their mother. "I want an apron," Madelyn declared. "Just like yours."

"Maybe," Faith said, her smile so wide her cheeks must have ached. "We'll see."

Grammie settled the children at one of the long tables in the side room, Quincy supervising, while Faith and I sat at the other to talk. She had a great resume, with years of retail experience at various shops around the area.

"Over the past few years, I've mostly worked part-time," Faith said. "But now that all three are going to school, I can take on more hours."

With children in school, opening the store wasn't a problem. But staying to close at five might be. When I inquired about that, she told me that she had childcare lined up. "Not the person who was supposed to help me today," she assured me.

"That all sounds good," I said. "There's one more thing. Can you stitch on a ruffle for me?" At my other two interviews, we hadn't even gotten that far. As a sewing test, I wanted her to add a ruffle to the armhole of a pinafore apron.

"Of course." Faith glanced at the nearby sewing machine, set up and ready. At my invitation, she sat down, checked the settings, and within a minute, had flawlessly attached the ruffle. I couldn't have done better myself.

I glanced over at Grammie, who was standing near the kids. Our eyes met and she nodded. "Faith, I'd like to offer you a job, if you're interested," I said.

"Yay, Mommy," Thomas said, waving a crayon. His sisters echoed him.

Faith beamed. "Yes, I am interested. I'd love to work here."

Quincy jumped down from his chair and came over to Faith. He rubbed her ankles, then leaped up into her lap. We all laughed.

"He likes you, Mommy." Grace put down a crayon and picked up another.

"The Quincy seal of approval has been bestowed," Grammie said.

After the O'Brien crew left, since store traffic was

light, Grammie and I poured fresh cups of coffee and sat in the side room. After discussing the menu for girls' night at the farmhouse this evening—grilled chicken and garden salad—we went over our notes concerning the museum project.

"A couple more work sessions and we should be ready for the opening," Grammie said as we looked at the exhibit plan for each room. The rooms were mostly ready but we were waiting on a few more donations to fill gaps. In addition, she had asked Bella, an inventory whiz, to set up a tracking system for the building contents. The database included donor name, item history and date, estimated value, and written description, as well as photographs.

"This is great, Grammie," I said, marveling at her efficiency. Good thing she was in charge right now instead of me, or we'd be way behind. Everything I knew, didn't know, and suspected about Lance's death and Alan's womanizing had infected my thoughts like a low-grade fever. I was floating around in a mental fog distracting enough that I couldn't fully concentrate.

"What's up, Iris?" Grammie asked. "I can tell something is bothering you."

Where to begin? Trying to gather my thoughts, I got up to fill my coffee mug. "A lot of things. Kyle getting hurt—and almost killed, for one. What if Madison and I hadn't arrived when we did?" I sat heavily, the thought making me weak. "The fact that we haven't found Lance's killer yet. That's huge. And, to top it all off, I think Alan is playing around on Bella."

"What?" Grammie's tone was sharp. "I thought they were trying to reconcile. He'd changed, blah, blah, blah."

I lifted my mug and sipped. "Me too. But last night I accidentally found Gretchen Stolte's hair clip in his car. You know Gretchen, right? The dental hygienist at

Dr. Pedersen's office. Or she was. She either quit or was let go."

"Of course I know Gretchen," Grammie said. "She's an odd one. She and Alan dated?"

"They sure did. A while back and not for very long. But I saw her wearing that hair clip the day I had my filling fixed. It's really unusual, maybe even an antique." I explained how I'd come across the clip while searching for my phone. I also told her about his secretive conversation with Donna at the resort.

"None of that sounds good, I'm sorry to say." Grammie set her lips in a thin line. "But maybe you should talk to him first. We could be jumping to conclusions."

"Like the police are about Bella?" I acknowledged her point. "You're right, all I have is circumstantial evidence." My chest eased a trifle. Although I still had serious doubts about Alan, I didn't need to act on them yet.

Grammie flipped her notebook to a new page. "So what's the latest on the other suspects?"

"Nothing conclusive about anyone so far," I said. "We have Donna, Peter, Derek, and yes, even Kyle."

She wrote each name in her neat script. "You don't think Kyle's accident clears him? Donna said he knew something about Lance's death, right?"

"She *said* he did. But what if Kyle killed Lance and then someone decided to take revenge? Maybe it was an impulse. They saw him working under the car and decided to kick out the jack and blocks." I winced at the cruel image.

"Who has an alibi for when Kyle was hurt?" Grammie asked.

"Bella does, thank goodness," I said. "She and Florence were together. So maybe the police will start looking at other people."

"That is good news," Grammie said, "although I'm sorry someone else almost died before they widened their focus."

"Me too." I pointed at the list of names. "We know Donna was in the area, because she came along right after we found him. Derek is a possibility too, since he wasn't at the garage when we picked up Bella's car. And Peter lives right up the street, so it would have been easy-peasy for him to do it."

"All of them are still in the running, then." After making a few notes, Grammie glanced at the wall clock. "Are you still going to the yacht club for lunch?"

"I don't know," I said. "I'm pretty content right here." Frankly, I was exhausted, both mentally and physically.

Grammie stood, picking up her empty mug. "Oh, go ahead. The fresh air will do you good. Plus you'll get to see Ian." Her eyes twinkled.

"True." Spending time with Ian was always a bonus, even if he was going to be surrounded by little kids. "Maybe I will."

CHAPTER 18

When I pulled into a parking space at the yacht club, I realized the man locking an Audi a couple of spots away was Peter Pedersen. Great. With the memory of our last encounter fresh in my mind, I really wasn't in the mood to talk to him. I thought about hiding in my car until he walked away, but of course he noticed me. Or noticed Beverly, rather. That was the downside of owning such an eye-catching and beautiful vehicle. It was hard to go incognito.

As he continued to stare at me, I climbed out, taking only my phone and keys, since I wouldn't need my handbag. "Hey, Peter," I said as I locked the car. "Here to do some sailing?"

"I am," he replied, falling into step with me as I crossed the parking lot toward the yacht club building where lunch was already underway. "The office is closed today so I'm taking advantage of the great sailing conditions."

It was a perfect sailing day, I had to agree. Overnight, the air had cleared and the humidity had dropped, and with this frontal passage, the wind had also picked up.

"I don't blame you," I said, torn between getting away from the man and hoping he might say something to incriminate himself. "Got to take advantage of it while you can."

"That's right. Before winter sets in." His brow furrowed. "That tooth okay now?"

I put my hand to my cheek, thankful that at least one annoyance in my life had been resolved. "It's fine, thanks." Since we were on the topic of the dental practice, I asked, "Are you taking over for your dad? I heard a rumor that he's retiring."

He didn't answer right away, and when I glanced over, I saw him staring toward the *Lucy Ann*, which was docked nearby. Gretchen was standing on the top deck, tanned and attractive in a pair of khaki shorts and a white T-shirt, coiling a length of rope. Her long hair was in a ponytail, and I wondered if she had missed the dragonfly clip yet.

"To be honest, everything is up in the air right now," he finally said, tearing his eyes away from Gretchen. "Yes, Dad is retiring, but I don't know if I'm staying in Maine. I'm ready for a change."

"Really? Where are you thinking of going?" My heart skipped a beat. Was his desire to leave town due to guilt about Lance? Or else, why go? The practice was very well established and, judging by the Pedersens' lifestyle, quite lucrative.

"I might be headed to Florida." He shifted his cap, navy with a Team USA badge, into a better position. "One of my buddies has a practice I can buy into. And I can sail all year-round down there."

"Well, if you do go, we'll be thinking of you next winter." While at our new dentist's office, no doubt, watching snow swirl past the windows.

We had now reached the main building, where a lunch station had been set up on the porch. Some kids were seated in little groups on the porch steps and the lawn, holding paper plates and juice boxes. Others were running around and screaming, a perfect after-lunch activity, right? Madison was seated cross-legged under a tree, a group of girls, including Bella's daughter, hanging on her every word. Two teenage camp counselors were also keeping an eye on the group.

One little boy darted over to us. "Hi, Lance," he said. "Are you going to be teaching us again?"

Peter took a step back in surprise. "I'm sorry, buddy. My name is Peter. I'm Lance's brother." He took off the cap so the boy could get a better look at his face.

"Oh. Hi, Peter." With that, the boy ran off, whooping as he joined his friends.

"Does that happen often?" I asked, intrigued by the child's mistaken identification. To me, the brothers didn't really look alike, plus Lance had had an ease and charisma Peter definitely lacked.

Peter chuckled. "Not often enough. I mean, because Lance was so popular with the ladies. But once in a while, especially in the summer when I get a tan and my hair bleaches out. He and I were the same height."

"Almost like twins," I said lightly. A thought teased in the back of my mind, but then Ian stepped out of the clubhouse and it went *poof*. "Nice seeing you, Peter, but I have to go."

Ian's face lit up when he saw me ascending the porch steps. "Iris. I didn't know if you were going to make it."

"Me neither, but here I am." We hugged briefly. "What's for lunch?"

Slinging his arm around my shoulders, he guided me over to the table. To my delight, I discovered the pizza was from Cheese Louise, one of my favorite places. I selected two slices, pepperoni and veggie, and a bottle of iced tea.

"Want to sit over here?" Ian led me to a pair of Adirondack chairs farther along the porch.

I sat as gracefully as I could in the sloped seat, placing my drink on the table between us. "You have time to visit with me?"

Ian checked the activity on the lawn. "Madison and the teen counselors have it under control. The kids are just burning off some steam before they head home. Today was a half day."

"Are you headed to a job after?" I took a savory, salty bite of the pepperoni slice. Cheese Louise's wasn't too greasy, which I liked.

"Not today." Ian sat back in the chair, placing his arms on the rests. "I'm going to help my parents with a couple of projects." He grinned. "Earn my keep."

Peter emerged from the clubhouse and, evading children, made his way down to the docks. But instead of going to where his boat was moored, he approached the *Lucy Ann*.

"That's interesting," I said, tipping my chin toward the scene. "I wonder what he wants with Gretchen."

Ian followed my gesture. "She's his hygienist. I had her last time I got my teeth cleaned."

I hooted in surprise. "I didn't know you went to Dr. Oslo. I've been going there since I was eight."

"Age five or so for me," Ian said. He smiled. "Does that mean something, that we have the same dentist?"

"It's destiny." I played along. Now Peter was waving at Gretchen, and although I couldn't hear him, I guessed he was asking for permission to board. "Anyway, she's not working for them anymore. I'm not sure what happened."

"I can't say that I'm sorry," Ian said. "Last time I was there, she seemed out of it. Dropping tools, almost forgetting one quadrant of my mouth." He grinned. "Giving me banana tooth polish when I distinctly asked for peppermint."

"Now that is a crime," I said. Maybe this type of behavior was why Gretchen had gotten fired. I wondered what precipitated it. "She always seemed okay to me." Peter and Gretchen spoke briefly on the deck, then disappeared belowdecks.

"I wonder who they'll hire to replace her," Ian said.

"Maybe nobody," I told him. "Dr. Oslo is retiring and Peter might leave town."

Ian's eyes widened comically. "No, tell me it's not so."

"Yep. We're all going to be looking for a new dentist." I finished the pepperoni and began working on the veggie slice. "Are you still painting the lighthouse tonight?"

"We sure are," Ian said. "We got a second lift and some more guys to help, so we'll probably knock out the job tonight."

I stared at him in amazement. "That's awesome. If it was just you and Jake, it would take several sessions, right?" I glanced toward the *Lucy Ann* again. Peter and Gretchen were still below, which seemed strange. But maybe they were still friends, even though she'd left the practice.

"At least three," Ian said, pulling my attention back. "So, on another topic. What's new with Bella and the investigation? Anything?"

"A few things. Kyle is still stable, I heard, which is good news. And Bella has an alibi for when someone sabotaged his car. I'm hoping they'll drop the charges or at least widen the net."

"They ought to," Ian said. "Maybe I can talk to Anton about it tonight. I know he's not happy that they're focused on Bella."

"It's too bad his hands are tied," I said.

Gretchen's head popped up in the hatch as she climbed back on deck. Peter followed.

"But if we can find some additional evidence regarding the real killer, I know he'll go to bat for her."

Ian's mouth opened and I knew he was about to warn me to be careful. But then he thought better of it and said instead, "I hope something breaks soon. The tension must be unbearable."

"I know. I feel so horrible and helpless. I can't even imagine how Bella must feel." Peter and Gretchen strolled down the *Lucy Ann*'s gangway in single file. Then, without speaking to each other, Peter veered off toward the club docks and Gretchen headed toward an older maroon station wagon. A moment later she was pulling out of the parking lot.

As she exited, a few other cars arrived. Parents, I guessed. Ian pushed himself to his feet. "Duty calls," he said, bending to kiss me. "I've got to go help the kids get ready to leave." He put a gentle hand on my cheek. "Soon as that lighthouse is painted, we are going out for a nice dinner. We're definitely not spending enough time together lately."

I laughed up at him. "Agreed. And I can't wait."

He swooped in for another kiss and then was gone, striding across the porch and down to the lawn. While he and Madison corralled the children with the help of the counselors, I worked on the rest of my pizza.

A familiar black BMW drove slowly down the drive, Alan at the wheel. I tossed the rest of my pizza onto the plate, my appetite gone. Should I go talk to him now? It really wasn't the best time, with his kids right here.

He pulled into a place near the *Lucy Ann* and got out. Rage ignited when, instead of going directly to where his children were playing on the grass, he stood and stared at the schooner. Then he turned and scanned the parking lot.

Who was he looking for? The answer thudded in my belly like a stone: *Gretchen.*

Without making a conscious decision, I found myself running down the porch steps and across the parking lot toward him. He must have heard my feet pounding on the pavement because he turned to face me.

"Iris," he said with a warm smile. "Here to do some sailing?"

Right. I was wearing a dress with a pinafore apron, not exactly sailing attire. But I didn't bother to refute his ridiculous assumption. "We need to talk."

He pulled his head back in alarm, as well he should. All men dread that particular statement, especially from an angry woman.

Then he made a partial recovery, giving me a placating smile. "What about?" He glanced toward the group of children. "I don't have long. The kids are waiting for me."

That further inflamed me. "But you had time to talk to Gretchen. She already left, by the way."

"Gretchen?" His expression was quizzical. "What do you mean?"

I stepped closer. "Don't play dumb, Alan. It's obvious you were looking around for her. I found her hair clip in your car last night, so I know you've been spending time with her."

Instead of denying my accusation, he held up the clip, which had been in his shorts pocket. "I was going to give it back to her."

Hot tears burned my eyes. "How could you, Alan? You almost had Bella convinced that you really have changed. What kind of person would do that, then stomp on her heart again?" To my horror, I heard a sob catch in my throat. So much for big bad Iris.

"Hold on," he said, putting up both hands. "It's not what it looks like. I promise. I'm not involved with Gretchen or any other woman. I love Bella."

"I wish I could believe you." And to my surprise, I really meant that. Then my heart hardened. "So when did she lose that clip, huh?"

His head went down. "A few days ago. I was down here while the kids were sailing and she wanted to talk to me. So we sat in my car." His tone became rueful. "Bad mistake."

"I'll say. So you two were rekindling something?" My tone also had an edge.

"Nope, we weren't." He ran a hand through his hair, giving a little laugh. "She was complaining about her job and some guy she's been seeing. Then she started talking about how good it was when we were dating. Asked me if I wanted to try again." His face screwed up into a grimace. "I tried to let her down easy. But she flipped out when I told her I'm hoping to reconcile with Bella."

"She hates Bella," I said. "Because of you, I think. She had high hopes when you first dated."

He winced. "I was such a jerk. She was my rebound relationship after the divorce."

"Yes, you were," I agreed. "So, I'm not one hundred percent sure I believe you, okay? But what might help convince me is you telling Bella about the clip and how it got into your car."

Alan thought about that for a moment. Then he nodded, almost seeming relieved. "Deal. It's the right thing to do. I want to be totally transparent with Bella."

"Good." I thought about bringing up his covert conversation with Donna at the resort but decided to wait. I wanted to see if he came clean about Gretchen first.

"Iris, I'm really worried." He inhaled a deep breath. "Cookie told us today that Bella might go on trial as early as this fall."

My heart jumped. "So soon? I'd better ramp up my efforts to exonerate her, then." Not that I hadn't been thinking about the case day and night.

"So, it's true," he said, lifting a brow. "Bella said you were investigating. According to her, you have quite a knack for it."

"Not just me," I said with modesty. "The whole gang helps." If I had trusted him more, I would share my suspicions about other suspects. Instead I thought of questions I had for him. "There is something I've been wondering. Why were you at the overlook that morning?" A truly wild conjecture was that he had been involved in Lance's death, jealous the sailor was dating Bella. But he wouldn't have used the Jeep, I was pretty sure.

Alan leaned back against the BMW, his lips twisting in a wry smile. "You're not the first person to ask me that. My original destination was Bella's house. After a long night tossing and turning, I decided to just get up and go talk to her. Pour out my heart, et cetera. Then I chickened out when I actually got there."

"Plus the sun wasn't even up," I noted. "Bad time to visit someone."

"That too. What an idiot I am." He shook his head. "Anyway, I drove right past her house and up to the overlook. To be honest, I didn't think about the Jeep not being at her house, didn't even notice. I was going to chill out for a while looking at the view and think about what to say to her instead of being all impulsive."

I had to admit I was thawing a little toward him.

This confession felt truthful. "Good plan. What happened next?"

His gaze went distant. "First thing I noticed was that old junker Jeep right in the middle of the road, driver door wide open. Then I saw"—he swallowed—"Lance. On the ground." His voice was a croak. "It was pretty obvious he was gone."

"Oh, Alan, that's awful." I couldn't imagine coming across such a horrific scene.

"So of course my first thought was Bella. Where was she? Was she okay? But when I called her, she was still asleep in bed." He sighed. "My next call was to the police. I never dreamed they would arrest her. Talk about naïve."

"Don't beat yourself up too badly," I said. "Of course you called them." I waited a beat. "I think someone framed Bella."

"Yeah, I do, too. And I hope you find out who." Shouts from the group of kids attracted our attention. "Listen, Iris. I'm glad we had this chat. But . . ." He gestured toward the children.

"I've got to go, too. See you later." Halfway to Beverly, I turned for a parting shot. "And don't forget to talk to Bella. I'll be following up." He nodded, waving that infernal clip. We'd soon find out how sincere he was.

CHAPTER 19

After a busy afternoon at the shop, Grammie and I arrived home around five thirty. Another change of weather had blown through and the evening air was soft and golden, the leaves on our giant maples barely stirring. It was a perfect night for a cookout.

"Can you pick stuff for a salad, Iris?" Grammie asked as we crossed the drive toward the house. "I'm going to get the grill started." One of Grammie's signature recipes, the chicken breasts had been soaking all day in a lemon-pepper marinade.

"Of course. Right after I get changed." Quincy was already cavorting about in the grass, playing hide-and-seek with a grasshopper.

Up in my room, which overlooked the back part of the property, I exchanged my dress and flats for shorts, a T-shirt, and sandals. While at the shop, I'd been able to push the whole Alan situation to the back of my mind. But now it came roaring back. Bella was coming to dinner, of course, and I was torn about what to do. Should I tell her about the hair clip tonight or give Alan the benefit of the doubt and wait a day or two?

That was the answer, I decided. Why ruin our meal? Feeling marginally better, I washed up, put on fresh lip gloss and combed my hair, then went downstairs, eager to get out into the garden.

Ever since I'd been a little girl, I'd loved helping Grammie grow vegetables. Planting seeds, watching plants emerge, watering the garden, and best of all, harvesting. Weeding, not so much. I found a wicker basket in the mudroom and, Quincy at my heels, went out to the patch.

Tomatoes were a must, so I chose several beauties. Then I foraged for cucumbers hidden under vines, plucked kale and lettuce and spinach, and picked bell peppers and green beans. Tugging gently, I pulled carrots, beets, and onions from the soft and loamy soil. Our salad tonight would be a cornucopia of fresh, healthy goodness.

Quincy, who had been watching my every move, followed me back to the house. We entered the kitchen through the porch door, and of course he went right to his dish.

I laughed. "He wants to see if we put anything exciting in there after he last checked."

"Not yet," Grammie said. "But if he's a good boy, he might get a taste of chicken later." She was using a big fork to turn the chicken over in the marinade.

While she put the chicken on the grill, I got to work washing and chopping and soon built a beautiful tossed salad in a big wooden bowl. For dressings, I decided to make Greek yogurt ranch and honey mustard. Homemade salad dressings were so much better—and quite simple to make, I had discovered.

Florence and Bella were first to arrive, both pretty in summery tops and Capri pants. "We have a treat for you," Bella sang out when they walked into the kitchen. Florence set two bottles of imported pinot grigio on the island.

"Lovely." Grammie picked up a bottle and read the label.

"No, not those," Bella said. "This." Beaming with pride, she set a footed glass bowl beside the wine. "Tiramisu. Family recipe." This creamy confection was a classic, flavored with liqueurs, coffee, and chocolate. She looked so gorgeous and happy, wimpy old me was relieved I'd decided not to bring up her ex tonight.

"How did you know I was craving tiramisu?" Grammie asked. "It's one of my guilty pleasures."

"Mine too," Florence said. "And I've got a new one." She opened her large handbag and pulled out a shiny new rose-gold tablet. "It's quite addicting."

"I've created a monster," Bella said, rolling her eyes. "She now has social media accounts and a whole slew of apps and games."

Florence held the tablet to her chest. "Plus my own e-mail account. I'm going to e-mail Chet but I wanted you all to help me write it."

How sweet. She was as shy and lovely as a teenager with her first crush. "We'd be happy to do that, Florence," I said.

The back door opened, accompanied by laughter and chatter, and a moment later, Sophie and Madison burst into the kitchen. "Good evening, ladies," Madison said, sliding a platter of antipasto onto the counter.

"That looks yum," I said, admiring the array of plump olives, cheese, salami, mushrooms, artichokes, and my favorite, peperoncini. I nabbed a hot pepper and popped it into my mouth.

"And I've got crusty rolls," Sophie said, adding her contribution.

Bella opened a bottle of wine while I set out glasses. "Did you check out the venue I sent you, Sophie?"

Sophie clasped her hands together, looking so

lovestruck that I laughed. "I did. And I can't thank you enough. We're booking it."

"What are you talking about?" Madison asked.

"Hold on," Bella said, pouring wine. "Once everyone has a glass, we're going to celebrate this good news." As the glasses were filled, I handed them around.

"All right," Sophie said, lifting her glass. "Is everyone ready?"

"We are," we chorused.

"I have found the absolutely perfect spot for my wedding." She paused. "Yes, including the ceremony. It's a place called Heart Island."

"I've heard of Heart Island," Grammie said. "But it's privately owned."

"That's right," Sophie said. "And it still is. But they are opening it up for weddings and other events. There's the most adorable little chapel and we've already spoken to our minister about performing the ceremony there. The reception will be held in the most perfect wedding barn I've ever seen." She grinned. "And Mom loves it, too. Even sight unseen."

"Oh, Sophie," I said. "It sounds perfect for you." My heart swelled with joy for my friend. She was going to get her dream wedding. I lifted my wine. "To Sophie and Jake. True love forever."

Everyone echoed this toast, and as I looked around the circle at their happy faces, I was filled with love and admiration for my tribe. My grandmother, a recent widow; Florence, a widow as well, separated from her first love for sixty years; Bella, struggling with divorce and a tenuous reconciliation; Madison, maybe on the brink of true love, maybe not. But their expressions revealed only pure delight in the good fortune of another.

While we nibbled on antipasto and drank wine, waiting for the chicken to finish grilling, Sophie showed us pictures of the island. Along with the church and barn, there were several cottages and a small hotel, remnants from when the island was fully occupied. These buildings had been refurbished, so most of the wedding party and guests would be staying there. "There's room for fifty," Sophie said. "And they provide a ferry to bring the other guests out for the day."

"I want to get married on an island," Madison said. Her fingers tapped at her phone. "Just added it to my bucket list."

Grammie raised her brows. "Do you have a groom in mind? Anyone we know?"

Madison ducked her head, cheeks flaming. "Not yet."

The fact that my gun-shy best friend was even talking about her own wedding was a major step forward. I wondered if our illustrious chief had something to do with changing her mind.

Once the chicken was done, we circled the island to fill our plates and then went to the porch table. The second bottle of wine accompanied us, as did Quincy. He had the promised tidbit of chicken in his dish. During dinner, discussion of Sophie's wedding continued. She'd picked out a dress, so naturally we had to talk about bridesmaid dresses. Madison, Bella, and I were going to be bridesmaids, along with Jake's sister and Sophie's cousin from Connecticut. She'd already started a page where she was collecting ideas for the wedding, including dresses she liked.

"I love your colors," I said. "They're perfect for a coastal wedding." Her palette included pale blush pink, seafoam, faded denim blue, and a vibrant berry pink.

"That's what I thought," Sophie said. "They'll look great indoors and out. The photos are going to be fabulous."

We'd used Sophie's tablet to view the page, passing it around the table. "The things you can do nowadays," Florence said when it was her turn. "We used to pin cloth to a board. And rip pictures out of magazines."

"This is just like that, only digital," Madison said. "So you can easily share it with other people."

"Your wedding will be lovely, dear," Florence said. "I hope you and your husband will be very happy."

"Thank you, Florence," Sophie said. "And I hope you'll come. I've added you to the guest list." Her grin was sly. "And a plus-one."

"A plus-one?" Florence's cheeks flushed. "Does that mean what I think it does?" At Sophie's nod, she said, "Well, I appreciate the thought but it's a little soon to think about that. I don't even know if Chet will want to see me."

"Let's find out," I said. "We'll send him an e-mail over dessert."

"I'll start coffee. Does anyone want tea?" Grammie said.

The rest of us pitched in to help clear the dishes and get dessert ready. Armed with heaping bowls of tiramisu and Florence's new tablet, we returned to the table. I helped her open the e-mail program. Her e-mail address was florencebailyricci@.

"That's good you included your maiden name, for people who knew you before you got married," I said.

"Like Chet," Florence said. She already knew how to open a message and did so, then carefully typed in Chet's address. "Now what? This is where I'm stuck."

"It's important to make a subject line that he will open," Madison said. "You don't want him to think it's spam."

We thought for a moment. "How about, hello from an old Blueberry Cove friend," Grammie suggested.

"I like that," Florence said. She typed in the subject line. "Okay." She rubbed her hands together. "Now we get to the really important part. I don't want to be too intense and scare him off."

"Maybe talk about visiting Blueberry Cove and the lighthouse museum," I suggested. "I'm sure once you get going, it will be fine. Sometimes the first sentence is the hardest."

"'Dear Chet,'" she said aloud as she typed. "'A mutual friend, Stan Perkins, gave me your contact information. I'm in Blueberry Cove visiting with my family right now, and guess what? They are starting a lighthouse museum in town. Naturally this made me think of you and all the good times we had there.'"

We gave her a thumbs-up, then concentrated on eating our dessert while she continued writing. The tiramisu was the best I'd ever had, and I told Bella that.

"I'll pass that along to my mom," she said. Her parents and siblings still lived in Milan. Bella went once a year to visit them and there was talk of the family coming to Maine. I hoped they would.

"All right," Florence said. "Say a prayer. I'm sending it." She squeezed her eyes shut and hit SEND, the e-mail departing with a *swoosh*.

"I can't wait to find out what he says." Sophie had stars in her eyes. "It's so romantic."

"This is the life," Madison said. The two of us were seated on the porch swing drinking wine and waiting for Anton and Ian to arrive. The rest of the gang had gone home after helping clean up, and Grammie was puttering around inside. Quincy was wedged between us, curled up and purring.

"Totally. I love summer." I leaned my head back and stared up at the star-freckled sky. The air was still warm even at nine o'clock and there was only the merest hint of a breeze. Late-blooming flowers in the nearby beds sent soft fragrance into the air.

Engines sounded out on the quiet road, the vehicles slowing to turn up our drive. Ian's truck pulled up in front of the barn first, followed by Anton in his personal SUV. As they made their way through the flower garden to the back porch, I saw Ian had a paper bag tucked under his arm. His favorite craft brew, no doubt.

"How'd it go?" I called. They had spent the evening painting the lighthouse.

Ian set the bag on the table then bent down for a kiss. "We got the tower done. Tomorrow we're going to touch up the cap." That part of the structure was black enamel.

"It's going to look gorgeous. I can't wait to see it." After another kiss, I said, "We have a couple more work sessions and we'll be done with the inside. Right on schedule."

Meanwhile, Madison had jumped up to greet Anton with hugs and kisses. "Missed you," she said. She took his arm and guided him to the table, where they sat close together. Had the talk of weddings bumped Madison's heat index up a notch? I thought maybe.

She glanced over at me and I laughed, guessing what she wanted. "Yes, I'll bring your wine." She'd left it on the table beside the swing.

Ian and I joined the other two at the table, Ian handing Anton a beer and cracking another for himself. I lit a candle lantern for a little more light. As for Quincy, he stretched out on the swing with a contented murmur, as if he'd been waiting for us to give him room. Brat.

"Want to play Phase 10?" I asked, showing them the fast-paced card game. It didn't require much concentration, so it was perfect to play while chatting. They all agreed, so I dealt the first hand and we began.

We were well into the game when Anton said, "Kyle is doing much better. They moved him to a regular room this afternoon."

Madison and I exclaimed in relief. "I'm so glad," I said. "I hope he mends quickly." Then I couldn't resist. "Did he tell you anything about Lance?" I was referring to Donna's belief that Kyle knew something incriminating.

Anton blew out a breath in exasperation. "Nope. He clammed right up. Claimed he had no idea what we were talking about." He drew a card from the pile and sorted his hand. "We couldn't press him too hard. Not while he's laid up. I wouldn't want to cause a setback."

"That's too bad, but I get it." I'd been hoping that Kyle would provide a missing piece of the puzzle. Had Donna been wrong in the first place? Or had Kyle decided not to talk for some reason? Then a shock ran through me. "What if the accident changed his mind? What if he feels threatened now?"

"It's a possibility," Anton admitted. "That's why I've got an officer stationed outside his room." He laid down some cards. "Phase two." We groaned. So far he was in the lead.

Anton's pager went off, and now *he* groaned. "There's my punishment." He called back. "What's up?" He listened for a minute. "Be right there."

"What is it?" Madison asked. If she was disappointed about our evening being cut short, she didn't show it. Interruptions were part of the deal when dating a police chief. And both her parents were doctors, so she certainly knew the drill.

"Remember the officer I told you about?" Anton clipped his pager back on his belt and picked up his phone. "He left his station for a minute and someone tried to get into Kyle's room."

worry if she woke... and noticed I was... when I

CHAPTER 20

"Ready, babe?" Anton asked Madison. The plan had been for him to take her home.

"We can run Madison home, Anton." Ian turned to me. "Want to go for a ride? We can swing by the lighthouse on the way back and check out my paint job." Madison's parents lived out on Hemlock Point, near the lighthouse.

Anton looked to Madison for confirmation that this was all right with her. "That works," Madison said. She jumped up and gave Anton a kiss. "Call me later with an update, okay? We're worried about Kyle."

"I will," Anton said. "See you later." He strode through the garden to his vehicle like a man on a mission.

"Do you want another glass of wine?" I asked Madison.

She shook her head. "No, thanks. I'd better get going. Early client meeting tomorrow."

Grammie was already in bed, so I sent her a text to let her know what we were doing. I didn't want her to worry if she woke up and noticed I was gone. Then I grabbed a jean jacket and packed bottled iced tea and cookies in a canvas tote bag. A late-night visit to the lighthouse with Ian sounded like the romantic outing I'd been longing for.

We took Ian's truck. As we passed the hospital, I wondered if they had caught the intruder. Had it been the killer, trying to strike again? The idea made me shiver.

"Cold?" Ian said. "I can close the windows." We'd been riding with the windows partway down, allowing the fresh air to sweep through the cabin.

"No, I'm fine," I said. "Just thinking about Kyle."

Madison leaned forward. "Isn't it scary? You'd think he'd be safe in the hospital."

"They must have security video," Ian said. "Hopefully they caught the person on tape."

"Good point," I said. "It's not that easy to sneak around a hospital nowadays."

We left downtown and were soon turning onto Hemlock Point. A winding, scenic road looped around the entire peninsula, with the lighthouse located in the middle at the end. Side roads to the interior branched off here and there, leading to homes, with the more spectacular estates located along the waterfront.

Madison's family lived up one of the side roads, in a small development featuring sprawling, comfortable homes. Ian pulled into the drive. "Thanks for the ride," Madison said as she climbed out. "I'll send you a text when I hear from Anton."

"Please do," I said. "See you soon."

Ian waited until she was inside the house, then backed down the driveway and pulled away. *Alone at last.* A sweet, warm atmosphere settled over the truck's interior and I reached for his hand.

Happy in our little cocoon, we rode in silence around the loop to the lighthouse access road. As authorized, Ian had a key to the gate, and he climbed out to open it. I drove the truck through and he shut it behind us, latched, not locked, but deterrent enough to the casual eye.

Being the only ones inside a gated area made it feel even more special, as if the lighthouse belonged to us. And it did, for the hour or so that we would be here.

As we drove up the access road, the newly painted tower was revealed in the glow of security lights around the base. At the top, as it had for more than one hundred years, the light flashed in its regular pattern.

I inhaled a sharp breath. "It's beautiful, Ian."

"Wait till we get the trim done," he said with pride. He pulled the truck up close to the lighthouse door and switched off the engine. "Feeling brave tonight? I thought we could climb up to the observation deck."

I'd done it once, so I could do it again. "Great idea. Long as you're there to catch me."

"Always, Iris," he said, his eyes suddenly intense.

My heart began to thump as the tension between us ratcheted up a notch. But I tried to play it cool as I picked up the tote bag of snacks. "I'm ready when you are."

He unlocked the tower, allowing me to go inside first. The space was dim and cool, smelling of old stone and metal. Ian switched on the light and we began to climb. This time was so much easier. My knees only wobbled once or twice. Plus I was so deliciously aware of his warm bulk behind me.

The evening was warm and still enough that we went outside to the deck circling the tower. Here we found a spot to sit, huddled shoulder to shoulder looking out to sea. Below us, waves crashed against the rocks, each one a little smaller. The tide was going out.

After a few smooches, I broke out the tea and cookies. "Raspberry filled?" These old-fashioned cookies were one of my favorites, especially when Grammie used homemade raspberry jam for the filling.

He demolished half of the cookie in one bite. "I love these." He took a swig of tea to wash it down. "You know what? Everything is so much more fun when I do it with you," he said. "Even eating cookies."

I felt exactly the same way. Due to both of us being burned in previous relationships, we'd agreed to go slow when we started dating in May. At one point, my emotions got ahead of me, but I reigned in the unruly little rascals.

Now I sensed a shift, as if the two of us were on a seesaw. Ian had all the signs of a man about to make a declaration of some sort. And I don't mean about cookies.

He capped the bottle of tea and set it on the metal decking. "Iris," he said, turning to me. He leaned in for a kiss, the long, luxurious, toe-curling kind.

We broke apart, breathless.

The lighthouse beam flashed overhead like a strobe revealing a slice of the bay.

"What's that?" I cried, pointing.

A small white sailboat was drifting, sails down, broadside to the waves pushing it toward shore—and the jagged rocks waiting to greet it.

"What the—" Ian scrambled to his feet for a better look. "I sure hope someone isn't on that boat, injured. Or fell overboard." The way the boat was wallowing spoke to the captain being incapacitated or worse. He pulled out his phone. "I'm calling the Marine Patrol and Coast Guard." Since emergency services were coordinated, he dialed 911.

As he waited to be put through, I watched the boat

approach and recede with the waves as revealed by the flashing light. The fact that the sails were down was puzzling. The night was calm, so they hadn't been lowered during a storm or squall. Had the captain been using the motor to travel, only to have it quit? Although you'd think he or she would raise the sails in that case. The motor quit and they got sick, had a heart attack, maybe? That seemed far-fetched.

Or had the boat escaped its mooring? Rare when there wasn't a storm or heavy seas, but it did happen. That was a better scenario than man overboard or ill, although the boat was about to become a heap of splinters when it hit the rocks.

"They're coming right out," Ian said. "Fortunately the boat isn't that far offshore, so they should get to it fast." The good conditions tonight would make the rescue operation fairly straightforward, although the valiant Marine Patrol and Guard had undertaken many dangerous sea rescues. They are brave and wonderful, true heroes.

He tucked away his phone. "I'm going to run down for my binoculars. Will you be all right here?"

"I'm fine," I said, bringing my knees up to my chin. The excitement of the situation had knocked my fear of heights clean out of my head. From my perch on the tower, I watched official watercraft approaching across the water at speed, spotlights beaming. As they drew closer, the beams traveled over the nearby water and the boat itself, no doubt looking for the captain and any passengers. To both my relief and horror, I didn't see any bobbing heads or hands waving for help. I prayed the boat had been empty.

Footsteps thumped up the metal staircase and Ian appeared in the doorway, binoculars in hand. He stood at the rail and trained them on the rescue operation, adjusting the focus. "I don't see anyone in the water," he confirmed. Then he gave a grunt of surprise. "Take a look at the boat's hull."

I stood up for a better look, taking the binoculars he handed me. As the boat wallowed in the waves, the name painted on the hull became clearly visible under the glare of the spotlights. *Nixie.* Peter Pedersen's sailboat.

My heart thumped in dismay. "What does this mean? Did Peter fall overboard and drown?" The officers were now attaching a grappling hook to the craft so it could be towed out of danger. I didn't see anyone on the deck, either.

Ian put an arm around me and squeezed. "Hang in there. Let's not jump to any conclusions." Releasing me, he took the binoculars for another look at the sailboat. "The sails are still fully furled and tied. So I'm guessing this is a drift situation."

We watched, enthralled, Ian filming on his phone, as the team secured the boat, searched it, and began towing it back to port. Once they were almost out of view, Ian asked, "Ready to head out?"

The tender yet electrifying mood between us wasn't so much gone as supplanted by the adrenaline rush of the boat rescue. Now that surge of energy had ebbed and I was exhausted, although still anxious about Peter's whereabouts.

"I guess so," I said. "Do you think we can get an update about Peter somehow? I'm really worried."

"I have an idea," he said, tucking his binoculars in my tote. "We'll drive down to the docks and talk to the Marine Patrol."

By the time we arrived at the main wharf downtown, the Marine Patrol boats had reached the harbor.

Officers were moving about the dock where they had moored the *Nixie*. Ian parked in the public lot and we went to join them.

A familiar figure waved as we approached. Anton. The Marine Patrol always coordinated with the local force. "Hey, you two. I heard Ian called this in."

"We did," I said. "We were up in the lighthouse when we saw the boat drifting, about ready to hit the rocks." Under the lights, the *Nixie* appeared undamaged, without even a scratch on her glossy surface. "Any word on the owner?"

"We placed a call to him," Anton said. "Peter Pedersen. He should be down here any minute."

Overcome by a rush of relief, I gripped Ian's arm. "I'm so glad. We were afraid that he had gone overboard."

Anton turned to study the sailboat. "We think she came loose from her mooring. There's no sign that someone was trying to steal it and then abandoned ship." That was another possibility, if the engine had quit. But then where did the thief go? Swimming in cold Maine water—yes, even in August—could be deadly.

"That must be him," I said. Car headlights had turned off Main Street and a vehicle raced through the parking lot toward the wharf. He was traveling much too fast, but I didn't think Anton would scold him under the circumstances.

An Audi I recognized as Peter's jerked to a stop and the dentist jumped out. He bolted the rest of the way, feet flying and arms pumping. "Hello, Chief," he greeted Anton, barely glancing at us. "How's my boat?" Judging by his wrinkled shorts and T-shirt and his messy hair, he must have dressed in haste.

"Come see for yourself," Anton said with a gesture. The two men walked down to the *Nixie*, where they conferred with Marine Patrol officers under the glow of a security lamp.

Ian and I had a choice. Duty done, burning question about Peter answered, we could slip away and go home. *Nah.* "Let's go down and find out what's going on," I said.

We strolled down the dock to join the others. "I secured the boat the way I always do," Peter was saying. "I've been doing it since I was a kid. Never lost a boat yet."

Resting his hands on his hips, Anton regarded Peter with a thoughtful expression. "Are you absolutely positive?" he asked. "You've been under duress lately and that can lead to mistakes." Duress caused by the untimely death of his brother.

With a laugh, Peter ran a hand through his rumpled hair. "I can't swear to it. And no, I didn't document it with a photo. But I'm ninety-nine percent sure I did what I always do. I love that boat. And I'm so grateful she didn't founder." "Founder" was a nautical term for a ship taking on water and sinking.

Anton pointed at us. "Thank these guys. They spotted your boat and called it in."

Peter's eyes widened. "Oh, I know you two. I can't thank you enough for saving *Nixie*."

"I'm glad we were there to see her," Ian said. "She was about ready to end up on the ledges below the lighthouse."

"We were really worried that you had fallen overboard," I added. "I'm so glad to see that you are all right."

Peter shifted his stance. "I was home in bed and the call was a real shocker, I tell you." He crossed his arms. "And I know I tied that boat securely this afternoon. I always use an extra line, just in case."

"Why don't we go take a look at the lines," one of the Marine Patrol officers suggested. "They might have been tampered with."

I locked eyes with Ian. Had someone cut her loose? A criminal act, if so.

"Good idea," Peter said. "I was moored out in the harbor near the yacht club. Someone took my usual spot at the dock." He studied the sailboat. "Are you sure she's okay? Not taking on water or anything?"

"No, she's perfect," the officer said. He climbed aboard the *Nixie*, followed by the other officer and Peter. We watched while they traced the lines and pulled them out of the water.

Peter gave a cry of satisfaction. "Look at that. Someone cut the pennant." The pennant was the rope usually attached to the mooring ball, but now it was dangling from the sailboat's lines. Sailors threaded their lines through the pennant loop and then back to the boat, where they cleated the lines to secure them. Cutting the pennant was probably faster than untying the lines, a consideration when sabotaging a boat.

"Looks like malicious mischief to me," Anton muttered.

"Me too," I said. "I wonder who did it." And another key question was why. Someone with a grudge against Peter? Or the Pedersen family in general? Maybe Derek had transferred his anger about the failed loan to Peter since his brother was no longer available. I'd have to ask Peter if Derek had approached him for money.

Anton didn't respond to my question, of course. Thinking about Derek reminded me of his cousin. "I never did hear from Madison tonight. How's Kyle doing?"

"Kyle is fine," he said. "Still under guard. But the security footage was inconclusive. Meaning they spotted the intruder on camera, but he or she was unrecognizable."

It had been someone savvy enough to evade identification, then. "That's too bad," I said. Nothing about this case was easy, it seemed.

His lips curved in a crooked smile. "Can you give Madison the update on Kyle for me? I was supposed to text her earlier but I got slammed. One of my night officers went home sick. And then I got called out for this."

I was sure she would rather hear from him but I understood his time crunch. "Any other message you'd like me to pass along?" I said in a teasing voice. "Kisses and hugs, perhaps?"

He made a scoffing sound and didn't reply. "Good night, guys," he said, starting off toward the *Nixie*. "I'll be in touch."

We were on our way back to Ian's truck when a bicycle veered into the parking lot and raced toward us with its headlight bobbing and reflectors flashing. The rider wore a headlamp too, for extra safety.

"What the—?" Ian exclaimed. "Kind of late for a bike ride."

"I think I know who it is," I said with a sinking feeling. "Lars Lavely. He's like a tick. Once he digs in, it's hard to pry him loose."

"I heard that, Iris," Lars said, halting with a screech of tires. He braced the bicycle with wide-planted feet. "Don't tell me. You were the one who called in the drifting sailboat."

I crossed my arms, hoping my body language would convey my reluctance about doing an interview. "We did. We were at the lighthouse when we spotted it drifting in the waves, really close to the rocks."

Ian pointed toward the docks. "You probably ought to go talk to the boat owner and the Marine Patrol," he said. "I think they'll be wrapping up pretty soon. That's where the real story is."

Lars glanced back and forth between us and the others standing near the *Nixie*. "Good point. But I'll be calling you tomorrow for quotes." He pedaled away.

"Is that a threat or a promise?" I muttered.

Ian laughed as he slung an arm around my shoulders. "Both. Come on, let's go home."

CHAPTER 21

Anyone owned by a cat knows that the cat sets the schedule. And whenever I sleep too long for Quincy's liking, I get the treatment. Loud purring in my ear. A soft paw batting at my nose. And, when those don't work, the big guns: nipping my toes.

"Ouch. Quincy." I shot straight up in bed, as he intended. I threw back the covers and looked at my foot. He hadn't broken the skin or even left a mark. He never did. But it certainly got my attention.

Unrepentant, he blinked at me. Still dazed with sleep, I swung my legs around and glanced at the clock. Wow. No wonder he was bugging me.

Grammie rapped softly at the door. "Iris? Are you up?"

I yawned. "Barely. Come in."

She peeked into the room. "I'm making blueberry pancakes. Thought you might like to know." She grinned, knowing full well they were one of my favorite breakfast foods.

"Oh yeah," I said, forcing myself upright and reaching for my robe. "I'll be right down."

As for Quincy, he beelined for the crack in the door, giving Grammie his *I'm starving* cry. "Ready for breakfast, baby?" she crooned. "Follow me."

By the time I got down to the kitchen, he was chomping away on kibble and Grammie was sliding steaming hot pancakes onto a plate. "Maple links?"

"Absolutely," I said, pouring myself a cup of coffee. After adding cream, I sat at my usual place at the island.

Grammie set my plate in front of me. "Guess what? Florence heard from Chet."

I paused in the act of pouring maple syrup on my pancakes. "Already?" She'd only e-mailed him after dinner last night, which frankly felt like centuries ago. Quincy, now done with his breakfast, leaped up to the adjacent stool, no doubt hoping for a stray tidbit.

Grammie returned to the stove, where she ladled another set of pancakes onto the cast-iron griddle. "I know, it *was* fast. She sent me a text this morning saying that he had written back before she got to the resort."

"What did he say?" I used my fork to cut into the fluffy stack, a perfect triangle that would fill my mouth. Grammie made the best pancakes, light as air and crispy around the edges.

"He was very happy to hear from her." Grammie teased up the edge of a pancake to check its progress. "And he wants to come to the museum opening."

"Yay. That's awesome." My heart lifted like a balloon. To think that an accidental discovery in an apron pocket had led to sweethearts being reunited—after more than sixty years.

"I think it's thrilling," Grammie said. "I've always been a sucker for happy endings." She flipped the cakes.

"Me too." Sophie had gotten hers, Madison and I were on our way to happy endings—I thought—and hopefully things would resolve for Bella regarding Alan. One way or another. "Oh, I have news, too."

While we ate, I told her about the adventures of the night before.

"I knew I should have stayed up a little longer," Grammie said, pretending to grumble. "How fortunate that you and Ian spotted Peter's boat when you did."

"Yeah." I swirled a piece of sausage in a puddle of syrup and melted butter. "By this morning it would have been a heap of matchsticks on the rocks." I pictured the sailboat scattered in pieces below the lighthouse, another victim of the sea's mighty force.

"That's a mighty evil thing to do to someone." Grammie shook her head. "Sounds like Lance wasn't the only one who had enemies."

Exactly what I had been thinking. "Kyle is doing better, Anton said. But he had a scare last night, too."

Grammie's mouth dropped open. "After I went to bed, right?"

I nodded. "Anton got the call while we were playing cards. Someone tried to sneak into Kyle's room at the hospital. But they weren't able to get an identity from the security video."

Her expression was grim. "Someone trying to finish the job? Oh my, this is getting out of hand."

A wave of helplessness flashed over me. "I know. And we don't seem to be getting any closer to solving this thing."

We sat in glum silence, our delicious food sitting untouched for the moment. "All we can do is keep moving forward," Grammie said. "Oh, and by the way, there's a celebration of Lance's life tonight at the yacht club. Kind of short notice but I think we should go."

"I think so too." Maybe we could uncover some clues by talking to Lance's family and friends. Whether one criminal or two, we needed answers fast, before someone else died.

* * *

Parked cars lined the road to the yacht club on both sides when Grammie and I arrived. "Wow, great turn-out for the memorial," I said, pulling into the first space I found. We would have to walk down from here.

"I'm glad, for Oslo's and Elsa's sakes," Grammie said. "Plus Lance was the closest thing to a celebrity we had."

There was that. No doubt the media, including Lars, would be on hand, too. He'd called earlier today for a quote right when we were slammed, so I babbled something to get rid of him. I couldn't even remember what I'd said and was fully prepared to cringe when the article was published.

After I locked Beverly, we strolled down the lane, waving to other mourners and checking the vehicles to see who was already here. I saw Jake's truck, Alan's BMW, Madison's Mini, and, happily, Ian's truck. I picked up the pace a little, eager to see him.

Crowds swirled on the grass in front of the club and stood in clusters on the porch. Under a large white event tent, uniformed servers moved about, setting up food and drinks on buffet tables. At a silent signal, the guests began making their way inside. The service must be about to begin, I figured, so we got in line. Captain Greg was standing at the front entrance, handing out programs.

"How are you tonight, ladies?" he asked when Grammie and I reached him. "I heard the news about Chet coming back to town." He winked. "Can't keep a good soldier down."

"Or a determined woman," I said, taking a program. "Thanks for your help with finding him. I know Florence is thrilled to see him again."

"And so am I. Chet is good people." He turned his

attention to those pressing close behind us and we took the hint and moved along.

Inside, the ceiling fans were spinning full force to ventilate the room, which while large with high ceilings, was already warm from all the bodies. Rows of folding wooden chairs had been set up facing a podium. A screen overhead flashed pictures of Lance through the years.

Madison's arm waved in the crowd and we edged around the back to where our gang was sitting. "Saved you seats," she said. We were on the end, with Grammie on the aisle and me next to Ian. Beyond Madison were Sophie, Jake, and Florence. No Bella, which I understood. She was out on bail for Lance's murder and showing up here would not be a good move.

"How are you doing, babe?" Ian asked, giving me a kiss. "Did Lars get hold of you?"

I rolled my eyes. "Of course. I can't wait to see my quote. Not." I spotted our intrepid journalist standing on the other side of the room, talking to other reporters. He'd gotten a scoop with Bella's bail hearing and no doubt was leveraging his insider standing to benefit his career. I didn't begrudge him that. Maybe he would get hired by a bigger paper and move away. We could only hope.

Madison leaned forward. "That was quite the excitement you two had last night."

"No kidding," I said. "Peter was this close"—I held up two fingers an inch apart—"to losing his boat on the rocks."

The room continued to fill and a woman began to play soft, mournful music on a portable organ. Peter guided his elderly parents, one on each arm, up the center aisle. Elsa and Oslo shuffled along, eyes fixed straight ahead and shoulders bowed. My heart went out to them. Normally vital and energetic, they both seemed to have aged a decade since their son's death. This must be unbelievably hard. I grit my teeth with determination. We needed to find the killer *now*.

While we waited for the service to begin, I started watching the slideshow. Lance was an adorable boy, as was Peter. Pictures showed them in their first sailboat, riding bicycles, hiking up a local mountain. Family occasions, like Christmas and birthdays.

And then pictures from the teen and young adult years began. Lance became an instructor at this club, standing proudly with his students. One teen girl with a mane of tangled hair looked so familiar . . .

I grabbed Ian's arm. "I think Gretchen was one of Lance's sailing students."

His brow furrowed. "Is that important?" His tone implied not.

The show had moved on, so it would be a while before the picture came back around. "Oh, it probably means nothing. I was surprised, that's all." I'd had no idea that Gretchen's ties to Blueberry Cove went back more than a decade. And so did her acquaintance with Lance. And Peter too, no doubt.

The crowd fell silent as Peter took the podium. In contrast to his dishevelment the night before, he was dressed immaculately in jacket, slacks, and open-collar shirt. "Thank you, everyone, for gathering with us today. This is a very sad occasion for my family but it heartens me that so many of our friends and neighbors have gathered to pay their respects and remember my brother."

The slideshow had paused on a great headshot of Lance. With windswept hair and a huge grin on his tanned face, he embodied health, humor, and good cheer. The kind of person you wanted to get to know, to count among your friends. Studying that magnetic man, I could see why people, Bella included, had been drawn to him.

Peter went on for a while, his heartfelt speech sparking tears and sniffles in the audience. If only I could be sure his emotion was one hundred percent genuine. A few other people got up to share memories of Lance, but the best—and most surprising—was a recording made by Kyle from his hospital bed. Funny and irreverent, almost a roast of his famous friend, it was the perfect final touch to the formal portion of the event.

"Wasn't that great?" Peter said from the podium when Kyle's clip ended. "I hope you'll all stay and enjoy some refreshments. They're outside in the tent."

With a scrape of chairs, the audience stood. Chatter burst out, echoing in the cavernous room, and the group began to move en masse toward the door.

"Do you want to stay?" Grammie asked me. "I wouldn't mind." She waved at Florence, who was waiting for us to walk that way.

"Sure. For a little while, at least." I was hoping to find Gretchen, if she was here, and ask her about her relationship with Lance. When I'd broached the subject before, thinking that she'd known him through her job, she'd been strangely avoidant. Although murder investigations did made people more wary than usual. That might have been why.

Outside the club, people were lining up under the tent for the buffet tables. "Do you want to get something to eat?" I asked Ian.

He shook his head. "I'm sorry, but I've got to get back to the inn. Dad and I need to tackle a plumbing project." He grimaced. "Guest room."

I stood on tiptoes and gave him a kiss. "Say no more.

Talk later." After he left, with a detour to offer condolences to Lance's parents, I circled the grounds, looking for Gretchen. Grammie and Florence were seated on the porch, chatting, and Madison, Sophie, and Jake were standing in line for food.

I found Gretchen down by the docks, sitting on a bench and staring out at the view. Sailboats gently rocked at harbor, halyards clinking against the masts with every swell. The lowering sun was touching the water with gold, and in the distance, islands floated in a warm haze.

"Nice spot," I said, sitting beside her. Although my eyes were on the view, I felt her stiffen. Was she going to get up and leave? Trying to show her that I was totally harmless, I sat back with a sigh. "It's so relaxing to just sit and look at the water. I don't do it often enough." That was the honest truth.

Gretchen threw me a sharp look. "What do you want, Iris? We're not exactly friends."

True. "But we are both here to pay respects to Lance."

She ducked her head and began to play with her skirt. Like most of the other guests, she had dressed up for the occasion. "Yeah. Poor Lance. Talk about wrong place, wrong time." She spoke in such a low voice, I had to strain to hear her.

"It's a tragedy for sure. I didn't know him well, but he was quite a guy."

Gretchen snorted softly. "That's an understatement. He was the biggest thing to ever come out of this town. I mean, he was a world-famous athlete."

"Can't argue with that," I said. Though a well-known author or two and some respected artists lived in Blueberry Cove. They tended not to appear in the tabloids while dating supermodels and partying on yachts, though.

An uneasy silence fell, broken only the incessant *ting-ting* of the halyards. "I never had Lance as a sailing instructor when I took lessons here as a kid."

"He mostly worked with teens," Gretchen said. "They used to hold intensive two-week sailing camps for age fifteen and up."

"And you attended those." No response. "I saw the group photo in Lance's slideshow. That was you, wasn't it?"

She gave a little laugh. "Good eye. I was what, sixteen? Such a long time ago." Her voice was tight and I sensed she was holding back a tidal wave of emotion. "I was a mixed-up kid from Portland. And my parents thought sailing camp would be the best thing for me. Get me away from the crowd I was hanging with."

"Sailing is a great sport," I said. "It uses both your brain and your muscle. Lance was your instructor, I take it."

Gretchen tucked a strand of hair behind her ear. "Yeah," she admitted. "I had a little crush on him. We all did."

"I can understand that." He had been, what, three or four years older, not only gorgeous but an expert sailor. "And to think he went on to the Olympics. You couldn't ask for a more talented instructor."

Gretchen clenched then unclenched her fists, giving a huff of agitation. "If you don't mind, I'd rather not talk about it anymore." Pushing herself to her feet, she stalked away with her head down, so lost in her own world she almost bumped into Donna, who was coming the other way.

Donna stopped to watch Gretchen go, shaking her

head at the near miss, then continued toward me. "Hey Iris." She sat in the place recently vacated by the other woman.

"Hey," I responded, thinking this was a great opportunity to talk to her, since we were alone down here. "Sad day, huh?"

"Sure is." Donna sighed, slumping lower in her seat. "I still can't believe he's gone. Lance was so . . . so *alive*, you know? The kind of person that made you feel like you could do more with your life, as well. Made you want to try."

"Did he encourage you to go pro?" I asked.

She nodded. "He was the first person to tell me I had what it takes." Her laugh was rueful. "I didn't make it all the way to the U.S. team, but hey, I gave it a shot."

"That's what counts," I said, wincing at this lame platitude. I changed the subject. "I'm glad Kyle is doing better. His speech today was so funny."

"It was," Donna said. "Vintage Kyle at his best. And yes, such a relief that he's out of the woods." She sighed deeply. "I was super worried for a while."

"Me too." I turned to face her. "Do you think it was the same person who hit Lance?"

Her skeptical gaze asked who else it could have been. "My theory is that he saw something, which makes sense since he lives right next door to Bella."

"But not Bella." This was a statement, not a question.

Donna ran a hand through her short hair, ruffling it. "Not Bella. Although I was pretty sure at first that she was guilty."

I remembered how sure she'd been during her breakdown in the bathroom, but there was no point in debating Bella's guilt, since she had just admitted she'd been wrong. "I'm glad we agree on that. Any ideas who, then?"

She leaned closer, her dark eyes glittering with a crusader's zeal. "I think it was Alan."

CHAPTER 22

Stunned by her accusation, I rocked back in my seat. "Alan? You're kidding." Although Alan had been first on the scene and no doubt had resented Lance for dating his ex-wife, I'd never seen him as the killer. Our conversation yesterday had only reinforced his innocence in my eyes. Concerning the murder at least, I amended. The jury was still out on the Gretchen situation.

"Why would he frame Bella by using her loaner?" I asked. That to me was the real clincher.

A sly smile hovered on Donna's lips. "I think he made a mistake, didn't think things through all the way. Stupid, yes, but every killer makes at least one mistake."

I still thought her theory was out to lunch but I was curious about her thought process. "Why don't you take me through it, step by step?"

"Sure." She reached into the pocket of her flowing pants and pulled out her phone. "Okay. I'm like you. At first I discounted Alan as a suspect. But then I began to put some things together." She shifted on the bench. "One. He and Lance had a heated discussion one day when Alan came to pick up the kids."

This was news. "Really? What about?" While I still

hoped and believed that Alan wasn't guilty, I wanted to hear this.

Donna plucked at her lip, thinking. "I'm not exactly sure. I did hear Bella's name a couple of times." She slid a glance toward me. "And I also found out through the grapevine that Alan wants to reconcile with Bella. So it makes sense he wouldn't want another man to mess that up."

After overhearing Donna and Alan talking in secret, I'd wondered if he had been hitting on her. But now I revised that assumption. In light of what Donna was telling me, she had been trying to learn more from him about Lance's death. And it was highly possible he also been probing for information since she worked for the police department. "Bella told me that Alan wants to get back together," I said. "So you're right about that."

She nodded. "It's a great motive. Man wants to save his family, and an attractive, rich, famous athlete is dating his wife. Quite the competition."

Bella wasn't the type to be swayed by externals, but I didn't bother to argue. "Besides, he was wrong. You and Lance were dating." *Or thinking about dating*, I thought. "That night I saw you two together on the yacht club deck," I added helpfully, in case she had forgotten.

Her face was a thundercloud. "Listen, I loved Lance, but he was stringing us both along. He told me his involvement with Bella was casual." Her spine straightened. "But that's not the point. What counts is what Alan believed, not what was true."

"I guess he didn't get the memo," I muttered, still thinking her case was weak. "All right. Alan was jealous of Lance's involvement with Bella. Then what?"

She displayed a picture on her phone. It was of a car key, an old-fashioned metal kind, inside a plastic bag. "What am I looking at?" I asked.

"The key that was found in the ignition of the Jeep," she said triumphantly. "Placed there to look like a joy-rider stole it."

"That's not Bella's key?" A second key was news to me. I'd assumed that they thought Bella had used her set.

"Nope, it's not. It's a copy. Probably Alan took her keys and made one."

Or someone had. The Beast had been borrowed by all kinds of people, and the likelihood of spare keys floating around was high. Because face it, no one wanted to own that thing permanently, so theft wasn't an issue. Until now.

"Say you're right. Alan had a key. How did he do it?"

She settled her bum on the bench and took a breath. "Okay. Bear with me. Alan drove down to town from the resort in his BMW and left it up at the overlook. Then he went down the walking path to Bella's, where he stole the Beast. After that, he parked somewhere up the hill, waiting for Lance to run by."

"How did he know Lance was going to run by?" Bella had said that Lance wasn't an early morning runner.

Donna gnawed at her lip in response and I sensed this was a weak area in her case. "He knew that Lance went running early in the morning. Maybe Bella said something. Or he overheard it. Alan's been at the yacht club a lot. Plus everyone in town who runs goes up the hill and along the overlook. It's even recommended on running websites."

I accepted this scenario for the moment. "Lance runs by. And what? Alan follows him and then runs him over? Abandons the Jeep and hops back into his car?"

Her mouth dropped open. "Wow, you're good. I figured you got lucky the other two times." She was referring to the two murders I, along with the gang, had solved earlier this summer.

I didn't bother to address her backhanded compliment. "That's all plausible. So why didn't they arrest Alan? He was first on the scene, which normally is looked at very closely." Some criminals call in a crime so they could enjoy watching the police at work, all the while smug in their supposed immunity.

Her shoulders sagged. "That is a weak spot, I admit it. They didn't find any trace of Alan in the Jeep. But they did find Bella's hair and DNA."

Of course, since she was openly using the loaner. I thought of something. "Maybe the killer made sure they didn't leave any DNA or hair." The moment I said this it had the ring of truth. This didn't get Alan off the hook, but it also meant that someone else might have evaded detection somehow. Had they worn gloves, booties, and a jumpsuit like those worn at crime scenes? And who would have access to that kind of safety gear? Yes, Donna, since she worked for the police. Was she trying to send me on a wild-goose chase by blaming Alan?

"Are you investigating on your own?" I asked her bluntly. Another thing I'd been wondering about. Anton would probably hit the roof if he knew she had pictures of evidence in her phone.

Donna wove her fingers together and squeezed. "I guess you could say that."

"Why?" I left it at that, not wanting to put words into her mouth.

She tipped her head back and forth, thinking, then turned to me, her eyes narrowed. "I want justice for Lance. He didn't deserve what happened to him."

"True. But is that all?" Because it didn't feel like it to me.

She looked away. Swallowed. Twisted her fingers again. "I'm trying to help. Our force is stretched thin and so are the state police. I thought . . . I really want to—" She sighed. "I want to be a detective, 'kay? I'm trying to help so Anton will see my potential."

Not the way I'd go about it, but good luck to her. Someone called my name, and I turned around to see Grammie coming along the path. "There's my cue," I said to Donna. "I've got to go."

She lifted a hand in a wave of farewell, not budging from the bench. "See you later, Iris. Have a good night. Oh, and think about what I said." If she was lying, she was certainly good at it. I couldn't discern a trace of uneasiness in her demeanor.

I cut across the grass to meet Grammie. "I take it you're ready to go home? I am." I thought briefly about grabbing something from the buffet, but my talk with Donna had stolen the little appetite I had.

If Donna's theory was right, and I prayed it wasn't, then Bella was thinking about reconciling with a murderer. And here I'd thought Alan being a serial philanderer was bad enough.

Needless to say, I had a restless night. And this time I annoyed Quincy, not the other way around. After the third time I got up for a drink of water, he jumped down with a squawk and went to sleep with Grammie, every line of his body quivering with outrage.

Once he left, I gave up on getting back to sleep and switched on the light, reaching for the notebook and pen I kept on the nightstand. When I wasn't worried about a killer, I often got great ideas for original aprons in the middle of the night. I had learned the hard way that no, I wouldn't remember them the next morning.

I flipped through, looking for a blank page. So far

we were making classic pinafores only, but I'd thought about expanding our line. Pretty organza half-aprons made wonderful bridal-shower and birthday gifts, for example. And not to leave the men out, I had designed a great grilling apron with pockets. Once I had time to make a prototype, I would ask Ian to test it for me.

The thought of Ian made me smile. I couldn't wait to solve this case and get things back to normal. I sighed. What wouldn't I give for my sweet boring former life, where the most exciting thing that happened was dealing with a cranky customer? Not that we had many of those. Our customers were wonderful.

And so was our new employee. Faith was coming in tomorrow to train on the point-of-sale system. Her first day would be the Tuesday after Labor Day, when the children were back in school.

I was stalling, big time. Clicking the pen open, I doodled hearts and flowers in the notebook. Was Donna right about Alan? Now that she'd made the suggestion, the question of his guilt nagged at me like a stomachache.

Could he really have miscalculated that badly, thinking that Bella wouldn't be blamed for Lance's death? I had a hard time believing that. Alan was a very intelligent man, savvy and sharp-witted and worldly. According to Bella, the family import business had grown to a new level of sales and profitability under his leadership.

But if he had killed Lance, he must be going out of his mind right now trying to figure out how to get his ex-wife off the hook—while evading arrest himself.

The worst part about all this was that I couldn't discuss Donna's theory with anyone, especially not Bella. I'd even put Grammie off on the way home, claiming I was tired when she noticed how preoccupied I was.

But these accusations, once released, would be explosive. If Alan *was* innocent, I certainly didn't want to be responsible for tainting his name—and putting yet another hurdle between him and Bella. And if they were false, she might never forgive me for casting aspersions on her children's father.

Maybe I should shelve this line of thinking for a while, since it was only snarling me into a ball of confusion. Donna was probably totally wrong, and there were definitely a couple of holes in her theory. Alan obtaining a second key to the Beast, for one. Had he copied Bella's? And how had he known that Lance was going running that particular morning? According to Bella, he wasn't in the habit of going every day.

And what about Peter's boat? Did someone cutting it loose have anything to do with Lance's death or was it unrelated?

I had a really twisted thought. What if Peter had set his own boat adrift, thinking that would divert suspicion elsewhere?

No, Peter was still on the short list, as was Donna. And I couldn't forget Derek Quimby. He definitely had access to keys for the Beast, plus he had been away from the garage when Kyle was hurt. He hadn't been at the memorial service tonight, I'd noticed. Was it because he still held a grudge against Lance—or was the reason more sinister?

I always got my oil changed at Quimby's, and I thought Beverly was about due for another. The decision to call for an appointment tomorrow—actually only a few hours from now—made me relax. I now had a plan, something to do besides stew in suspicion and fear. With a yawn, I put aside my notebook and pen and switched off the light.

A short while later, when I was in a twilight half

sleep, little paws padded on the floor. Quincy leaped up onto the bed and curled up next to me. His purring seemed to say he was glad I'd come to my senses. Nighttime was for sleeping.

Morning brought a surprise. Madison showed up for breakfast with two dozen very fresh eggs from Briar Rose Farm. "Collected this morning," she said, opening the box. The eggs were large and a variety of colors—white, buff, brown, and blue. Gorgeous.

"Oh, lovely. Thank you." Grammie picked up one of the boxes and carried it to the stove. "How do you want your eggs?"

I took a sip of coffee. "I've been craving poached. On some of that homemade bread, toasted." Going to the breadbox, I pulled out the loaf. "I'll be on toast duty."

Madison poured herself a cup of coffee. "I'll take poached, too. Thanks, Anne." She glanced around. "What can I do?"

"How about getting out the silverware and napkins?" Grammie looked down at Quincy, who was winding around her ankles. "And top off Quincy's dish."

Madison took a healthy swig of coffee then got to work. After many years of eating meals at our house, she knew where everything was.

Working together, we soon had breakfast ready and were digging in. "I can't get over how orange these yolks are." I poked one egg with my fork, allowing rich yolk to run down over buttered toast.

"Healthy chickens," Madison said. "Briar Rose has free-range hens." She took a bite and chewed, then said, "They're my newest marketing clients. The farmers, I mean, not the hens."

"Do they pay you in eggs?" Grammie teased.

"Yes," Madison said, playing along. "And goat cheese, fresh veggies, and berry preserves."

"I love their stand," I said. "I haven't made it out there nearly often enough this summer." While we had a pretty extensive garden, Briar Rose and other farms had items we didn't grow or produce.

While we were eating, I had come to a decision. I needed to confide in Madison and Grammie about my conversation with Donna. With the possible exception of Ian, they were the two people in the world I was closest to. If I couldn't trust them, I couldn't trust anyone.

After pouring refills of coffee for everyone, I said, "I had a very disturbing conversation with Donna Dube yesterday."

Madison and Grammie exchanged glances. "I noticed you talking to her at the memorial service," Madison said. "What was it about? She's pretty intense even in the best of times."

"Intense is the right word," I said. "She has a very interesting theory about Lance's murder." I took them through our discussion pretty much word for word, since after thinking about it all night, I practically had it memorized. By the time I was done, Madison and Grammie looked sick.

"I didn't see that coming," Grammie said. "And you know what? I think she's wrong."

"So do I." Madison scowled. "Alan is far from perfect; in fact, he's a real jerk sometimes. But a killer? Uh, no."

"Thank you for saying that." Until it lifted off me, I hadn't realized how much anxiety Donna's accusation had provoked. "There are a couple of holes in her theory. When did he have time to make an extra key? And how did he know when Lance was going to go running?"

"Those are both good points," Grammie said.

Madison spun her cup on the island top, her expression thoughtful. "I wonder what her deal is. Why is she trying so hard to solve this case?"

"She said she wanted to avenge Lance while moving up in her career," I said. "But maybe she's only trying to point suspicion away from herself. For one thing, I find it very strange that she arrived at Kyle's when she did."

"Maybe she's trying to get Bella off the hook," Grammie suggested. She always tried to see the best in everyone.

Madison and I looked at each other with skepticism. "Doubt it," I said. "She wanted Lance for herself. Plus at first she really thought Bella did it. She told me so."

"Plus accusing Bella's ex won't help Bella or the kids," Madison added.

Grammie laughed. "I take it back. Then I can't guess what she's up to."

"Me neither. And I do have a few more ideas to hash over." I opened my notebook, which I'd brought downstairs, then noticed Grammie doing the same with hers.

Madison laughed. "You two really are peas in a pod." She held up a hand. "But hold on. I can't believe I forgot to mention this. Kyle Quimby can have visitors now. Approved by the police, of course. Who wants to take him flowers?"

Grammie insisted she could handle opening the store—with Quincy's help, of course—so Madison and I went to the hospital at ten, when visiting hours began. On the way, we picked up an arrangement from a florist.

Our local hospital was set on a hill overlooking the harbor, pleasant and modern and sparkling clean. The receptionist directed us to Kyle's room on the second floor, and at Madison's insistence, we took the stairs. "Got to get our steps in," she said, charging ahead of me, her lanky legs flying.

"I get more steps per day at the store, I bet," I called, defending myself. Carrying the bouquet, I followed, my movements much slower since I preferred gentle exercise to vigorous workouts. Being out of breath had nothing to do with my pace.

"No doubt," she said from above, her laughter floating down. "I ordered a standing desk, did I tell you?"

"Good idea." I climbed the last rise. "Hold on before we go in. How should we approach this? The last thing I want to do is upset Kyle and set him back."

"True." Madison tapped a finger on her lips. "Anton said that Kyle won't talk about Lance's death. I think we need to play it by ear, see what we can find out." She winked. "I'm sure Kyle will find us much more fun to talk to than Anton."

Which meant she would be using her wiles to get him to spill. I didn't have a problem with that, especially since an officer was still stationed outside his door, if we needed one for some reason.

On the second floor, we followed signs to the patient rooms, then stopped at the nurses' station to check in. The nurse behind the desk smiled at us. "Kyle is in room two twenty-four." She pointed. "Down the corridor and to the left." She took in the bouquet, an extravagant array of lilies and daisies. "How pretty. Our patient is getting lots of gifts this morning. It's really cheering him up."

We thanked her and proceeded down the hall, looking for Kyle's room. Some of the rooms were occupied, the open doors providing a glimpse of feet in a bed. I quickly averted my eyes, feeling intrusive.

"That must be it," Madison said, waving at an officer

seated outside one of the rooms. He didn't look familiar. She approached him with a big smile, introducing us. In turn, we learned that he was assisting from another town, since the Blueberry Cove force was already stretched.

"Go ahead in," he said. "But keep it brief, okay?"

We nodded agreement, and with a knock on the partly open door, entered the room. Bracing myself, I followed Madison around the drawn curtain. To my relief, Kyle didn't look too bad. Although he was hooked up to an IV, the only visible injury was a bandage on his forehead.

"Good morning, Kyle," Madison said in a cheery voice. "We thought we'd stop by and see how you're doing."

"We hope you're feeling better." I added, placing the flowers next to another arrangement and a large gift basket filled with snacks.

Kyle winced as he shifted in the bed. "Getting there. Going home in a day or two, I hope." He cracked a crooked smile. "I understand I owe you two my life. What's my first assignment?" He was referring to the fictional trope of a rescued person owing a life debt to their Good Samaritan.

"Continuing to heal," Madison said. She pulled two chairs close to the bed. "We won't stay long. The officer outside made us promise."

"But what if your visit is helping me get better?" he asked in a joking voice.

Madison glanced toward the door while settling into her chair. "We'll beg him for more time."

He continued to smile at us as he picked up a small box of chocolates from his tray table. "Want one?" At our denial, he picked one and took a bite. "Fruit-filled. My favorites."

"Your speech about Lance was great," I said. "Everyone at the memorial loved it."

Kyle pursed his lips and took another chocolate. "That's good to hear. Recording it actually helped me quite a bit. I was finally able to put aside my resentment toward Lance and remember what I loved about the guy." He blinked, a hint of moisture in his eyes, so we gave him a moment. "What else is new?" he asked. "What'd I miss being stuck in here?"

There was so much, I had trouble deciding what to talk about. But it was too soon to bring up the murder investigation. "Peter Pedersen's boat got loose the other night," I said. "Ian and I spotted the *Nixie* drifting from the lighthouse observation deck. Thankfully the Marine Patrol showed up before she crashed on the rocks."

"Seriously? Peter must have freaked out." Kyle struggled to sit up a bit but then flopped back, wincing. "I always forget about my injuries." To my alarm, I noticed his voice was slower, almost slurred, and his eyelids were drooping.

Madison noticed, too. "Are we tiring you out, Kyle? We can go."

He rolled his head back and forth, indicating no. "Don't have to." He groaned softly and closed his eyes.

I jumped up from the chair. "Something's wrong. He's either drugged or ill." Had the killer gotten to Kyle a second time?

CHAPTER 23

reached for the call button clipped to the bed and pushed it. Hopefully a nurse would come right away. If not, I would go get one.

"I'll tell the officer," Madison said, rushing for the door. She put her head around the doorjamb and spoke to him.

He came right in, as did a nurse a moment later. Frowning, she checked his vitals, lifted his eyelids, and examined the bags on his IV. "He shouldn't be having these symptoms." She turned to us. "Did he have anything to eat or drink that you know of?"

My gaze fell on the small box of chocolates, now half-empty. "Just those. He was eating them when we came in."

The officer picked up the box and studied it with curiosity. "An allergic reaction or something?"

"Or something," the nurse said, her tone grim. She made a shooing motion as she unclipped her phone from her waist. "Everyone out."

In the hall, Madison took my arm, her dark eyes huge with concern. "Thank goodness we were here and noticed something was wrong. Do you think he'll be okay?"

"I sure hope so." A deep chill in my core made me

shiver. Someone had tried to get to Kyle before and been rebuffed. Had they resorted to delivering a poisoned gift? What if Madison or I had eaten a piece? If the poison was strong enough, all three of us could have died.

The officer emerged from the room, his face ashen. "I'd better call the chief," he said, fumbling for his phone.

"Please do," Madison said. "He needs to know about this." To me, she said, "Want to wait? I think we'll need to give a statement."

"I agree." I glanced around, noticing a small waiting room a few doors away. "We can hang out in there." While we walked down the corridor, I took out my phone and sent Grammie a text updating her about the situation. She assured me that all was fine and what we were doing was a priority.

An hour later, we'd paced every inch of that room a hundred times. Nothing is more claustrophobic than being stuck in a tiny and airless space while awaiting news, hopefully good but perhaps bad. Other medical personnel rushed down the hall to Kyle's room and I wondered if they had figured out what was wrong. Had he survived that horrific assault only to succumb here in the hospital?

Finally we saw Anton pass by the open doorway, and Madison darted out to intercept him. "Any news on Kyle?" she asked.

"He's going to be okay," Anton said. "Thanks to you two." He shook his head. "I don't know how you do it, but this is the second time you've come to his rescue."

"And thank goodness for that," I said, my heart soaring with relief. Our determination to clear Bella had been our motivation for talking to Kyle, but I didn't mention that part. We kind of had an unspoken agreement with Anton that we would help investigate when his hands were tied. At times he got a little annoyed, especially when I scooped him, but I think he appreciated our help. As private citizens, we sometimes had flexibility he didn't. Plus people often talked to us more freely, since we weren't wearing uniforms.

Anton pulled out his tablet. "While I have you, why don't you give me a rundown of the incident?" He typed away as we took him through our visit to Kyle, what had been said, and what we observed. He tucked away the tablet. "Depending on what the lab says, we might need more formal statements later. We'll give you a call if so." Meaning whether or not a criminal act had been committed.

"So we can go?" I picked up my handbag, eager to leave. "Talk to you later, Mads." We'd driven to the hospital separately.

Giving the two lovebirds some privacy, I rushed out of the waiting room and headed toward the elevators. I really didn't like hanging around in hospitals.

Faith O'Brien was already at the shop when I arrived. She and Grammie were working together to hang up new inventory while they waited for me. I was supposed to train her on the point-of-sale system today.

"My great-grandmother made aprons out of sacks," Faith said, holding up a flour sack full apron. "She used to tie one around me when I helped her in the kitchen."

"What a sweet memory," Grammie said. "Aprons are so much more than a piece of clothing." She turned to smile at me. "How did it go?" Then she frowned. "What's wrong?"

I'd put on a bright smile to welcome our new employee, but Grammie obviously saw right through it. "Kyle Quimby had a setback today," I said, not sure how much to say in front of Faith. I put up a hand when both women exclaimed. "But he's going to be okay."

"Whew," Faith said, fanning her face with her hand. "Isn't Kyle the young man who got hurt by that falling car?" Her brow furrowed. "As the wife of a policeman, I hear about everything. Well, everything he can tell me," she amended. "What happened to Kyle was horrible."

"It was," I agreed. I glanced at the time, remembering that I'd wanted to get an oil change today—and talk to Kyle's cousin, Derek. With this second attempt on Kyle's life, it was imperative that we find the culprit. "I'll be right with you, Faith. I just need to make a quick call."

"Take your time," Faith said, hanging up a blue-and-white seersucker bib apron. She twitched the skirt into place. "I'm having so much fun checking out the inventory."

I heard them chatting happily and took my phone into the side room, where I poured a cup of coffee. Quincy was sleeping on one of the chairs, so I stopped to pat him.

"Quimby's," a woman said. I recognized Gladys' voice. "Can I help you?"

"This is Iris Buckley," I said. "I need an oil change, today if possible." Then I specifically asked if Derek could do it. "I have an antique car and he's always done my maintenance," I said. "He knows all of Beverly's little quirks."

Her attitude underwent a definite change when she heard it was me, Bella's friend. After some hemming and hawing, she told me to come in at two. "Be on time," she said. "Otherwise we'll have to give your slot to someone else."

All righty then. I hoped her bad attitude wasn't going to continue because I might have to go elsewhere. And if Derek *was* guilty of murder, I would also be changing mechanics, I reminded myself. Dentists, mechanics, what's next?

I set Faith up with a login for the system and, after a tour of its features, I let her ring up some customers. She was a quick study, plus she was great with the customers. They all left with smiles on their faces.

"I'm ordering lunch from the Mug-Up Deli," Grammie said, placing a take-out menu on the counter. "What would you two like?" She smiled at Faith. "My treat."

"In that case"—Faith picked the menu up with a laugh—"I adore their tuna melts."

Claiming she needed a walk and fresh air, Grammie went down to the deli to pick up our lunch. Faith and I continued to price inventory and put it out.

"I love this design," she said, holding up a tea towel with a folk-modern chicken print.

"That's Robert Darr Wert," I said. "He was a great mid-century designer from Massachusetts." To my delight, I had discovered a fantastic trove of screen-printed linens by Wert at an auction. Now my hope was to create special designer spotlights of work by him and other wonderful designers like Vera Neumann and Pat Pritchard.

"Look at these." I unfolded a set of "Give Us Our Daily Bread" placemats. The turquoise and gold design depicted kitchen tools and loaves of bread.

"Love them." Faith sighed. "I can see where my paycheck is going to go."

"Employee discount," I said with a smile.

We worked in quiet harmony, with me taking things out of the boxes and Faith putting them on display. I could see that we'd made the right choice in hiring her and I was so grateful Anton had made the recommendation.

"I've been thinking," she said as she clipped a dish towel to a line. "The person who stole the Beast. Did they take the Jeep because it was convenient or because they wanted to implicate Bella?"

"Good question," I said. Did any of the suspects have a grudge against Bella? Only Donna, because Bella dated Lance—and had blown up at him in public the night before, which gave her a visible motive.

Interesting. Was Donna investigating Lance's death to deflect suspicion, the way she claimed Alan was doing? Was Donna the person Kyle was protecting? Had she pulled away the jack and left him to die, then circled back to be sure she'd completed the job? She also had access to protective gear through her job, for when she stole the Beast. The more I thought about it, the more convinced I became. Donna Dube had some 'splaining to do.

At quarter to two, I left the shop to drive out to Quimby's for my oil change. Faith had gone home after lunch and would be back next week, the Tuesday after Labor Day. She and I would work all that week together while Grammie took time off. She'd already lined up a visit to an old friend down in Boothbay Harbor, and they were planning to take an excursion out to the islands in the bay.

Good for Grammie. What would I do with time off, if I had any? Well, hopefully Ian would be able to join me. A trip to Acadia National Park sounded good to me. We could stay in a cute bed-and-breakfast and hike, kayak, and eat lots of great food in Bar Harbor.

I thought back to our visit to the lighthouse. I'd been almost positive Ian had been going to make some kind of declaration. Was he going to admit he loved me? That thought made my skin tingle. But like you do when you wait to eat dessert—delayed gratification—I decided I wouldn't push to find out. I'd let things unfold naturally and enjoy the anticipation.

The garage loomed up on my left and with a surge of panic, I signaled, preparing to turn in. I had just wasted my prep time with some very sweet but distracting daydreams. What was I going to say to Derek? How should I approach the topic of Lance? Should I bother if Donna was guilty? But I could ask him who else had borrowed the Beast. If Donna had, that would be another nail in the coffin.

I pulled into a spot and turned off the engine. I wanted so badly to run my ideas past someone else, to test this theory out. I almost called Madison but then decided against it. I'd see how it went with Derek first.

Inside the office, the desk was empty. Whew. I wouldn't have to deal with Gladys. I rang the bell on the counter and a minute later, Derek opened the door leading to the garage. "Hey, Iris. Here for your oil change?"

He appeared so friendly and normal that for a moment I experienced a brief wave of cognitive dissonance. How could the mechanic I'd known for years be a possible killer? By that logic, how could anyone? Unfortunately real killers don't wear T-shirts announcing their murderous intent. Instead they move among us, neighbors and friends. And police dispatchers and auto mechanics.

"Sorry," I said. "Lost in thought there for a moment." I held out the keys. "I'm parked on the side."

"I'll get 'er right in." He took the set of keys. "Are you waiting? Or should we call?"

"I'll wait," I said, moving to the row of plastic

chairs. "I have a couple of things I want to talk about once you're done." Let him think our conversation was about Beverly. It wouldn't be the first time we'd discussed my vintage beauty.

"Good enough. There's fresh coffee if you want it." With a jingle of keys and a whistle along with the classic rock song playing over the system, he headed out the door.

I sat in one of the seats and fished through the pile of magazines: *Car and Driver*, *Road & Track*, and the ubiquitous *Reader's Digest*. *Reader's Digest* won, but I ended up flipping through the pages blindly. Besides wondering what I was going to say to Derek, the radio station kept distracting me by playing the worst songs ever. Can anyone tell me why "Muskrat Love" was a hit?

After about twenty minutes, Derek appeared in the doorway again, wiping his hands on a rag. "You're all set, Iris." Through the front window, I saw another mechanic backing Beverly out of the garage.

"That was quick," I said, coming to the counter to pay him. "Oh, by the way, Madison and I went to visit Kyle yesterday."

In the middle of writing up an invoice, his hand stilled. "Oh, yeah? The poor guy had a setback, I heard. Must have been after you visited."

Was that what the police were telling family, that it was only a setback, not another attempt on his life? Probably a good strategy, until they knew more. Why tip off the killer? "Actually, we were there when he got sick. We were really worried."

He cocked a brow, regarding me with assessing eyes. "Huh. Any idea what was up with that?"

So they hadn't revealed the full story yet. And I wouldn't either, in their shoes. "I'm not sure. The nurse hustled us right out of there." Thinking it was now or never, I glanced around the garage. "This is such a great business. I heard that you're planning to take it over."

His gaze dropped to the desk and for a moment, he concentrated on finishing the bill.

To encourage him, I said, "I love owning my own business. It's a lot of work, sure, but there is nothing like it."

Derek ripped off one of the layers and slid it toward me. "I *want* to buy it, but I'm kind of stuck right now. The bank will only do so much and my other backer fell through."

I glanced at the total and pulled out my bank card. "Oh, that's too bad. Maybe you'll find another investor."

He still wasn't looking me in the eye as he ran my card. "Yeah, maybe. My last guy burned me pretty bad. Almost makes me afraid to try again. Who needs to keep getting shot down?"

"True," I said. "I'm really sorry to hear that."

"Me too," Derek declared. He pressed his lips together and shook his head. "It was that hotshot sailor dude. Lance Pedersen. He liked to toy with people, I guess."

Bingo. "Ugh." I made a disgusted expression. "I hate to speak ill of the dead, but that's not right." I meant it. As a small business owner, I understood how devastating it could be to get jerked around.

The machine finally burped out a receipt, and Derek ripped it off and handed it to me, then pushed a pen my way. "No, it's not. I was pretty angry for a while."

Angry enough to kill? "It was pretty shocking that whoever it was used the Beast to hit him. And no, I don't think Bella is guilty." I signed the receipt and handed it back.

"Me neither. She's a sweetheart." Derek opened the register and tucked the receipt inside, then gave me a copy. "And if I find out who stole my Jeep and used it like that, they're going to be in a world of hurt." His voice rang with sincerity, no false note I could detect.

I moved Derek down the list of suspects, not that he'd ever been as high on my list as other people. "I'll see you in—" I was going to say, *three thousand miles*, but a blast of music drowned me out. The jingle for Pirro Auto. *We're on fire . . .*

With a muffled curse, Derek turned the radio down. "Never understood why the ads are so much louder."

"They sure advertise a lot," I said. "I'm tired of hearing that jingle."

"Yep, they certainly do." He pointed a finger at me. "I even complained to Kyle's girlfriend about it. She's from that family. But she blew me off, said that's why they do well. Market saturation."

"Kyle has a girlfriend?" I asked. "Not that it's any of my business." I'd never seen him with anyone, but that didn't mean much.

"Sort of," Derek said, straightening things on the counter. I could tell he was ready to get back to work. "It's real casual. Gretchen something. Pirro was her maiden name."

CHAPTER 24

Gretchen Stolte was a Pirro? As I walked out to my car, I realized there was a connection between Lance's death and Kyle's attempted murder that I hadn't seen before. Both had involved the use of a vehicle as a murder weapon. While growing up, had Gretchen been active in the family business, learned how to jack up a car, for example? It was possible. Thanks to working with my grandfather on his car restoration projects, including Beverly, I knew quite a bit about automobiles myself.

But why would Gretchen kill Lance? If she had, was that what Kyle was hiding from the police? Had he witnessed her doing or saying something incriminating? The fact that they were dating might be enough to make him leery about pointing the finger. Or maybe he'd been afraid she'd come after him next. Which she had, maybe, first kicking out the jack and then delivering tainted chocolate candy.

In a daze, I climbed into Beverly and started the engine. Before I took off, I sent Grammie a text. *Everything okay at the shop? If so, I'll be gone a little longer.*

Everything is fine. See you soon.

My conscience eased, I put Beverly into gear and pulled out onto the highway, planning to take a nice long ride to clear my head. A few miles up Route 1, I turned off onto a side road that hugged the shore. This was one of my favorite excursions, and a tiny beach covered in pebbles was one of my favorite places to stop.

The small parking area was empty, and I was glad to have the place to myself. I got out, the slam of my car door loud in the silence, and crunched my way down to the water. The afternoon air was almost perfectly still, with barely a breeze, and the incoming tide merely rippled and splashed on the shore.

Allowing my mind to clear, I strolled back and forth, bending down to toss rocks into the water or to retrieve a pretty shell. My companions were the gulls and other sea birds stalking along the wet sand at the water's edge, their heads bobbing as they searched for something to eat.

The facts were plain. Someone had killed Lance and tried to kill Kyle. Introducing Gretchen as a suspect only put a spanner in the works, as a mechanic might say. In both cases, her motives seemed weak—a grudge held for twenty years against her former sailing teacher and anger toward a man she was casually dating.

There had to be more. My spirits sagged at the idea of starting over, of digging into what may well prove another dead end. Her connections to the victims were real but not exactly strong.

Then, as sometimes happened, a thought dropped into my mind like a stone plunking into still waters, sending out ripples that commanded attention.

What if we'd been working from the wrong assumption all along? What if *Lance* hadn't been the intended victim?

What if someone had tried to kill *Peter* and made a terrible mistake?

Both brothers were tall, with streaked blond hair and lean but muscular physiques. People sometimes confused them, like the little boy who thought Peter was Lance. In addition, Peter was the one with the regular running habit, according to Bella, not Lance. They both wore sailing ball caps and running shorts.

In the early morning light, with his back to the driver, wouldn't Lance have resembled Peter?

Closing my eyes, I conjured the scene. The runner huffing as he trotted along under the trees, body and face mostly in shadow at that time of day. The driver of the Beast creeping up the road, moving slowly until the target was in view. Then pressing his or her foot on the gas and racing forward—ugh. I couldn't continue.

My phone rang, making me jump. I pulled it out of my pocket and looked at the number. Not one I recognized, so I hit decline.

After gathering my interrupted thoughts, I began strolling again. The more I thought about it, the more my uneasiness grew. If Peter *was* the intended victim, who had killed him? Who had a motive?

I really had no idea. Gretchen was the only person who had a possibly negative encounter with him that I knew of, and it might not even be important. Maybe she'd quit her job, not been fired. How could I find out? *Hey, Peter, did you fire Gretchen? Because if so, she might be out to get you.* Yeah, that'd go over well.

But . . . what about Peter's boat? Whoever cut it loose must have an issue with him. Gretchen spent a lot of time at the yacht club. Had she set the *Nixie* adrift so it would wreck on the rocks? If so, that plot had been foiled by Ian and me.

Wow. I was more confused than ever. Deciding that I needed to go back to the store and hash it out with Grammie, I started walking toward the parking area.

My phone rang again and to my annoyance, I saw it was the same number calling back. With a shrug, I declined it again. Maybe they would get the message this time.

Glad I'd left Beverly's windows open since it was roasting hot inside the car, I slid gingerly onto my seat. As I inserted the key, a beep announced that I had a voice mail.

Maybe I should listen to the message and find out who was bugging me, then block the number. Putting the phone on speaker, I called voice mail and set the phone in my lap so I could hear it while driving.

Hey, Iris. This is Alan. Alan? *I'm calling from Alice's phone because mine is dead.* Oh, that explained the unfamiliar number. *I'm, um, wondering if you've seen Bella.* No. *She said she was going to stop by your store this afternoon.* So? What did he want? *Please call me back when you get this.*

I didn't feel like talking to Alan at the moment, so I pulled over and dialed the store instead. Maybe, just maybe, he wasn't a murder suspect anymore, but he still wasn't my favorite person. "Hey," I said when Grammie answered. "I'm on my way back. Did Bella come into the store by chance?"

"No, I haven't seen her," Grammie said. "If she does come in, I'll tell her to wait for you."

"That's not it," I said. "Alan called me just now, looking for her. Twice. I have no idea why he's calling my cell."

"Maybe because I just got off a long call with a customer," Grammie said. "He must have gotten a busy signal."

"All right," I said with a groan. "I'll call him back once I get to the store, although I doubt it's an emergency. He didn't say it was."

After we disconnected, I decided to give Anton a call to discuss my new theory. Maybe his hardheaded voice of reason could clarify my thoughts. I dialed his cell phone, not the station, since I didn't want to go through dispatch. Unfortunately, but as I expected, it went right to voice mail. Should I leave a message? *Oh, why not.* He was good about returning calls, so I'd hear from him soon as he was free.

"Anton," I said, "it's your favorite person. Or second favorite. Anyway, I was thinking . . . what if Peter was the intended victim, not Lance? He was a regular morning runner and they kind of looked alike. Wore the same type of clothing. I know, crazy idea, right? But I thought I should run it by you. Call me when you get a chance."

Feeling marginally better, I began driving again. And then my phone rang. *Anton?* Without looking, I picked it up and said hello, then signaled to pull over. One definite disadvantage of a vintage car was the lack of a hands-free system.

"Iris?" Oh, no. It wasn't Anton.

I sighed. "Hi, Alan. Bella hasn't been to the store. I'm not there either, but I asked Grammie if she'd seen her."

He gulped audibly. "I was afraid of that. I'm sorry to bother you with all my calls, but I'm really worried."

Something in his tone made me sit up and pay attention. "What do you mean? Is she having a hard time? Is she depressed?" My friend had put such a brave face on her ordeal that I hadn't even considered that she might be struggling.

"No, it's not that. She's fine emotionally." He paused. "I think. Well, anyway, she was supposed to run over to her house earlier and then do a couple of errands.

But she's not back and she's not answering her cell. It's going right to voice mail."

She was probably declining his calls, the way I had. "Maybe she wants some alone time. I'm sure she'll turn up soon." I imagined her taking a drive, the way I had, allowing the wind to blow through her hair as she decompressed.

He was silent a second, then said, "I get what you're saying. Yes, she might avoid me. But she wouldn't do that to the kids. We're staying on Isleboro tonight, and I rented a boat to take us out there. We were supposed to leave an hour ago."

Alan was right. Bella wouldn't disappoint Alice and Connor by ruining such exciting plans. Heck, I'd love to hitch a ride out there with them myself.

"What were her errands?" I asked. "I can drive around and check to see if anyone has seen her." This effort might be totally futile, because she could be anywhere by now. But it was something concrete I could do to set his mind at ease. Hopefully. Maybe she would show up at the resort any minute, full of apologies about being late.

"Do you mind?" he asked, relief heavy in his voice. "I'd do it but Florence isn't back from her lunch yet. I expected her by now but you know how it is when old friends get together."

I did. "Got it. You said she went home. Then what?"

"Her next stop was Dr. Pedersen's office, believe it or not. Alice is getting braces, and she needs her X-rays for her next appointment with the orthodontist. For some reason they didn't e-mail them so Bella had to pick them up."

A trickle of unease slithered down my spine. "Bella is the prime suspect in Lance's death. Wrongly, of course, but why on earth would they expect her to go by their office? I would think she's the last person they'd want to see."

"I wondered the same thing," Alan said. "But it wasn't Dr. Pedersen or his wife who called. It was someone from the office."

The uneasy feeling ramped up to a screech, like the music in the classic movie *Psycho*. "Who called from the office?" I asked, dread in my belly like a lump of lead.

"I don't know," Alan said. "But Bella said, 'She told me to swing by.'"

She? Gretchen. "Okay, Alan, I'm going right over. If you don't hear from me in fifteen, call the cops." I disconnected over his squawks, threw the phone aside, and hit the gas, peeling off the shoulder with a spray of gravel.

I don't even remember the ride to town. The beautiful scenery whipped past my windows, tourists lollygagged in front of me, trucks tailgated and then passed with throaty roars—although I was speeding—and I barely took it all in.

The only thing tempering my panic was the thought that I could be completely wrong. Maybe the Pedersens had hired a new office employee to distribute records and help wind down the operation.

Maybe. But the deepest part of me doubted it. The elder Pedersens were out of town, at their camp. I had no idea where Peter was. I hadn't seen him since the memorial. He could be away as well, at the camp, perhaps.

Or—the killer could be finishing the job.

Sometimes in a crisis, I go on autopilot, functioning

as if normal but actually numb. Thankfully this was one of those times. I couldn't afford to curl up in a ball and scream.

Bella needed me. Alice and Connor's mom needed me. Tears sprang into my eyes as my shell began to crack. I blinked them back. *Focus, Iris, focus.*

All looked calm as I approached the dentist's office. The large house drowsed in the sun, birds and bees playing in the extensive flower gardens. Slowing to a crawl, I eased into the driveway and toward the small lot at the rear.

I braked in confusion. The lot was empty. No sign of Bella's car—or Peter's Audi. All the garage doors were shut, and the house appeared deserted, shades down and curtains pulled. She wasn't here. No one was here.

My route had taken me past Bella's house and she hadn't been there, either. So where was she? Was my theory totally and completely wrong?

I sure hoped so. Where to next? I wished I'd gotten the full list of Bella's errands from Alan. Now I'd have to call him back and lose more time. At least I could reassure him that she hadn't run into trouble here.

What was that? A low rumble caught my ear. It sounded like an engine running. Maybe someone was idling a car on the adjacent street, which I could glimpse beyond the garage.

The rev of an engine in front of the Pedersen house caught my attention, but I couldn't see the vehicle from where I was. Then tires squealed as someone pulled at high speed into the driveway and raced toward me.

Alan, at the wheel of his BMW. He jumped out and ran toward me, engine running. "Have you seen her?" His normally perfect hair was standing on end and one side of his polo shirt collar was up. Looking into his handsome, distraught face, I knew. *He loves Bella.*

I got out of the car before I answered. "No, Alan. She's not here." I gestured toward his car, which was still running. "If you move, I'll go check Bella's other errands. Or you can, since I'm guessing Florence is home."

His answer was an inarticulate groan. "No, Iris. Something is wrong." He pulled his phone out of his pocket and held it up, facing me. "Listen. I have no idea why this voice mail took so long to come through. Plus my phone being dead didn't help." He hit a button.

I had to move closer to listen. "Alan . . ." Bella's voice was garbled. "Help . . ." That word came through clearly. "She's—" Her voice cut off suddenly, but before the voice mail ended, there was a strange rumbling sound.

Exactly like the one I could hear right now. "What is that?" I asked Alan.

"A car engine," he said. "Where is it?" He glanced wildly around then pointed. "The garage. It's coming from the garage."

I stared at the big building with its four bays. The doors were the type without windows, so we couldn't actually see inside—from the front, at least. Maybe there was a window around the side.

"Come on, let's go." I began running toward the garage. The engine sound grew louder the closer we got.

Alan pressed his ear to the one of the doors. "It is coming from in there." He reached for the handle and tugged, but the door was locked. I tried another, and between us we attempted to raise all four. All were locked tight and wouldn't budge.

"I don't understand what's going on," I said to Alan. "Why would someone run a car inside a garage?

Wouldn't the exhaust—" Then I got it. That was how Gretchen was trying to kill Bella—and perhaps Peter as well.

Alan ran both hands through his hair, frantic. "There's got to be a way in." He darted toward the side of the garage, with me hot on his heels.

We found a regular-size door with a partial window. It was also locked. The garage was dark but I could see the shapes of two vehicles inside. I gasped. Bella's Volvo was one of them. And the sickening odor of auto exhaust was beginning to escape the cracks around the door. Our theory was right. This was another case of attempted murder by automobile—and with my friend's life on the line, I was determined to let it go no further than "attempted."

Alan was scanning the area frantically, running toward the back and then into the adjacent flower beds.

"What are you doing?" I asked. Then I saw. He picked up a garden gnome with both hands and carried it toward the door.

"I'm going to break the glass and unlock the door," he said. Then he looked at me. "We need to be smart about this. Do you have anything we can use to cover our noses and mouths?"

I thought about the contents of my car, which included a couple of children's aprons I'd been planning to deliver to a customer in town. Her order was now going to be further delayed.

"I do," I said, bolting toward the car. "Hold on. I'll be right back." As I ran, I thought about calling 911. But even if I did, that wouldn't change what we had to do. We needed to get Bella out of there and shut off the car engine. Waiting for help could mean the difference between life and death.

I grabbed the aprons and ran back. "Tell me what

to do." I tied one around the lower half of my face and he did the same with the other. "How are we going to coordinate this?" I realized he might not guess the rest of the story. "We might have two victims in there, not one." His glance was quizzical, so I explained in as few words as possible.

"Okay," he said. "Get the person in the driver's seat out and then we'll drive the car outside so we don't have to carry two people." He swung the gnome toward the glass, which broke with a satisfying tinkle, dropped the statue, and reached inside.

Exhaust began to pour out through the opening, making my eyes water. He had the door open now, and I inhaled what I hoped wouldn't be my last breath of relatively fresh air and followed.

Bella's car was first, cold and still. Through the haze of gray smoke, I saw Alan skirting the Volvo's rear and moving farther into the garage.

The only other vehicle inside was Peter's Audi, and yes, it was running. Alan ran around the far side and opened the driver's door. I did the same on the passenger side, my heart almost bursting from my chest when I saw Bella, leaning back in the seat with her eyes closed.

Was she already—no, I couldn't think about that. Instead I made my way to the garage door and fiddled with the handle, trying to unlock it. Behind me I was vaguely aware that Alan had pulled Peter out of the Audi and placed him on the floor.

The door wouldn't budge. I didn't know if it was me fumbling ineptly or if someone had done something to it.

Alan shouldered me aside and turned the handle, then hoisted the door up. Fresh, fresh air poured into the garage, blowing gray, choking exhaust aside. He turned and pointed to the Audi, gesturing that I should drive the car outside. While I did that, he ran over to Peter and checked his vitals.

I hopped into the driver's seat and put the car into gear, happy it was an automatic. Although I could drive a stick shift, right now I'd probably stall out. "Hang in there, friend," I whispered to Bella, who was still lolling like a boneless doll in the other seat.

That Audi had never left the garage so fast in its life. We shot out the door into the driveway, where I braked sharply, throwing out my arm barely in time so Bella wouldn't flop forward.

Then I saw it. A note taped to the dashboard. "Dear family and friends," it began. I didn't bother to read the rest. I turned off the key and reached over to Bella, gently shook her shoulder. "Bella. Bella. Are you all right? Please wake up."

She groaned softly, moving her head back and forth and flexing her arms and legs. *Hooray!* She was alive. Now I prayed that she would recover fully.

My phone was still in my pocket and with shaking fingers I dialed 911. Then movement to one side caught my eye. Gretchen, launching herself onto Alan, still bent over Peter. She raised something above her head, and whack, Alan was down.

"Nine-one-one. What's your emergency?" I almost wept upon hearing that monotone voice.

"Two ill from carbon monoxide," I said, sliding down in the seat and hoping Gretchen wouldn't see me. Of course Beverly parked in the drive was a dead giveaway that I was in the vicinity. I gave the address. "Send police and two ambulances. No, make that three. There's a head injury, too. Oh, and Lance Pedersen's killer is on the loose. It's Gretchen Stolte."

Her voice rose in inquiry but I didn't bother to explain. "Hurry, that's all. *Hurry*."

Now what? Gretchen was standing with arms held wide, a tire iron dangling from one hand. Her eyes were glittering and her tawny hair hung loose in a tangle. She looked totally and completely unhinged.

She turned toward Alan and Peter, both sprawled on the floor of the garage, and lifted that tire iron again.

Without conscious thought, I opened the car door and bolted toward her. I was not going to allow her to hurt them again.

I had no weapon, nothing to use against her except my body weight. So use it I did. With a guttural growl, I launched myself through the air and landed square on her back. She fell flat onto the concrete and the tire iron went flying, landing with a *clang* somewhere in back.

"Get off!" she cried, bucking up against me and trying to scratch and kick.

I pressed my body down even harder, holding her wrists. "No way. You are not going anywhere. Give it up, Gretchen. The police are on their way." She squirmed and complained. "No, I am not letting you up."

"It was an accident," she said. "Honestly."

I reared back in surprise and she redoubled her efforts to get free, almost dislodging me. Then I remembered the apron still draped around my shoulders. I sat back and tied her wrists together with it. Then I grabbed the one Alan had used, lying on the floor nearby, and used that to tie her feet. After making sure she was snugly secured, I left her lying on the concrete beside Peter and Alan.

I went over and checked on them both. To my relief, they were still breathing and Peter's normal color was returning. Then I went out to check on Bella. She was conscious, her eyes at half-mast. "What's going on?" she muttered sleepily.

"Don't try to talk," I told her, patting her shoulder. "Help is coming."

I ran back into the garage to confront Gretchen. "Now what was that about an accident?" My voice was tight with rage. "You deliberately tried to kill Peter and Bella. And Alan."

She shook her head wildly. "No, no, no, not them. Lance."

"Lance was an accident?" The pieces fell into place. My crazy theory was right. "You were trying to kill Peter." It wasn't a question. "And Kyle figured it out."

"Yeah. He noticed I was gone early that morning and put two and two together." She let out a string of curse words. "Why didn't he mind his own business? Then I wouldn't have had to do that to him."

Classic victim-blaming. I glanced toward the street. When *were* the police and ambulances going to get here? "Why did you want to kill Peter? Because he fired you?"

She made a scoffing sound. "No, that was just the icing on the cake. We were involved. He even talked about marrying me." She scowled. "Then he changed his mind. He said I was unstable. So did my ex. I can't help it if they made me angry."

And Peter was right. "Got it. So why Bella?" My own anger rose up, choking me. "She didn't do anything to you."

"Alan loves her," was the quiet answer. "And that's why he dumped me earlier this year. He was my first choice . . . not Peter." She sneered toward the unconscious dentist. "I thought if she was out of the way, it would give us a chance. I tried to pin the hit-and-run on her but then I got worried they would let her off. So, today . . . happened." As if she wasn't responsible.

Alan lifted his head. "No way was I ever going to be with you, Gretchen. Never. She's my wife. And I've been a total ass." With a groan, he lay his head back down.

He was right about being an ass, although I had a feeling that today's events might help redeem him in Bella's eyes. If he hadn't called me so insistently, Gretchen's evil plan would have worked. And we would have lost Bella.

"You had a key to the Beast," I said. "Brilliant." I figured a compliment would encourage her to spill. "And I gather you wore something to prevent your DNA from showing up?"

Her smile was smug. "Kyle actually gave me the idea of using the Beast. He had a key that he forgot to give back to his cousin. So when I saw Bella had borrowed it . . . everything fell into place. And yes, I wore protective clothing. I'm not dumb."

That explained the white bathrobe. And no, she wasn't stupid, only murderous.

Sirens echoed down the hill, growing louder as help approached. *Finally.* I ran down to the bottom of the driveway to welcome them.

Anton was first on the scene, behind the wheel of the police SUV. He rolled down his window and stared at me in shock. "Iris. I just barely listened to your message. What's going on?"

I motioned him to keep driving. "Later. Three down. Two with carbon monoxide poisoning and one head injury. You're going to need a third ambulance." His gaze raked me up and down, and I added, "I'm fine." I stood back to let him enter the drive, followed by an ambulance. Then I ran to back Beverly up into a space out of the way.

"Iris," Bella said. "What's going on?" She still sounded super groggy but I could tell she was improving fast.

"You, my dear," I said as I put Beverly into reverse, "are now a free woman."

Somehow, with Anton directing, two ambulances were able to park near the garage, ready to accept patients. Hopping out of Beverly, I called to a pair of EMTs. "Over here. Carbon monoxide poisoning."

I ran toward the garage, where Anton and Officer Rhonda Davis were regarding Gretchen with bemusement while the other two EMTs were checking Alan and Peter over. Both were conscious now, I was glad to see.

"Untie me," Gretchen ordered, trying to roll over. "I'm sick of lying on this cold, hard floor."

Anton peered at her bonds. "Are those *aprons*?"

"I used what I had," I said. "And don't release her. She tried to kill Peter and Bella. And bashed Alan on the head. I saw her do that. This is after Alan and I rescued them from the Audi, which was running. I had to jump on her to subdue her."

Both officers regarded me with amazement. Anton opened his mouth to say something, then thought better of it.

Gretchen began to struggle. "Let me go. You're going to take her word for it? She's lying. I demand an attorney."

"I heard the whole thing," Alan said. "Give it up, Gretchen."

She continued to wail and kick as Rhonda read her rights and cuffed her, removing the aprons. Rhonda and another officer were helping her up, preparing to take her to a cruiser, when she shouted out, "I cut your boat loose, Peter. It's probably in splinters by now. How does it feel to lose something you love? I loved my job."

"Um, no, we rescued the *Nixie*," I said. Another loose end tied up, this time literally.

As they helped Gretchen into a cruiser, Anton said, "Don't move, Iris. I need a statement from you." He patted my shoulder. "Like I've said before, you ever want a change of career . . ."

"No, I'm good," I said. "I love my business. Solving murders is just a sideline." At his startled look, I added with a little laugh, "An inadvertent one, trust me." Pulling my phone out of my pocket, I dialed the store. I was going to be late once again, but I was pretty sure Grammie would understand.

CHAPTER 25

"Knock, knock." Cradling a huge bouquet in one hand, I knocked on the doorframe of Bella's room. Madison and Sophie were right behind me, their arms laden with Bella's favorite treats. Peter, Alan, and Bella were all expected to recover fully, but all three had spent the night in the hospital.

Bella smiled at us from her bed. Although makeup free and dressed in one of those hideous blue-and-white johnnies, she was radiant and gorgeous, no trace of her ordeal visible. "You didn't have to bring all that," she said as we set down our gifts. "I'm getting out later today."

"I know," I said, dropping a kiss on her forehead. "But we wanted to show that we care."

She took my hand. "No surprise there. You saved my life yesterday." She squeezed my fingers. "You and Alan." Her voice was husky. "I'll never be able to thank you enough."

"How about that Alan," Madison said, her eyes twinkling. "He turned out to be quite the hero."

"He sure did," I said. "But before we discuss *him*, tell us how you are doing." Not letting go of her hand, I perched on the chair beside the bed. After hugging Bella from her other side, Madison and Sophie arranged themselves on the window ledge and standing against the wall.

Bella lifted her free hand and let it drop. "I'm actually feeling pretty good. The doctors figured out that Peter and I were sedated with injections before Gretchen tried to kill us with carbon monoxide." She reached a hand to the back of her head and grimaced. "When I showed up at the dentist's office, she was out in the garage. After I went to talk to her there, she knocked me down and then injected me. I still have a bump where I hit my head."

"So that's why you were unconscious," I said, relieved. Last night, I hadn't been able to resist researching carbon monoxide poisoning, and I'd learned that many people who breathed in enough to pass out ended up with brain damage or dead.

Bella nodded. "I didn't even know Peter was in the car with me until the police told me. I never saw him." Her lips twisted in disgust. "Despite the charming note claiming we'd made a suicide pact because of our remorse over killing Lance to get his money. Lance left his brother a big chunk of change."

"So ridiculous," Sophie said. "No one would have believed it." She opened one of the bakery bags and passed it around. "Cookie? Toffee chocolate chip made fresh this morning."

"You know what?" I said, crunching the delicious treat. "Before I got Alan's call, I had actually started to wonder if Peter was the intended victim, not Lance. I even called Anton and left a message to that effect."

Madison chewed and swallowed. "I know, he told me. He said at first he thought the idea was absurd but right after, you called nine-one-one." She grinned. "That will teach him to doubt your genius."

"True." I gave her a thumbs-up. "It had started to bug me that Peter, not Lance, had a daily running habit. So how did the killer know Lance would be on that route on that particular morning? Oh, and one of the kids at the yacht club thought Peter was Lance."

Sophie handed the bag around again. "They did look quite a bit alike. Same height and coloring. If Gretchen was watching from Kyle's house, she could have seen a tall man in shorts and a ball cap and assumed it was Peter."

"You're right," Bella said. "From what Gretchen said in her ravings, I gathered Peter had figured that out too, that she'd mistaken him for Lance. So she decided to try to kill him a second time." Her lips twisted. "I was just a bonus."

I shuddered, as I did every time I thought how close we had come to losing Bella. "I understand she gave a full confession down at the station."

"She did," Madison said. "Of her own volition but not without a tantrum or two, I understand."

"I feel so bad for her poor son," Bella said, ever tenderhearted. "But I understand he's doing really well with his dad and stepmother. Gretchen basically cut him out of her life." She shook her head. "The woman has issues."

"She certainly does," I said. "I hope she gets help." After a beat, I asked, "What's next for you, Bella?"

She smiled. "Florence and the kids are coming to pick us up soon as we're released. We'll be staying at the resort a few more days." She sighed deeply. "I've already got another spa day booked. This time I'll really enjoy it, not being under suspicion and all."

"Us?" Madison asked, one eyebrow quirked. "Any more to say on that front?"

Sophie laughed. "I'm glad you asked that, Madison. We're all dying to know: Are you going to take Alan back?"

Bella smoothed her blanket, not meeting our gaze. "I've given it a lot of thought, believe me. Driven myself crazy with the pros and cons." She swallowed. "The last thing I want to do is hurt my kids. Or get my heart broken again. But we've been talking . . . debating . . . arguing, even, and this is what we came up with. For the next six months we're going to meet with a therapist, together and separately. And we're going to have regular meetings with our minister." She looked up, her eyes shining with what looked like hope. Joy, too. "Maybe it's too soon to tell, but I have a really good feeling about it. People can change, right?"

"They sure can, if they want to," Madison said.

"Sounds like he does, from what you're telling us," Sophie chimed in.

"Tell you what," I said. "I saw his face yesterday when you were in danger. And he loves you, Bella, he really, truly does." To break the tension, I clenched my fist and added, "And we're always here as backup if you need us." We all laughed.

Bella grinned. "You're all on my speed dial, believe me. Now tell me, ladies: What other treats did you bring me?"

CHAPTER 26

"Where do you want this, babe?" Ian stood in the kitchen doorway, mannequin gripped in his arms. She wore one of my 1950s shirtdresses, topped with Florence's apron.

I pointed. "Over there, near the stove." The lighthouse committee was frantically doing some last-minute tasks before the grand opening at four this afternoon. A catering tent had been set up and grills were heating up, ready to feed the crowds we hoped would show up. On Saturday of Labor Day weekend, Blueberry Cove was certainly busy enough, full of visitors eager to enjoy the last of summer before school started.

Ian set the mannequin in place and I tweaked her garments into place. Behind her on the wall was the enlarged photograph of Florence's mother cooking at this very stove.

"The displays really bring it to life," Ian said. With folded arms, he checked out the table set for a meal, the collection of sea glass and shells along the windowsills, and the cast-iron pans and percolator on the stove. "I feel like I can step right into the past."

"That's the idea," I said. "Want a quick tour?" He'd

been busy with the final touches to the lighthouse tower and hadn't seen the cottage exhibits yet.

"Love one." He gathered me into a hug and kissed me. "With the prettiest docent ever."

I kissed him back. "We're all pretty good-looking." I gestured for him to follow.

The cottage living room was now cozy, with an overstuffed sofa and matching club chairs. We'd found a wonderful antique radio and television console and lined the shelves with vintage books. We'd decided that this room would function as a reading room, with visitors allowed to browse a selection of local and maritime history titles.

"Good ahead, sit," I said, snapping a photo when he tested out the armchair closest to the fireplace, which was cold. But the chimney was safe so we were tentatively planning some special events over the winter.

We peeked into the office, which was neat now, the keeper's log set in pride of place along with other items. The university had been very excited to get digitized records for their archives, and we'd organized the logs and other documents for researchers to use. The mermaid figurehead was now mounted in the lighthouse, near a display of vintage gauges, lights, and equipment.

Next we went upstairs to the bedrooms. Two had been furnished with beds and bureaus, plus vintage quilts, and the third had been set up as an office. The historical society had taken a lot of the excess stuff we'd found, grateful for the additions to their collection, and we'd sold some to raise money.

Ian went to stand by a window overlooking the bay. "Imagine waking up to this every morning," he said. From here, the water was an endless stretch of blue, creamy-topped waves touched by the late afternoon sun.

"It certainly is a special place," I said, joining him. "And I'm so glad we were able to interview Florence. Wait till you see the video. Madison did a stellar job editing it." We would be running the interview continuously in the reading room while the museum was open, and it was posted on the museum's website and social media. She had also approached local television stations about running a segment, and one of the Maine magazine shows was coming next week.

The last room was the office, which had a view of the road to the lighthouse. So far, our vehicles were the only ones in the lot, but then I saw a Honda SUV approaching. When Florence and Bella moved away from the tent and walked toward the parking area, I knew. "Chet is here. I've got to get out there quick."

By the time I joined Florence and Bella, Grammie, Madison, and Sophie were also waiting with them. Ian excused himself and joined Jake and Anton at the grills. In silence, our little group watched the gray Honda wind its way to the lighthouse.

"This is intense," Madison whispered to me. She clenched her fists and wiggled. "I'm so excited."

"Me too." My heart was pounding. Finally, after sixty years plus, the two lovebirds were reuniting.

The SUV pulled into a space, and a comfortable-looking middle-aged woman climbed out of the driver's seat. After greeting us with a wave, she went around to the passenger door and opened it to help her father get out.

Chester Chapman, retired Air Force, was stooped and frail with age but still handsome enough to turn heads with his full head of white hair and craggy features. He wore a crisp, white short-sleeved shirt, a pair of gray slacks, and polished loafers. Once he was out of the car and fully upright, he scanned the crowd with keen blue eyes. We all saw the moment he recognized Florence by his widened gaze and the brief opening of his mouth.

Then he stepped forward, his eyes focused on her like a laser. She stood waiting, smiling, her eyes never leaving his face. She started to tremble, her shoulders gently shaking, and Bella put an arm around her.

On he came, step by step, while we waited, literally holding our breaths. Perhaps we should have made our excuses and left them alone, but it was too late for that. I glanced at his daughter, who was right behind him but giving him space. She wore a tender smile, and I was glad to see she didn't resent the reappearance of Florence in her father's life.

When Chet reached Florence, Bella dropped her arm and moved aside. We all dropped back a little but we weren't going to walk away now.

"Florence," he said, holding out one large, strong hand. "Is it really you?"

She took his hand, clasping it tightly. "It's me, Chet. Thank you for coming."

"I wouldn't miss it," he said. "After all these years . . . you're as beautiful as ever."

Florence laughed, putting a hand to her soft cheek. "I'm glad you see me that way." She reached up and smoothed his collar. "And you're still the handsome Air Force Lieutenant I remember."

Madison leaned her head on my shoulder for a second. "This is killing me."

"Me too," I said. Grammie was dabbing her eyes with a tissue, and when my eyes started to well up, I held a hand out for one, then passed another to Sophie, who was also teary-eyed. As for Bella, she was grinning, one hand covering her mouth.

Chet put an arm around Florence's shoulders. "What do you say the two of us get out of here?" He cast a bright, mischievous glance at his audience. "Just you and me, sitting by the water, the way we used to?"

"I know the perfect spot," Florence said, smiling up at him.

The elderly pair strolled away, his arm still in place around her, heading toward the bench with the best view on the bluff. The newly restored foghorn stood in pride of place beside it.

"Wow, that was so intense," Madison said. "Like something out of an old movie."

Grammie tucked away her tissue and approached Chet's daughter. "Hi. I'm Anne Buckley. How nice of you to bring your dad today."

The woman shook Grammie's hand. "Nice to meet you. I'm Sylvia Benson. I have to tell you, hearing from Florence really perked Dad up. I'm so happy to be here." She smiled at us and we all introduced ourselves.

The aroma of sizzling meat drifted from the grills. "Would you like something to eat?" Grammie said. "We've got hamburgers, hot dogs, and veggie burgers. And an assortment of salads and side dishes. We're going to eat a quick bite now, before the hordes descend." We'd be too busy leading tours and answering questions once the museum officially opened.

"I could go for a cheeseburger," Sylvia said. As we all made our way toward the tent, she said, "I can't wait to tour your new museum. And I want to know what led to Florence looking for Dad. I heard it had something to do with an old letter."

"An old letter in an apron pocket," I said. "I found

it while we were sorting through old trunks in the keeper's cottage." I began to tell Sylvia the story, beyond amazed and grateful that my discovery of Chet's letter in Florence's apron had set this reunion into motion. It was entirely possible they might never have seen each other again if we hadn't been so nosy—um, intervened, I mean.

Ian looked up and smiled when I reached him in line. "I take it things went well?" he asked, flipping a row of burgers.

"I'll say. Look at those two." Over on the bench, Chet and Florence were sitting close, hand in hand, and chatting. "I can feel the love from here." I sighed. My romantic heart was in seventh heaven.

"Me too." Ian's eyes were warm with approval as he gently placed my burger on a bun. I held out my plate so he could serve it. "Iris Buckley, you are an amazing woman. Anyone ever tell you that?"

I batted my eyes at him, flattered. "Not often enough," I joked. "Meet me later for a more in-depth discussion about my amazing self?"

"You bet," he said, his deep voice warm with promise. "After the museum closes. Lighthouse deck. You and me and a flask of Blueberry Cove cocktails."

"You and me," I echoed. How sweet that sounded. And as I carried my burger along to the salads, where my friends were gathered, my spirits soared. Even the sight of Lars Lavely huffing up the road on his bicycle couldn't dent my mood.

This night, this moment, this group of special people. What more could I ask for?

Not a blessed thing.